A Timeline Restored

Prevent the Past, Book 3

By Rebecca Hefner

To all of you, Dear Readers, who stuck with me on this passion project. Writing this twisty, steamy time travel series made my heart swell. I still can't read the epilogue of this book without crying, and I hope these characters make you smile and weep along the way as well. Thank you from the bottom of my science geek heart.

And to Nikki, my lifelong friend. You left us the same week I finalized this novel and I know you would've been the first to rush out and buy it. Your support and friendship was a guidepost, and your soul was one of the brightest I've ever known. I hope we meet in another timeline where we laugh and hug again. In the meantime, rest in peace my beautiful friend.

Table of Contents

September 2075

Eli Hernandez sat in the dim room of the New Establishment's compound, several miles from where Washington D.C. used to exist. Now, the former capital was mostly flooded, overtaken by the mighty Atlantic when the ice caps melted. The massive fortified headquarters had been built to showcase the New Establishment's supremacy over every speck of land left on the planet. Foreboding and menacing, Eli hated the compound with a violent passion.

A muscle clenched in his jaw as he observed his companions through narrowed lids. Tanner Cross, the leader of the Australian faction of the New Establishment, sat across from him at the round mahogany table. Four other high-ranking officers flanked their sides, but it was Tanner who worried Eli the most. Aside from himself, Commander Cross had the most nefarious reputation of any New Establishment leader. However, there was one huge chasm of difference between them: Eli was a spy, and Tanner was pure evil.

Feeling his lips twitch in a humorless grin, Eli recognized that sentiment wasn't completely accurate, for he'd committed many atrocities during his forty-three years on the planet. They were all compelled by his desire to establish his identity as a ruthless and merciless leader. Eli had learned long ago that cruelty inspired fear, and fear inspired subjugation. Once people were overcome with terror, a person could manipulate their actions with skillful ease. Ironically, performing terrible deeds in his youth had led to much less blood on his hands today.

But still, he had to keep up appearances, and dissenters must be punished or killed if they defied his orders. Unquestioned supremacy was the only way his plan would achieve fruition; the only option for defeating the New Establishment from within. When that day came and the good people of Earth defeated the enemy, Eli would leave the planet behind along with all the memories of past atrocities that haunted his nightmares.

"I'm still confused as to why you didn't let your men move into Dr. Randolph's hub when you seized it," Tanner said, his tone suspicious.

"The hub is small, and the men were better off outside," Eli responded, doing his best to relay a confidence and calm he certainly didn't feel within. "Overtaking Solera was our primary goal, and now, that is accomplished."

Tanner nodded. "Excellent job. The troops I left behind in Australia now rule that continent, and with your occupation of Solera, the New Establishment now controls the entire Eastern Isle. In effect, we have achieved world domination. To my knowledge, the only area that has rebel forces is the South American Isle, and they are scattered and unorganized. It is time for the final phase of the plan."

"Yes," Eli said, a muscle in his jaw ticking. "We'll use the knowledge we acquired at the scientific hubs to slowly introduce electricity and technology to the world. Our subjects will only be allowed to use it through complete surrender. Those who don't comply will be killed."

"Those who still believe in democracy and equality for all will perish. Earth no longer has use for willful idiots who believe in these false principles. Only the best of us will survive. Your father would be proud, Eli."

Hate coursed through his veins as it always did when Eli thought of Victor Hernandez. His father was born with a cruel, vicious streak Eli always feared he'd inherited against his deepest wishes. If so, it meant his soul was already lost. Sadly, that was most likely the case. He was a wasted shell of a man who strived to save the world but inadvertently was the embodiment of all he despised. Self-loathing threatened to choke him.

"Father always dreamed of the day the New Establishment prevailed."

"We still have several loose ends to tie up," Tanner said, rubbing his chin as he contemplated. "It seems the mission was botched when you raided the hub during the scientists' time travel attempt. Dr. Randolph, Captain Rhodes, Claire Finch, and Cyrus Montgomery all appear to have traveled successfully to the past. This will need to be dealt with."

"I'm already working on that with Dr. Longwood," Eli said, firm in his effort to keep the secret promises he'd made to Lainey. "You were right to bring him here on the high-speed ocean cruiser he reconfigured for you. He will help us locate the others in the past before they can manipulate space-time. I will ensure it."

"As you ensured the capture of all the dissenters at the hub?" Tanner asked, arching a sardonic eyebrow.

"It is unfortunate that Zach, Elle, Sara, and Marie escaped," Eli said, the lie smooth on his tongue since that had been his ultimate goal. "Alora is wily and a capable fighter for someone so slight. She killed three of my men before they could blink, allowing the others to escape."

"Then she needs to be exterminated," Tanner said, scowling. "She is a threat to our rule."

Eli took a measured breath, knowing he would only get one shot at saving Alora's life again. "I see a better option."

Tanner sat back in his chair. "I'm listening."

"I feel Alora can eventually be turned to our side. It would be an extreme waste if we killed someone with her cunning mind before we at least tried to sway her to the cause."

"And what advantage would we gain from turning her?"

"She has an extensive network on the South American Isle. Her family was highly revered before my father murdered them in front of her when she was a teenager." He smiled, cruel and sinister, pushing down the bile that rose in his throat. There was no place for sentiment as he strived to save the woman who hated him with every fiber of her being. "She would be an effective resource in getting others to follow us. I believe they will listen to her as we systematically employ our rule across the Isle."

"And how do you plan to turn her? From what I've heard, she has vowed to never align with the New Establishment."

"Why, isn't it obvious?" Eli asked, leaning forward and resting his forearms on the table. "I'll marry her. An allegiance between us will cement an alliance between a natural born leader of the South American Isle and the designated leader of the Eastern American Isle. I know you see the merits of this since it's the same reason you chose to marry Svetlana."

"True," Tanner said with a tilt of his head. "I married Svetlana because she was the daughter of a former head of state on the European Isle, and many were loyal to her. Although I find her repulsive, the alliance has been fruitful."

"And my alliance with Alora will deliver the same result."

Sighing, Tanner studied Eli while silence pervaded the room. "I see the logic, but Alora has quite a bit more...*personality* than Svetlana," Tanner said, waving his hand as he searched for the word. "I don't see her eagerly entering into a marriage with the son of the man who murdered her family."

"Let me deal with Alora," Eli said, already anticipating how furious she would be when she learned of his plan. "Taming her will be fun, and I've never shied away from forcing a woman to do something against her will. It will only cement my nefarious reputation."

Tanner's lips curled into a menacing grin. "Indeed."

Eli tamped down his shiver, determined not to show any weakness. Tanner's reputation included instances of many misdeeds, including assault of women, and Eli needed to project the same willingness to violate others. Inside, the flames of self-hate burned in his gut. Although he'd committed disreputable deeds in his clandestine attempt to save the world, Eli would never sexually assault a woman. Knowing it was imperative the others at the table believed him capable of the act, he threaded his fingers together, clenching his hands.

"It will be a pleasure to crush every ounce of fight from Alora. I'm excited to break her. There's nothing like taming a spirited woman."

"All right. I agree to your alliance with her if the others do as well." Tanner regarded the other men at the table, all of whom nodded in consent. "With that resolved, what about the others who escaped?"

"I will marry Alora and bring her along on the mission to find Dr. Randolph's team. She knows them well, and her insights will help me track them down. I'll take a small battalion with me and anticipate it should only take a week or two to locate them."

"They've most likely been trained in evasion by Hunter and Cyrus," Tanner said.

Eli shrugged. "No matter. I'll find them. And, unlike Alora, they won't be so lucky. They have no ties to the outside world. No scattered rebels who revere them. Once I locate them, I'll murder them."

Eli had other plans, of course, but it was imperative no one at the table knew them.

After several more minutes of discussion, the meeting adjourned, and Eli ran a hand through his thick black hair. Expelling a ragged breath, he began the trek to the cellblock that sat below the sprawling compound. Alora was being held in one of the secure units, and he felt it best to break the news to her as soon as possible.

After all, it wasn't every day one was forced to marry their greatest enemy against their will. She would be *livid*.

A strange sense of anticipation lined his gut, and his lips twitched into a grin. Although Alora hated him with her entire being, Eli found the stunning woman a magnificent foe. Filled with a strange excitement about their confrontation, he admitted his washed-up soul felt alive when he was around Alora. Sparring with her. Absorbing the biting insults from her cunning tongue. He reveled in every ounce of hate she sparingly threw his way.

Perhaps because they were the only snippets of emotion he ever granted himself to *feel*.

Ready to face the woman who consumed his thoughts, he trailed down the stairs toward the cells.

Chapter 2

Alora lifted her head at the shuffling sound in the distance. Two men murmured a hushed conversation before she heard the footsteps approach. Standing, she walked toward the metal bars, clenching them and straining to see in the dimness.

A man's silhouette formed in the waning light, and Alora gritted her teeth. *Eli.* She recognized his broad shoulders and tall, muscular build. For some reason, it had always been ingrained in her mind. Perhaps she'd memorized it when he stood still, all those years ago, as his father slaughtered her family.

"Alora," he said, giving a slight nod. As he stood before her, she noticed the yellow flecks in his deep brown eyes. They shone with clarity and a slight bit of hesitation. Was the all-powerful leader wary of her? Impossible.

"What do you want?" she asked, fingers squeezing tighter on the metal bars.

"We don't have much time to discuss what I've come to say, so I need you to remain calm. I sent the guard to get coffee, but that will only take him minutes."

"What could you possibly have to say to me?" Scowling, she pushed her hatred down to the pit of her stomach, determined not to lose her cool in front of him. He was the only person who'd ever incited her to lose her meticulously cured control, and that frightened her to her core.

"Tanner wants to kill you. I've convinced him to let you live."

"On what terms?"

His lips quirked, causing her to note how full they were, set perfectly in his handsome face. For someone so evil, he was wickedly attractive. How categorically unfair and annoying.

"Tanner secured a successful marriage to Svetlana, and it has paid off handsomely. It helped the New Establishment attain domination over the European Isle. He wants to accomplish the same on the South American Isle. As you know, there are still many rebel factions there. The regime controls the major compounds but needs a respected native of the Isle to gain true acceptance."

Alora swallowed, her mind racing as she attempted to understand. "So Tanner wants to marry me too? The New Establishment is into polygamy now? I didn't see that one coming."

He breathed a laugh. "No, they haven't yet crossed that bridge as far as I'm aware."

"Then how...?" Realization swept over her, heavy and cold. "No," she breathed, nostrils flaring, as ice ran through her veins.

"I'm afraid so," he said, dropping his gaze before he lifted it back to hers. Running a hand through his thick black hair, his expression was deathly serious. "You're going to marry me, Alora."

A demented laugh sprung from her throat. Unable to control the strange reaction, her hands fell from the bars, and she crossed them over her stomach as the stilted, angry laughter pervaded the cell. Unable to believe he thought her capable of even considering the idea, she gazed at him in disbelief.

"You've got to be fucking kidding me."

"It's not ideal, but it's the best solution I could come up with," he said. "It will keep you alive so we can find the others. Then, hopefully, we can reconnect with Lainey, and she can transport you all to 2035."

Alora's arms dropped to her sides, limp and numb. Working her jaw, she tried to form words from her almost frozen body. Taking a stilted step forward, she stared deep into his eyes as she spoke in a low, rage-filled tone.

"You have the audacity to think for *one moment* that I would marry the man who stood by and let his father murder my family?" Grasping the bars, she asked through clenched teeth, "Are you insane?"

He gave a dismissive eye roll. "I don't have time for dramatics, Alora. It's the only solution we have. Otherwise, Tanner will kill you. He's already pissed you killed the soldiers when I raided the bunker during transport."

"Some double agent you are," she hissed. "You should've warned us—"

"Tanner showed up at the headquarters with Nelson in tow. I had no idea he would arrive so quickly after seizing the Australian Isle. I thought I had more time and was busy overtaking Solera. He threatened to attack the hub himself, and I urged him to let me instead. I had no choice."

"What if Lainey, Claire, or Cyrus died?" she asked, worried for her friends. "We have no idea where they are. And Marie is out there with Zach, Elle, and Sara. They're all alone. For someone who was supposed to protect us and be our ally, you did a pretty shitty job."

His eyes narrowed, and he leaned forward. Alora could feel his warm breath across her cheek as he spoke with restrained frustration.

"The others are still alive. So are you, but not for long unless we play their game, Alora. You need to marry me, and then we'll track them down. I've convinced Tanner you'll be helpful in the search."

Scoffing, she suppressed the urge to spit in his face. "I'll never hunt them like animals and turn them over to the regime."

"Of course not," he said, his expression maligned with a thousand shades of frustration. "We'll find them and hopefully reconvene with the others who traveled back. When I raided the hub, I gave the appearance of destroying the Sphere, but I secretly tried to leave it as intact as possible. With Zach's help, I think we can get it back online and send you all to 2035."

"And what about you? Tanner will kill you for your deception."

"Yes," he said, resignation crossing his face. "That will most likely be the end for me. I once thought I might have a chance at happiness in this timeline, but I understand now, that was never an option. My suffering is meant to prevent the suffering of many others. When death comes, I will die knowing this, and it will bring me peace."

Something strange curled in her gut, and Alora realized it was sympathy. The sticky feeling pervaded her bones as she stared at the man before her. She'd always seen him through one lens: demented, evil murderer. And then, only weeks ago, she'd learned he was a spy; someone who'd been approached as a child by Lainey and asked to embody evil so he could infiltrate the New Establishment and vanquish it. In effect, he'd never lived his own life. Eli had only ever lived the life dictated to him by Lainey.

"Why did you do it?" Alora asked softly.

Dark eyebrows drew together. "Do what?"

"Listen to her?" she asked, inching closer to gaze at him between the bars. "You could've said no and lived your life as a normal human being instead of a deranged psychopath. I don't understand your choice."

Mahogany irises darted between hers as he contemplated. "Lainey was very convincing. She came to me multiple times when I was seven, and on a few other occasions as I became a teenager. Eventually, I became embroiled in the cause. She relayed a genuineness that called to me. I'd never met someone with so much...*purpose*, and I wanted to be a part of it." Glancing down, he swallowed thickly, his Adam's apple bobbing under his olive skin. "I don't think I understood the gravity of the terrible things I would have to do when I took up the mantle. Once it set in, I was already on my way to becoming a respected figure in the New Establishment. My father cultivated me, and I strived to keep the line between good and evil from blurring. Sadly, I failed long ago."

"Yes," she whispered, unsure of why her voice was so gravelly.

"I can't change the past. In this timeline, at least," he said, shrugging. "All I can do is stay the course and try to save you and your friends. If Lainey prevents President Randolph's actions in 2035, the young version of me will hopefully live a better life, free of the grave misdeeds I've committed in this one."

A door hinge creaked in the distance, causing them both to snap their heads. Turning back to her, Eli said, "The ceremony will be tomorrow. This won't work without your full cooperation. You can remain resistant—after all, Tanner will be suspicious if you turn too easily. But he also understands your cunning nature and will believe you see an advantage to aligning with us to stay alive."

She gave him an incredulous look. "Eli, I'll never marry you. This is absurd."

Tentatively, as if he thought she might strike him, he slid his hand over the back of hers curled around the bar. His skin was slightly rough, causing her to shiver.

"It will be in name only, Alora. I know you detest me, but it's your only option. I would never force you to consummate the marriage or tolerate me in any capacity except to keep up appearances."

"I won't do it," she said, her vision blurring as wetness clouded her eyes.

"I'm sorry," he whispered, shaking his head. "It's the only way I can keep you alive. I'll be back tomorrow. You can dissent, but don't fight it. Remember to balance your emotions. Your hate is believable, but you're also fighting for your life."

"There has to be another way..."

Pulling back, his face resumed the unemotional mask she was used to seeing. "Enough. It's done. Be ready tomorrow." With a dismissive nod, he pivoted and stalked away.

A plethora of heavy emotions swamped her as she backed away from the bars. Rage, frustration, disbelief. Was this really what her life had become? Forced into marriage to the one person she despised above all others? A humorless laugh escaped her lips as she crouched to the floor, arms hugging her bent knees as the stark reality set in. Unable to process it, she rocked back and forth, attempting to find another solution...any solution.

For hours, she contemplated, praying to God to help her out of the mess she was in. Sadly, God was nowhere to be found, and the silence of the cell was her only response.

Chapter 3

Alora opened her eyes to the fresh morning sun. Although it was bright and airy, a sense of dread washed over her. Sitting up in her plush bed, she searched her bedroom. All seemed in order, from the canopy with flowing white fabric above, to the sounds of horses nickering outside. Throwing off the covers, she rose and donned her robe, tying the sash around her waist.

Tentatively, she walked toward her bedroom door, the creaking ominous as she slowly drew it open. Her father was speaking to someone outside, and she approached the open front door, her bare feet quiet on the wooden floor.

Peeking outside, she observed her father standing tall, chin thrust high under his thick black hair, as he addressed a man who listened with a scorn-filled expression.

"Our settlement is peaceful, Victor," her father said, his hand encircling her mother's wrist and slowly drawing her behind his body. It was a primitive form of protection, and Alora's heart began to pound. "We do not wish to fight the New Establishment. We just want to be left alone to raise our families in what's left of the world."

Victor's lips formed a cruel smile. "You were one of the youngest and most respected governors in Colombia before it was destroyed, Alejandro. People throughout the isle have a reverence for you and your family. It's why you've been able to build such a thriving compound. The New Establishment asks for your full allegiance. We require your help to bring our systematic rule to every person across the Isle."

"I don't believe in the principles of your regime, Victor. I do not wish to fight you, but I will not help you. In your quest to save the world, you destroyed it. All we want is to rebuild in peace."

Victor's head turned to address the man beside him. Barely a man, from Alora's observation. She guessed him perhaps seventeen or eighteen, the whiskers on his chin barely-there. His tall frame and broad shoulders mimicked Victor's, although his body was lanky.

"It's time to prove your loyalty, Eli," Victor said, motioning his head toward Alejandro. "If he won't align with us, he must die. Dissenters must be made examples of."

The gangly teen pulled his handgun from his belt and studied it, seeming to contemplate. Turning the weapon in his hand, he considered it for what seemed like a small infinity to Alora and then replaced the safety. Placing the gun back in the holster by his belt, he shrugged.

"If it's loyalty you wish to see, it would be more prudent for me to command the men to do my bidding." He tilted his head toward the men dressed in black who encircled them, most with rifles slung across their bodies. "Killing someone is easy. Commanding others to do it shows true power."

Victor's lips quirked. "Perhaps." Turning to face Alejandro, Victor pulled his own gun from his belt. Cocking it, he aimed it at her father's heart. "My son is still young and learning the ways of world domination. I am more resolute." Taking a step forward, he said, "Pledge your loyalty to the New Establishment, Alejandro. Just a few words. That's all it will take to save your wife and your three pretty daughters."

Her mother, Gloria, began to weep, and her father's fingers squeezed upon her wrist. The gesture was poignant, offering comfort in a severely untenable situation. Alora noticed her sisters frozen several feet behind her parents, hands joined as they seemed to accept their fates.

Alora's fingers clenched the door so fiercely her knuckles turned white. Would this man truly murder her family in cold blood? How had she gotten stuck in this terrible nightmare?

Alejandro shook his head, the motion slow and resigned. "I cannot pledge my loyalty to you, Victor. I would rather spend eternity with God above knowing I made the moral choice than lead an entire isle of people to follow a cause I know is corrupt."

Victor took one final step forward, his face a mask of resigned admiration. "Then you will die with honor, friend. I'm sorry it has to be this way. We will kill your family quickly, so they don't suffer."

"Thank you," Alejandro whispered, throat bobbing as he swallowed. Addressing Eli, her father said, "I see your struggle, son, and urge you to choose the light. Although darkness tries to prevail, the light will always carry you through."

Eli's spine was straight as he contemplated Alejandro in silence, a strange, invisible energy seeming to tether them together. Crying out in immense pain, Alora charged the scene, determined to save her family from slaughter.

Sadly, she was too late. Several pops sounded as she ran, and she collapsed over her father's body, her lungs failing to secure the oxygen she so desperately needed.

"Papi!" she cried, her hands stained red from the trails of blood she attempted to curb. Tears clouded her eyes as she crawled toward her mother, her brown eyes glassy as they stared back at her, lifeless. "Mami," she mewled, noticing her sisters' motionless bodies behind them before pulling her mother into a firm embrace. Cradling her, she rocked back and forth. Burying her face in Gloria's soft hair, Alora waited for her own imminent death.

"I'd give you the opportunity to shoot her, Eli," she heard Victor's muffled voice say, "but I'm disheartened by the sentiment in your eyes. I thought you'd gotten past this, son." Victor's tone was laced with slight annoyance. "Killing those that disagree with our cause is noble. Your mother's nature makes you weak. I'll remind you that you searched me out and begged me to bring you into the regime's fold. I was content to let you live the rest of your days with the worthless woman who bore you. Don't make me question my decision. I already doubt you are up to the challenge of assuming my mantle if any of our enemies succeed in killing me."

"Sometimes, letting your enemy live is more effective than murder," Eli said. "If we leave the princess here alive, she will spread the story of the New Establishment's desecration of her family across the Isle. Perhaps even across the world. It will bolster our cause more than one single death."

Silence stretched as Victor contemplated. Lifting the gun, he cocked it and aimed at Alora.

"Father," Eli said, striding forward and placing his body between Victor and Alora. "I've studied subjugation and warfare extensively. Let her live. I'm convinced her retelling of this day will cultivate more fear than her death. Trust me," he implored.

Lifting her head, Alora gazed up at Victor, the morning sun burning her tear-soaked irises.

The sinister man pushed his son aside and crouched. Sliding his fingers under Alora's chin, he violently grasped it when she tried to pull away. Holding her firm, he stared into her soul.

"My son has different perspectives on things than I," he said, eyes narrowing as he contemplated her. "But perhaps he is correct. I see the logic in letting you live. Go forth, little Alora, and spread my son's message to the world. Eli? What words should she take with her?"

Victor stood as Eli twisted to gaze down at her. Alora noticed his clear black pupils, as dark as the soul that must dwell within.

"People who defy the regime will always be made examples of, Alora." His voice was smooth and deep for someone still so young. "We're leaving you alive so you can spread the word to everyone on the Isle. If they resist the New Establishment, their family will die." Giving a firm nod, he pivoted and rejoined his men.

Victor shot her one last sneer and followed his son. The battalion climbed atop their horses and rode away, leaving Alora surrounded by the bodies of her family.

Throwing her head back, she gave a final wail, cursing God in heaven above, not caring that He would most likely punish her for it.

And then she stood, hands fisted at her sides as she stared down at the lifeless bodies.

"Mi niña," a soft voice said.

Alora flinched as a soothing hand stroked her arm.

"We must prepare the bodies and warn the others in the surrounding compounds. I'm so sorry, but now is not the time to grieve. That will come later."

"Later," she muttered, not even understanding how words could form on her lips when she was in so much pain. "Yes, I will destroy every man who was here today and every last person in the New Establishment. Only then will I allow myself to grieve. Thank you, Rosa," she said, facing the woman who'd helped raise her and her sisters. Rosa had been a fixture in her life for as long as she could remember. Part au pair, part house manager, and a fully adopted family member, Alora took solace that she had been left alive. At least there would be one person left to remember her family as she secured her revenge.

And revenge she would have. No matter the cost. There, under the blazing sun, she vowed to search the Earth until she found someone powerful enough to defeat Victor Hernandez and the New Establishment. She would align with them and stop at nothing to achieve her goal.

As Alora stewed in the intense agony, the sun was covered by darkened clouds, and she stared at her blood-soaked hands. Eyes narrowing in confusion, she slowly rotated them, not understanding why the red stains were slowly disappearing.

"Are you daydreaming again, Alora?" Lainey asked, smiling as she sat beside her in the clearing by the hub.

"Lainey?" Alora asked, confused. "How did I get here?"

White teeth flashed under her friend's smiling amber eyes. "I'm pretty sure you're dreaming. About the distant past, and now, the recent past. You're remembering why you found me and pledged your loyalty to my cause."

"Yes," Alora said, eyebrows drawn together as she combatted the strange sensation of being in a false reality. "You will prevent the rise of the New Establishment. I'm so honored to pledge myself to your mission." Training her gaze on Lainey, she asked, "Are you back in 2035? Are you going to come back for us? I don't care so much about me, but the others are in danger."

"I will do my best to find you all," Lainey said, clutching her hand. "Several are lost, and I fear we won't succeed unless we all find each other before we confront my grandfather."

"Cyrus and Claire?" Alora asked, worry snaking through her veins. "Are they with you?"

"Everyone is right where they need to be," her friend said, her tone calm and sure. "Even you."

"How can I marry him, Lainey? I hate him so vehemently."

"Your hate has the capability to fuel you and grow into much more. You have a deep capacity for love, my friend. Eli has never had a choice. I robbed him of one. It was selfish but necessary to save so many others. Your heart will come to understand this."

"I doubt that immensely."

Lainey's image began to fade, and Alora desperately clung to her hand. "What's happening? Please don't go."

"You're waking up, Alora. To a future you can't escape. It calls to you, and you must answer. I will see you soon. In this timeline or another."

With a gasp, Alora's eyes shot open. Jackknifing on the bed, she clutched her throat as she panted, realizing she was still in the dark cell of the prison beneath the New Establishment's headquarters.

And, whether she liked it or not, today was her wedding day.

Chapter 4

Eli threaded the comb through his thick black hair and tossed it onto the dresser. The chambers he inhabited at the New Establishment headquarters were as lavish as one could have in their sparse dystopian world. The bedroom had all the amenities he needed: a warm bed, basic furniture, and a large tub in the adjoining bathroom. Glancing at his reflection, he unbuttoned the top button of his collar, tugging it apart so he could breathe. Even though it was his wedding day, there was no reason for formality.

Perhaps because the woman he was marrying hated his guts.

For so long, Eli had convinced himself that he could be saved; that if he held onto a sliver of hope that goodness still dwelled in the deepest parts of his soul, he would one day deserve a wife and family. His mother, Ingrid, had instilled the traditional values in him when he was so very young.

"You're such a good boy, Eli," she would say, stroking his hair. "The light of my life. One day, you will have your own children, and you will understand the depth of my love for you."

Although he wasn't sentimental, Eli found himself mired in the memory. It was most likely spurred by the nuptial he would enter into in less than an hour. Although it was a sham, it incited an unwanted shaft of longing inside his blackened heart. He couldn't remember when the dream of having a family had died. Sometime over the past few years, when he realized the New Establishment was close to world domination. He'd committed so many terrible deeds to ultimately bring them down, and his hands would only get bloodier before their demise.

Blood-soaked hands had no place in the dreams he'd eventually discarded.

But still, he needed to marry Alora today. It would guarantee her safety and allow them to work together to find the others. Already, he'd begun putting pieces into place so they could travel unaccompanied by New Establishment soldiers to find the stragglers from the hub.

Was there a part of him that wished the alliance was real? That the stunning woman who so vehemently detested him would somehow see him worthy of her trust and admiration? Scoffing, Eli regarded his derisive expression in the mirror.

"Never going to happen, Hernandez. Get your head out of the clouds and your shit together, man."

Giving his reflection a nod, he straightened his spine, steeling himself for the confrontation that lay ahead. Alora was an extremely intelligent woman and most likely understood the gravity of her situation. She wouldn't refuse to complete the ceremony; that would get her killed. But there would be animosity in her stunning brown eyes as she said the vows that would tie them together for whatever time Eli had left on this godforsaken rock.

Exiting his chambers, his body pulsed in anticipation as he strode down the hallway to the compound's grand ballroom. There were never any balls held there, of course, but it was expansive, and that was what expansive spaces had been called before President Randolph destroyed the world. It would accommodate enough onlookers to complete the show and convince everyone that Alora was aligned with their cause.

She was an effective fighter and cunning strategist, known for her calm collectiveness in tense situations. Eli had heard stories of her ability to pull secrets from New Establishment soldiers for years. But when he'd confronted her at the hub weeks ago, the tight rein she held on her control had slipped. Her apple-ripe cheekbones had flared red, and her body had seemed to vibrate with anger. For someone like him, who was feared by so many, it was nice to be challenged. Repudiated. Engaged in passion. Oh, how passionate she'd been when she'd stared up at him with such scorn...

Eli was an excellent liar, but he couldn't lie to himself about one inexorably true fact: he was extremely attracted to Alora.

Not just her beauty—although it was undeniable—but her quick wit and crafty tongue were just as alluring. After such a tragic loss in her youth, she'd not only figured out how to survive, but how to thrive in their world while she searched for vengeance. She'd carved out a life that most others would've ended along with their families who lay slain beside them. It was admirable as hell, and Eli wished he'd been able to alter the past. Sadly, when he'd stood beside his father on that terrible day, he hadn't seen an opportunity to save them. But he'd figured out how to save her, and that had given his soul peace, if only a kernel.

And now, he'd saved her yet again. The infuriating woman should be kneeling before him, thanking him with unbridled enthusiasm. Instead, they would have a silent battle of wills during the ceremony. Of that, he was sure.

Smiling, he turned the corner and headed into the grand ballroom. The sight of Alora on her knees in front of him with her fingers laced, pleading, was something he'd never see. The image kindled a jolt of pleasure inside his chest. Truthfully, he loved her fighting spirit and would be extremely disappointed if she ever capitulated. No, the princess of the South American Isle was the perfect sparring partner.

Now, Alora on her knees in other ways...? he thought as he trailed to the makeshift altar at the far side of the room. With those full ruby-red lips open, her almond-shaped eyes swimming with lust as she begged for his cock? Yeah, that was definitely a vision he could get down with.

Realizing blood was now surging to his crotch, Eli closed his lids and told himself to get a grip. The likelihood of Alora begging him for anything was about as probable as them preventing the apocalypse. Even though they were still going to try. Good lord, they were all completely insane.

Once they were married, Eli and Alora would track down the others. Then they would attempt to put the Sphere back together and travel to 2035 to find Lainey and prevent the apocalypse. Eli was sure he'd be killed once his deception was discovered and carried no illusions about traveling back with Lainey's team. He was prepared to die knowing he'd committed far too many terrible deeds in this timeline. Hopefully, his younger self would grow up to be a vastly different man, free from the burden of saving the world. The man he wished he could be. A man who actually deserved a future.

"Eli," Tanner said, tilting his head. "Ready for the big event?"

"Ready as I'll ever be," Eli said, scanning the room.

Several men stood around the large room, all high-ranking officials in the New Establishment. They would all need to observe the nuptials to confirm the validity.

"Who ever thought I'd officiate your wedding? The two top generals in the regime, one officiating for the other."

Eli's expression remained stoic, a trait he'd perfected long ago. Tanner would love nothing more than the be the *only* general in the regime, but that wasn't the plan. Once the others were sent back to 2035, Eli would kill him. It would be the last act in a life marked with death before Eli conceded to his own demise. Inwardly contemplating the tasks ahead, he noticed something from the corner of his eye.

Turning, his gaze locked with Alora's. She wore a simple white dress that fell to her calves. Eli had instructed one of the soldiers' wives to lend her a dress and ensure she received a warm bath in the woman's chambers before the ceremony. The frock was so plain it should've been ugly, but never on Alora. Nothing would ever look unseemly when it adorned her luscious curves and smooth, creamy skin. Long black hair shone silky and glossy as it almost touched her waist. God, she was *magnificent.*

She gave the woman who'd escorted her a brief smile and headed toward the altar, head held high. Stopping to assess them, she said, "Hello, Eli. Tanner." She nodded to both. "Shall we proceed?"

"Your vows will require you to pledge your loyalty not only to Eli, but to the New Establishment. Are you prepared to speak them aloud?"

Her nostrils flared slightly as a raven-black eyebrow arched. "Yes."

Tanner's eyelids formed suspicious slits. "I won't tolerate dissention, Alora. I sense your displeasure. Although your father's name will carry influence in the South American Isle, your death would also be a stark reminder of our power."

"I am prepared to help you overtake the Isle. I believe it can be done relatively peacefully and with compassion, and I realize that will only happen if I am around to control the outcome."

Tanner scoffed. "Control is something you lost when Eli captured you in the hub. But it is true that people are more easily herded into submission when things are...*calm*. I don't care whether the Isle is taken with compassion or war—I just want every inch occupied. Although we control the main compounds, there are rebels that still fight for freedom. From what?" he asked, palms facing up as he shrugged. "We've won. Occupying the land is just a formality at this point."

"Then there is no need for more senseless death," Alora said. "I will be able to sway the rebels so we can prevent more desecration of human life."

"Fine," Tanner said, appearing as if he didn't give a damn either way. "Let us cement our alliance." He called to the other men, stepping toward the center of the room and waving them all toward the altar.

"He's going to make you pledge your allegiance in front of the men," Eli whispered. "I know how much your word means to you. Know that you lie for a good cause."

She glowered up at him. "Said by the best liar of all time."

"Why, Alora," he said, placing his hand over his heart, "you flatter me."

"It wasn't a compliment, *huevon*," she hissed as tiny flecks of spittle landed on the skin of his neck, spurring tingles of desire throughout his body.

"Careful. Good Catholic women aren't supposed to call their husbands assholes." He waited for puffs of smoke to exit her nostrils like it did from the bulls in the cartoons he'd watched as a child.

"Don't speak of religion when you're about to force me into this travesty. You're a wretch!"

"Is everything okay?" Tanner asked, having finally gathered the men around.

"Yes," Alora said, slinging her long hair over her shoulder. "Let's proceed."

"Here," Eli said, reaching toward the nearby table and picking up the bouquet he'd had prepared. "You can't get married without a bouquet. I think it's bad luck or something."

Sighing, she took the flowers and turned to face Tanner. "Bad luck. God forbid," she muttered, making the sign of the cross before clutching the bouquet above her abdomen.

Suppressing his chuckle, he stood by her side and proceeded to clearly state his vows so she would have a future. It was an easy price to pay to ensure her fiery light wouldn't be extinguished.

Chapter 5

Alora had never been so exhausted in her thirty-nine years on the planet. Stifling a yawn, she lifted the glass to her lips and drank another sip. The wine was good, being that they were now stationed in the large dining room of the massive compound, and she felt she deserved at least one decadent vice after today's fiasco.

Lifting her hand, she slowly rotated it so the simple gold band Eli had slipped on her finger glinted in the glow of the multitude of candles that adorned the table. She'd taken it off when she used the latrine earlier and had noticed a worn inscription on the underside that simply read "IH." Understanding they were initials, she wondered who'd given Eli the ring. Obviously, she would give it back to him once the sham marriage was over, but it actually looked quite pretty on her hand. Alora was always a sucker for pretty, shiny things and figured it wouldn't hurt to wear it to further the lie.

Glancing around the table, Alora noticed several of the men shooting Eli looks filled with undisguised lasciviousness. Revulsion curled deep in her gut when she realized they were urging him to take her to bed—with force if necessary. All the high-ranking members of the New Establishment were men, something that proved how short-sighted and stupid they all were. She'd been so lucky to find Lainey— who possessed the most brilliant mind on the planet—and the other women who comprised her team. She liked their chances against these idiots. Lust-filled men with a sense of false power and complacency. Alora couldn't wait to decimate their timeline and would revel in their deaths.

"It's time to head to my chambers," Eli murmured, glancing down at her. "Drink up, and let's go."

"To the happy couple," Tanner said, saluting them with his glass from the end of the table. "I was barely able to consummate my marriage on my wedding night, but I muddled through. Somehow, I don't think you'll have the same problem, Eli."

"It's a shame Svetlana couldn't be here to celebrate with us," Eli said, standing and offering Alora his hand. She took it only because she knew it would sow suspicion if she didn't.

"The woman is much happier on the European Isle, several thousand miles away from me. That's for damn sure," Tanner said, taking a huge gulp of wine. "Let's see a kiss between the newlyweds before you consummate the marriage."

Alora's eyes narrowed as vitriol for Tanner coursed through her veins.

"That's not necessary," Eli said. "My mother always taught me intimacies between partners should remain private. I'm a possessive man and trust you'll all remember that. Now that she is a Hernandez, Alora is under my protection, and I expect you to treat her with the respect I've cultivated in this regime."

Tanner rolled his eyes, drunk and sloppy. "Come on, Eli. One kiss won't hurt—"

Wanting to seize control, Alora gripped Eli's chin and jerked his head toward her. Lifting to her toes, she cemented her lips against his. They were surprisingly soft for a man who was so hardened inside.

It had been a while since she'd kissed a man, and her body sparked with desire. Unnerved by the unwanted reaction, she broke the kiss and stared at the surprise swimming in his eyes...along with a pulsing desire.

Alora was a confident woman and had learned the ways of seduction long ago. So her new husband was attracted to her? Good. She'd sure as hell find a way to take full advantage of that little nugget of information. He held the upper hand in their world and in their relationship, but she was determined to claim the higher ground.

"Well then, gentlemen," Eli said, clearing his throat. "Good night. I'll see you all at our meeting at oh-eight hundred hours."

They exited down the darkened hallway, Alora yanking her hand from his as soon as they were out of sight. In the dimness, she thought she saw him flex his fingers as if he missed her touch. The thought was absurd. Eli was a heartless bastard who had no propensity for feeling or emotion. Perhaps he was still racked by their kiss— after all, she certainly hadn't expected her body to jolt with arousal at the innocent peck.

When they reached his chambers, he closed the door behind them and opened the drawer of the nearby table. Pulling out some matches, he lit a few of the candles that adorned the surfaces in the sitting room.

"I can take the couch," he said, gesturing to it with his head. "You can have the bed. Figured you might want to sleep on something soft after all those nights in the cell."

Well, that was thoughtful. Rubbing her upper arms, Alora felt a sense of...hesitancy? Strange, since she was usually fearless.

"Thank you, but I don't want to put you out."

He smiled and blew out the match. "I've slept on surfaces much less appealing than this couch, believe me."

"As have I," she said, chin lifting. "And I insist. I don't want favors from you, Eli. This isn't a friendship or an acquaintance. This is two people who detest each other working toward a common goal."

Something flitted across his face. Was it sadness? Tough to tell in the glowing candlelight, but Alora convinced herself it couldn't be.

"What is your plan to locate the others?" she finally asked, uncomfortable with the silence that had blanketed the room. "We must go alone and try to send them back in the Sphere."

"Yes," Eli said, stuffing his hands in the pockets of his black pants. The gesture relayed a sense of defeat, as did the hunch of his broad shoulders. "I have a band of seven men who are extremely loyal to me. They're my most trusted soldiers. They were a team of ten until you shot three of them dead when I raided the hub."

"I was protecting my friends," she said, defensive.

"I know, but it would've been nice for you to give me the benefit of the doubt. I was going to shut down the Sphere and bring you all above ground. My men were going to tie the bonds too loose so that everyone could make a run for it."

"And how was I to know this?" she asked, lifting her hands in exasperation. "You stormed the bunker with armed men."

He took a measured step toward her. "Because I'm your ally, Alora. Lainey was clear. You have to trust me. That's the only way this will work."

She ran her hand through her hair, the long tresses spilling over her shoulder. "I'm sorry. I reacted impulsively. I always seem to around you."

"I've noticed," he said, inching closer. "Why do you think that is?"

She breathed an angry laugh. "Perhaps because you slaughtered my family when I was fourteen?"

"No," he said, slicing his hand through the air. "I didn't kill one person that day, Alora. My father slaughtered your family, and he would've murdered you too if I hadn't been able to sway him."

"Oh, so you are absolved of guilt then?" she asked, consumed by angry mirth. "An angel among us?"

"I am the wretch you accuse me of being," he said, a muscle ticking in his jaw, "but I won't let you accuse me of atrocities I didn't commit. Lord knows, I've committed enough on my own, and I don't need extras added to the tally."

"Whether you pulled the trigger or not, you're still a murderer," she said, realizing he was now close enough that she could feel the heat emanating from his muscular body. "No alliances or good deeds will erase your past. Monsters will always be evil, no matter how much they attempt to reform."

Thick silence stretched between them until he said softly, "I know." Dark irises roved over her face. "But in the meantime, before I burn in eternal damnation, I can help you and your team. Four of my men who are stationed at Solera will release forty rebel prisoners tomorrow. Those prisoners will fight to take back the compound. It will be futile, but it will give me the opportunity to convince Tanner to send every available soldier to Solera to reclaim the commune."

Alora's eyebrows drew together. "And you will ask him to let us go alone to find the others?"

"Yes," he said. "I'll convince him that the two of us can track them more efficiently on our own and that every man needs to be sent to Solera to ensure dominion over the compound. Once we find your team and return to the hub, hopefully, Zach can fix the Sphere and send everyone to 2035."

"And you'll stay behind?" she asked, not understanding why her throat tightened at the thought.

He nodded. "Someone has to destroy the Sphere for real once you all transport back. I can't have it fall into the New Establishment's hands. Especially since Tanner brought Nelson back from Australia with him."

"Is he okay?" Alora asked, consumed with worry for the kind scientist. "Did they leave Lorna behind?"

"Yes. She'll remain in Australia until Nelson helps Tanner. He was planning on taking Nelson to the hub soon to start harnessing the technology and rebuild the Sphere, but that will be delayed with the new unrest that will erupt at Solera."

"I'd like to see him before we go."

"No," Eli said, shaking his head. "It's too dangerous to look sympathetic toward him. You're aligned with the New Establishment now, Alora. You can't—"

"I get it," she interrupted, holding up her hand, palm facing him. Sorrow swept over her since she wanted so badly to comfort Nelson and let him know the others were okay. Well, most of the others. She had no idea about Lainey or Hunter, or Cyrus and Claire.

"I'm sure they're fine," he said, placing his hand on her upper arm to gently console her. "It's best we don't dwell on unknown possibilities. What's meant to be will be."

The slide of his palm against her skin was mesmerizing, causing Alora's heartbeat to quicken. He'd slithered into her space so skillfully, their breaths were now mingled. Warm and airy, his soft exhales glided over her face; made the hairs at the back of her neck prickle. Wet arousal coated her core, slick and warm. Mortified, she took a step back, breaking their touch.

"I don't need comfort from you. I'm tired and wish to rest."

His arm dropped to his side as he gave a resigned sigh. "Since you won't take the bed, let me at least get you something to sleep in. Be right back." He headed to the next room and returned holding a folded T-shirt and shorts. "They'll be too big for you, but they'll be comfortable. There's a blanket on the arm of the couch and a small latrine through that door there," he said, gesturing with his head. "Probably not as fancy as the functional bathrooms and indoor plumbing system you had at the hub, but it's serviceable."

"Thank you," she said, taking the garments, annoyed at the spark of fire she felt when their fingers brushed.

"If my plans succeed, we'll head out to find the others tomorrow. You might want to bathe in the tub when you wake since we'll be camping for the foreseeable future." With a slight nod, he pivoted and headed toward the bedroom. Halting, he turned, placing a hand on the doorframe as he spoke. "I don't wish to fight with you, Alora. I know you loathe me, but it will detract from our purpose. Hopefully, tomorrow, we can begin anew, with the anger of the past behind us. Once you're safe in 2035 and I'm long gone, you can hate me all you wish. Good night." The door closed softly behind him.

Feeling dismissed, Alora prepped for bed and admitted her new husband was right. Her antagonism was a waste of energy. Tomorrow would begin a new day in a world where she could no longer hate Eli Hernandez. The vow left a sour taste on her tongue as she tried to swallow it.

Chapter 6

Zach Bishop was out of his element—that was clear to anyone who observed him as he hiked alongside his companions. Sara was fierce as she stalked through the high grass, but the nurse had always been tough and practical. Marie was a force of nature as she stomped ahead, digging the base of her long walking stick into the ground with each alternating step and muttering to herself. Zach only heard every third word or so, but her speech consisted of alternating phrases such as, *"Stupid New Establishment bastards,"* and, *"Fucking asshole soldiers."* Somewhere close to eighty years old, Marie was an unstoppable whirlwind. She'd survived the apocalypse and was the most resilient person he'd ever met.

And then there was Elle. New to their composite family, she'd shown up a few days ago, and Lainey had deemed her an ally since she carried the letter Luke had sent through time warning them all of the dangers of the newly formed past. She was now part of their team and sequestered with them for the foreseeable future. She marched in silence beside him, her face an unreadable mask under her straw-colored hair. Pink lips sealed in a determined line sat below her pert nose and sky-colored eyes. They were perhaps the clearest hue of blue Zach had ever seen for the scant moments he'd stared into them. He found it difficult to maintain eye contact with the woman, mostly because his body seemed to enflame in a massive bout of raging hormones whenever she was near. It was extremely embarrassing, and he hoped like hell she couldn't sense the uncontrollable reaction.

Glancing at her from the corner of his eye, he convinced himself she had no idea. She must've sensed his gaze because her face tilted to his, and her lips curved into a heart-stopping smile.

"How are you doing?" she asked, her voice soft and sweet. "We've been hiking for hours."

"I'm fine," he said, returning her smile. "It will get dark soon, and then we'll have to find a place to camp."

"There are some woods about a mile ahead," Marie chimed in, back facing them as she led the group. "We'll camp there for the night."

"Sounds good, Captain Elders," Zach teased.

"Damn straight," Marie said with a huff. "I know this entire quadrant of the Isle better than any of those New Establishment soldiers. They'll never find us."

"How long until we reach the safe house?" Sara asked.

Lewis had set up a safe house years ago armed with supplies and rations in case they ever needed to flee the hub. It sat fifty miles east of Terrum and was extremely inconspicuous. Not even Nelson knew the location. Lewis had only given that information to Marie, Lainey, and Cyrus.

"Three days at least, considering the pace at which we're moving. You all need to get your butts in gear. I'm sure the bastards are already tracking us," Marie grunted as she dug her walking stick into the ground.

"Eli will find a way to help us," Elle said. "Lainey seemed firm in her trust of him."

"*Psst*," Marie said, waving her hand as she stomped ahead. "We'll see."

Zach uttered a chuckle at her muttering, and Elle smiled up at him. He was several inches taller and it made him feel a protective tug toward her.

"She's something else."

He nodded in response, his cheeks warming from their extended eye contact. Feeling like a dolt, he glanced toward the ground.

They lapsed back into silence and continued on their path.

Zach hadn't met many people in his life, and although he was comfortable with his family at the hub, he felt shy and gangly around Elle. What did she think of him? Although she was only three years younger, she'd experienced so much more than Zach during his twenty-seven years. Did she think him incredibly boring?

A sigh must have escaped his lips because she glanced up and gave him another encouraging smile. For the first time in his life, Zach felt the tug of desire, whether he was ready for it or not. Completely unable to combat the confusing feelings, he forged on, deciding he'd like to examine the new sentiments. It could be an experiment of sorts, and he understood experiments quite well. In order to do that, he'd have to stay alive.

Resolved to be useful on their journey, he decided he would build the fire to keep everyone warm once they set up camp. Since they'd escaped the hub during an ambush, they hadn't been able to grab any supplies. Zach wasn't a skilled survivalist, but he did understand science. Generating a fire was as easy as sparking a flame near kindling and flooding it with oxygen. Yes, he could find ways to be helpful on their journey.

Feeling his eyes dart to Elle again, he wondered if she would be impressed. Deciding there was only one way to find out, he tasked himself with building the most extraordinary fire ever lit once they finally made camp.

Chapter 7

The morning after the wedding, Eli bathed and prepared for the impending events in the large bathroom that adjoined his bedroom. His thoughts drifted to Alora, wondering if she was also using the tub that sat in the smaller latrine connected to the main room. Images of smooth, wet skin and curved hips flashed through his mind, and he scowled into the reflection as he shaved. Pushing them away, he concentrated on the mission at hand. If everything went according to plan, this would be his last shave under a roof for a while. His soldiers were set to surreptitiously release the Solera captives within the hour. Once that occurred, he and Alora would begin the quest to find the members of Lainey's team.

Dressed in black tactical gear, comfortable yet functional, Eli packed his supplies: a small tent, food rations he'd gathered from the compound's large kitchen, water, matches, a small blanket, a knife, and his Glock. Rotating it in his hand, he relished the security it instilled. Victor had given him the gun when he'd first joined the New Establishment decades ago. The evil men who formed the regime had systematically begun gathering all the firearms left on the planet, striving to build a complete arsenal. His father had trained him to always be armed—perhaps one of the lessons that, ironically, had hurt the least.

Slightly opening the door, Eli called to Alora. Not wanting to invade her privacy, he spoke through the crack.

"I'll be out in five minutes. Expect someone to show up at the door within the next ten minutes with news from Solera. I'll head to the conference room and convince Tanner to let us venture solo."

"I'll be ready," her sultry voice replied.

Even if the woman wanted to sound boring and staid, Eli realized it was impossible. That thick, honeyed tone with her lilting accent could inspire every man's wet dreams. Annoyed he couldn't stop thinking licentious thoughts about the vexing woman, he finished gathering his belongings, ready to leave the dreary headquarters behind.

A loud knock reverberated through the entire chamber, and Eli yanked open the bedroom door. Glancing at Alora, who was dressed in the black pants, boots, and tank top she'd been captured in—now freshly washed—he asked, "Ready?"

She gave a firm nod, and he stalked toward the chamber door, pulling it open. "Captain Parker," he said, addressing the soldier. "What's wrong?"

"There's been an uprising at Solera. Several Insurgency soldiers escaped, and the compound is in chaos. Tanner needs to see you."

"I'll be right there."

The gruff man gave a tilt of his head and pivoted to walk down the hallway. Turning to Alora, Eli said, "I think the meeting will be brief. Once the orders are given, we'll head out."

"I don't have any rations," she said.

"One of the staff is preparing a pack for you, and mine is stocked with food and gear. I'm also a pretty competent forager and can identify plants and berries for us to eat along the way."

Her thick eyebrow arched. "The prince of the New Establishment, a forager? I thought Victor would've assured you had underlings to do that task for you."

"Says the princess of the South American Isle," he murmured, giving her a droll look. "We've both had to learn clandestine skills to ensure our livelihoods. Don't prejudge my abilities, Alora. You'll be severely disappointed. I've only been able to count on myself, and that means I know many things others don't."

Something glinted in her expression before it disappeared. When she remained silent, he said, "See you in a few."

She nodded, crossing her arms over her chest to rub them. The action caused a protective swell in his chest, and he accepted that he felt a calling to defend her. Denying it was futile, and keeping her alive had many advantages since she was tough and experienced. His need to keep her safe would also assure his well-being, so he'd allow the vapid emotion even though it was unwanted.

Stalking down the hallway, Eli entered the meeting room, noticing a red-faced Tanner standing by the conference table.

"Those fucking rebel bastards," he grunted, running his hand through his thick brown hair. "I thought we had them secured."

"They were, sir," Captain Parker said. "I have no idea how they escaped. Each one was bound and kept separate from the others."

"It's possible we have a defector in our ranks," Eli said, wanting to float the idea before anyone else could. He'd learned through experience that if one postulated the idea of treason, they were much less likely to be accused of it themselves. "Perhaps the men we left behind weren't as loyal as we thought. This is disheartening, Captain Parker. You gave me your word the compound was under complete control."

"I swear, Commander Hernandez," Parker said, urgent earnestness in his tone, "I thoroughly vetted the men we left behind. If we have dissenters, they're not any of the men I deputized."

"Tough to believe if we have an uprising," Eli said, his tone harsh. "Perhaps we should throw you to the rebels to murder in the main square at Solera as a reminder that soldiers who fail the New Establishment will not be tolerated."

Captain Parker straightened. "Commander Hernandez, I assure you—"

"Enough," Tanner said, slicing a hand through the air. "At this point, we need all the men we have, even those who fail." He shot Parker a glare. "How soon can we get soldiers to the compound to stop the uprising?"

"We can march in ten minutes, sir."

"Fine," Tanner said, giving a gruff sigh. "Round them up, and Eli and I will address them before you leave."

Captain Parker gave a nod and trekked from the room.

"His incompetence is unacceptable, Tanner."

"Yes, but we need him. If we lose Solera, that will set us back months. Hopefully, we can reclaim it without too much effort."

Eli tilted his head. "I can march with the men to Solera if you wish."

"No," Tanner said, shaking his head. "I'll lead the men there. You need to find the rest of Dr. Randolph's team. Although you left some men to guard the hub, it will be disastrous if the scientists somehow repair the Sphere and travel back. She's much stronger with her full team. You and Alora should locate them and take care of them while I run things at Solera."

Perfect, Eli thought. "All right. We'll head out after you and I address the troops."

"Good." Tanner rubbed his forehead. "Do you truly think we have dissenters in our ranks? I thought everyone left was aligned with our cause. We've worked decades to reach this point and suppress the weak."

"If we do, we'll find them," Eli said, patting the man's shoulder. "And we'll murder them."

Tanner's lips formed a cruel smile. "For all to see, my friend. I'll murder every traitorous bastard I find. Nothing will inspire greater loyalty."

"Agreed," Eli said, still repulsed, after all these years, to be associated with men so evil. "Let's get to it then."

Together, they strode to address the troops before sending them to reclaim the compound.

* * * *

Alora and Eli set out on their journey, resolute to find the others. Although she still doubted his true intentions, she admitted he'd been kind so far. The bag upon her back had been packed by one of the servants at the headquarters, complete with supplies, clothes, and basic food like beans and homemade granola bars. Eli had ensured its preparation, causing her to admit he might not be the manifestation of Satan on Earth. Perhaps just his minion.

Lips twitching at the inner thoughts, she remembered the other kindnesses he'd bestowed so far. The bouquet he'd given her during their ceremony was beautiful, although she'd never admit that to him. What had possessed him to instigate the sentimental gesture? It seemed out of place for the stoic nature he projected.

Staring down at the ring she wore, she wondered about the warm metal as well. His expression had been thoughtful as he'd slipped it onto her finger. Did it symbolize something to the murderous leader of the New Establishment?

"What does 'IH' stand for?" she asked, unable to squelch the curiosity.

"Ingrid Hernandez," he said, lips forming a curt smile as he trailed beside her. "My mother."

"Oh," she said, stretching her fingers to gaze at the trinket. "It must hold meaning for you. I can take it off now that we're off the compound." When she reached to slide it off, he placed his hand over hers, stilling the action.

"Leave it. Please," he said, squeezing her hand. "My mother always wished I'd find a wife to wear it. I think she was hoping for a love match, never realizing that aspiration was wasted on someone like me. It would give her solace to know it's being worn by someone like you."

Feeling uncomfortable, her eyebrows drew together. "Someone like me?"

"Strong. Intelligent. Beautiful." He shrugged, gripping the straps of his backpack. "Chances are, you're the only woman who will ever wear it. Might as well fulfill some part of her wish."

"I can't," she said, reaching to remove it again.

"Please, Alora," he said, his tone soft and sad. "Just wear the damn thing. I saved your life twice. The least you could do is help me honor my mother's wishes."

Studying the trinket, she contemplated. Sighing, she nodded, deciding it didn't matter one way or the other whether she wore it or stuck it in her bag, so why not just wear the damn thing?

"It's very pretty. Simple. It fits my finger perfectly, actually."

"Good. It looks nice on you."

Alora had been complimented by many men in her life. Strong men. Drunk men. Sweet men. Savage men. Their compliments usually floated through the air, dismissed by her the moment they passed the giver's lips—which made her suddenly rapid heartbeat all the more perplexing. For some incalculable reason, the succinct comment tossed her way by the enigmatic man set her pulse aflutter. Deciding she was most likely going insane from her recent captivity, she pushed the unsettling feelings back into the pit of her stomach, determined to dismiss them.

They hiked for hours, setting the pace for what would be a physically taxing journey.

"I think we can locate them in a matter of days."

"Agreed," Eli said. "Do you know the exact location of the safe house?"

"No. Lewis only told Lainey, Cyrus, and Marie. But I heard enough to know it's somewhere north of the hub and east of Terrum. As we get closer, we should be able to pick up their trail and follow them easily enough."

"Bet you never thought you'd spend several days hiking the Isle with me, much less as my wife."

"My darling husband," she said, the words dripping with sarcasm as she blinked up at him, "I could never even begin to dream such a nightmare."

He huffed a laugh. "It won't be for long. Once you all travel to 2035, you'll be rid of me."

Alora remained silent, wondering why he was so dead set on ending his life in this timeline. The defeatist attitude went against everything she'd convinced herself about Eli. Was that truly his endgame? Did he have nothing to live for once Lainey's team successfully traveled back to 2035? Frustrated at the swirling thoughts, she forged ahead, reminding herself she didn't give a damn about Eli Hernandez's motivations.

<h1 style="text-align:center">Chapter 8</h1>

Elle studied Zach in the light of the fire he'd built. She'd overheard him telling Marie he wanted to build something large, but she'd urged him to make a small one since it would lessen their chances of being discovered. They'd settled into a dense thicket in the woods, and Elle felt they were safe for the night.

Regardless, she'd offered to keep watch while the others slept. Elle was an insomniac and didn't sleep more than a few hours a night anyway, so keeping watch was a welcome pastime. It gave her a purpose in the group, which she sorely needed because she was desperate to prove her trustworthiness. Traveling back to 2035 was an integral part of her plan, and the team needed to trust her in order to make that happen.

Zach shuffled next to her, hands crossed behind his head as he stared up at the darkened trees. Shifting her focus to him, she studied his tall frame in the dimness. Every so often, his lids would blink over his light green eyes, and she surmised he was lost in deep thought.

"You're not tired?" she asked softly, not wanting to rouse the others.

Grinning as his gaze found hers, he shook his head. "I should be, but I'm restless."

"You did a good job on the fire."

His pale cheeks reddened, causing her to wonder if she'd ever met a man who blushed. Most men she'd encountered in her twenty-four years had been devoid of innocence and empathy. But this man, with his soft demeanor and genius intellect, seemed so gentle. It was perplexing to Elle as she'd convinced herself men were inherently incapable of treating women with genuine kindness in their dystopian world filled with war and power struggles.

"Thanks," he said, rolling over to rest his head on his palm, elbow digging into the ground. "I want to try and pull some weight around here. I've really only ever been good at science, but I'm not sure how handy that is when your main goal is survival."

"I'd say it's really handy, actually. Science is the genesis of everything, isn't it? Without that, we'd be screwed."

His resulting smile was so bright it sent a warm rush of pleasure through her body. "Why, Elle, if I didn't know better, I'd say you were a science dork."

She bit her bottom lip, unable to control her grin. "My grandfather Will became enthralled by science once he met Luke. He passed down several books to my mother by Einstein, Hawking, Gott, deGrasse Tyson, and others. I found the theories fascinating."

"Those are some impressive physicists for sure," he said. "Have you read Michio Kaku? He published some really great books. There's one on parallel worlds that blew my mind."

"I haven't heard of him," she said, shaking her head as she trailed a stick through the dirt at her side. "Maybe I'll find a library in 2035 where I can get my hands on his books."

"In the meantime, I've got it catalogued here," he said, tapping his temple. "Want me to tell you about it?"

She nodded, excitement humming in her veins. She found abstract scientific principles like parallel universes, string theory, and time travel fascinating. If she lived in a different world, perhaps she would've been a scientist like Zach. Instead, much of her life had been lived with one goal in mind: *survival.* Would that change for her if they prevented President Randolph's actions in 2035? Not likely. There was a singular goal she was meant to accomplish in that timeline and having dreams of anything else was pointless. But still, it was a nice thought on the breezy late summer night as she sat beside the kind man she was coming to like very much. Listening to his melodious honeyed voice, she let herself be lulled by Zach's science stories.

And when he eventually nodded off, she reached over to gently brush a lock of his shaggy dirty-blond hair away from his eyes, compelled to touch him for just a moment. Wrapping her arms around her bent legs, she rested her chin on her knees, comforted by his soft snores beside her.

* * * *

Alora and Eli set up camp long after the sun had set behind the distant hills. Proud of the progress they'd made, she felt certain they'd locate the rest of the team soon. After starting a small fire, they sat in silence eating semi-warm beans from their packs. Alora was comfortable with silence and had no desire whatsoever to speak to Eli, so she was shocked to find conversational words escaping her lips, almost as if they had a will of their own.

"How long since you've seen Ingrid?"

His gaze flew to hers from where it had been fixated on the fire. Chewing, he stared at her, expressionless.

"Your mother?" she asked as if he was daft. "The owner of this lovely ring?" Holding up her hand, she wriggled her fingers, the band flashing in the flickering light.

"I saw her at her funeral in 2059."

Well, damn. She hadn't seen that one coming. *Awkward.* Clearing her throat, she said, "Well, I sort of meant the last time you saw her alive, but we'll go with that. Sorry to hear of her passing. How did she die?"

Finished with the dish, he set it on the ground and leaned back on his palms. "Her body deteriorated, most likely from cancer, although we didn't get an official diagnosis. I wasn't there when she died. Too busy sowing the seeds of evil." His lips twitched, although the gesture was humorless. "I would say that I regret not holding her as she slipped away, but I stopped counting regrets several years ago. The weight of the burden was smothering."

"It sounds like you loved her," she said, tracing her fingers through the grass beside her own now-empty bowl.

"Very much. Perhaps the only person I've ever loved. And certainly, the only person who's ever loved me."

Excruciating sadness pressed against every inch of her body. "What about your father?"

His scoff was harsh. "Victor was never a father to me. He saw my potential, and I exploited his vision so I could accomplish my goal."

"But he was your blood. That must account for something."

"Blood only matters when one has a heart to circulate it. His heart was dead for many years before I was born. As he aged, his rage and mental instability grew exponentially until he was a shell of a man. I didn't mourn his death."

"He died outside Terrum," she said, recalling the tales she'd uncovered from various soldiers during her reconnaissance missions.

"Yes," he said, nodding. "No one really knows exactly what happened. His body was found near the riverbank that flows outside the compound. Such a small whimper of a death from a man who hurt so many."

Shivers crossed her skin as the memories of her family's murder flashed through her mind.

"I'm so sorry, Alora," he said, the tone of his voice deep and reverent. "I know the words won't bring them back, and they're really quite pointless, but I figured I needed to say them at least once. Out loud. So you've at least heard them and can toss them away."

Wrapping her arms around her updrawn legs, she rested her cheek on her knees. "You're right. The words mean nothing."

Sighing, he crossed his legs in front of him, one ankle over the other, as they settled into the uncomfortable silence.

Eventually, she grew tired and washed their bowls with a damp towel. Spreading it by the dying fire to dry, she stood and walked toward the tent Eli had packed for her. He didn't have to do it—married couples usually shared tents after all—but he'd given her his word that the marriage would be in name only, and so far, he'd stayed true to that promise. Which was perhaps why she felt compelled to speak the soft words to him before she closed her tent to sleep.

"Eli?"

"Hmm?" Black eyebrows lifted as those dark eyes locked with hers.

"The words mean nothing, but I appreciate them anyway. Good night." Unable to look at the raw sorrow that permeated every feature of his handsome face, she drew the tent closed.

As the songs of crickets surrounded her, she began to realize something quite profound: Eli Hernandez possessed compassion. Although not extraordinary for most people, it was such an unexpected trait in the man who'd hurt so many.

"*Carajo,*" she muttered, punching the blanket she was using as a pillow. Telling herself to go to sleep, she forced her eyes closed, but the image of Eli's striking expression remained, blazing in her busy mind.

* * * *

Tanner Cross backhanded the Insurgency soldier across the face. "Tell me how you escaped! I won't ask you again."

The man licked his bloody lip. "Never! I'll never say one word to New Establishment scum like you!"

Eyes narrowed, Tanner lifted his gun and aimed high so the other men beside him could see. They were lined up outside Solera, four Insurgency soldiers Captain Parker's men had captured. "One last chance," Tanner said, his finger tightening on the trigger. "Who freed you?"

The man attempted to spit on the ground—tough because his teeth were now situated haphazardly in his mouth from the assault—and Tanner pulled the trigger. The man fell to the ground, still and lifeless.

Stepping toward the next soldier in line, Tanner held the gun high. "I don't have the patience for rebels," he said, noticing the sweat trailing down the man's dirty forehead. "Five seconds, soldier—"

"It was Eli Hernandez," the man said, shoulders slumped in defeat. "He's a spy. I'll tell you everything if you promise to let me live. My wife is pregnant up at Terrum, and all I want is to ensure her safety."

Tanner's face remained a calm mask although he raged inside. Something had been off with Eli recently, but Tanner had dismissed it. Furious he hadn't listened to his gut, he clenched his jaw, vowing to gather every speck of information from the soldier.

"You'll tell me everything?"

"Yes." The man gave a terse nod.

Turning, Eli shot the other two Insurgency soldiers between the eyes. Facing the soldier, he grabbed his arm and dragged him forward.

"Everything, soldier, or you'll share their fate. Do you understand?"

"Yes, sir."

Over his shoulder, he addressed Captain Parker. "We'll interrogate him together. Then we'll send a small faction to locate Eli, Alora, and the others and kill them. Once we reclaim Solera, we'll march toward the hub. Understood?"

"Yes, Commander Cross," Parker said.

"Good. We must move quickly. I want men who can cover a massive amount of ground, so the two groups aren't reunited. It will be easier to kill Eli and Alora separate from the rest of the group."

"I know just the men, sir."

"Good. Let's go. Take this traitor to the tent. I'll be there shortly."

As Captain Parker dragged the soldier away, Tanner addressed the troops, directing some of the men to dispose of the bodies. Pivoting, he headed to question the soldier before killing him. He didn't give a damn about the man's wife—traitors deserved to die a painful and arduous death.

His lips curved into a sinister smile. With Eli out of the way, Tanner would achieve true supremacy as leader of the New Establishment. The possibilities of his dominion over the Isles would be limitless. Already reveling in his newfound glory, he stepped into the tent, ready to learn every detail of Eli's deception.

Chapter 9

Alora and Eli trudged on, each day more grueling than the last, although she was determined not to give an inch. So what if she was exhausted? She had been kept in a cell for several days before beginning their trek and had lost some weight, which meant her body had less fat to burn. The meager meals they were eating weren't helping much either. Too many more days of this, and she'd begin eating her own arm just to get some meat.

"Look," Eli said, jarring her from her thoughts. Striding over, she noticed the banked ashes where a fire once burned.

"They were here," she whispered excitedly.

"Yes," he said, crouching down and rubbing the ashes between his fingers. "Still wet, which means they must've doused it with water this morning or last. We should catch up with them by tomorrow if we keep up our pace."

"Come on," she said, tightening her grip on the straps that hung over her shoulders. "I can go several more hours."

He glanced toward the sky. "The sun's already set. Aren't you tired?"

"I can sleep in 2035. Let's keep going."

Concern swam in his eyes. "Okay, but if you need a break, tell me."

With a firm nod, she pivoted and followed the trail the others had left behind. Their path was easy for an experienced surveyor such as Alora to spot. Broken sticks and pushed aside brush laid out their path. She'd have to remember to tease Marie when they reconnected about how sloppy the trail was.

They eventually made camp, only getting three hours of sleep. Resuming the pace, they continued north until Eli halted and placed a hand on her arm.

"Hear that?" he whispered.

Her ears perked as she heard the low-toned sound. Recognizing it immediately, her eyes grew wide. "It's Zach!" Elated at the sound of her friend's voice, she began jogging toward the riverbank, heart racing in anticipation of seeing him. When she came to the edge of the forest, she drew up short, holding up her arm as Eli almost plowed into her from behind.

"What are you—?"

Silencing him, she clamped her hand over his mouth. Jerking her head, she gestured toward the river.

His eyelids stretched open as he beheld the scene before him: Zach was shielding Elle, her small body pushed behind his, as three New Establishment soldiers held them at gunpoint.

Eli recognized the soldiers immediately. "They're Tanner's men," he murmured in her ear, so close she could feel the anger emanating from his firm body. "Son of a bitch, he must've sent them on his own."

"Which means he doesn't trust you," she said, turning her face toward his. If they were any closer, their lips would brush, and Alora wondered if her frenzied breaths were from his nearness or the danger her friends were in. Most likely both. *Mierda.*

"Better we find out now. Here," he said, handing her the gun holstered at his waist. "I'll try to get the jump on them and disarm them. Hopefully, I can get a hold of one of their rifles. If not, start shooting."

* * * *

Eli thrust the gun at Alora, and for once, the spirited woman didn't argue with him. Giving a nod, her eyebrow arched.

"What if I accidentally shoot you?"

Although the situation was in no way amusing, Eli couldn't stop his short laugh. "Just don't stomp too hard on my grave."

She huffed. "I don't make promises I can't keep."

Fuck, she was gorgeous. Eli had no idea what prompted his next move. Perhaps it was the knowledge he was heading to his possible death. Perhaps it was just pure, unadulterated lust. Grasping the back of her neck, he pressed his lips to hers, cementing them together. She was hard and soft at once, her body stiff. Drawing back, he slid his thumb over her flushed lower lip.

"Make sure I stay alive, and maybe next time, we can kiss each other at the same time, without one of us making a drastic move."

She shoved him, and he sensed her annoyance that he held firm. "I'd rather kiss a rabid dog."

"Liar," he breathed, tracing the pulsing vein on her neck that proved her words false. Releasing her, he stepped into the clearing. Lifting his hands, he called to the men. "Halt!" he said, forming a fist in the air. "By whose orders are you here?"

Two of the men turned, training their guns at Eli, while one remained pointed at Zach and Elle. "We're here on Commander Cross's orders, sir. He told us not to stand down even if ordered by you."

"Of course he did," Eli said, rolling his eyes in an attempt to downplay the differing orders as nothing more than a misunderstanding. "Tanner is new to this isle and doesn't understand the power dynamics. I assure you, I am still leader and will shoot any dissenters. Are you sure you want to disobey my orders?"

The men warily eyed each other. "Sir, we don't wish to disrespect you, but Commander Cross did say you would try to assert authority if you found us. We have been given direct orders not to obey you, and we will take you into custody if we must."

"Hmm..." Eli said, inching closer while keeping his hands held high. "With those rifles? It seems yours doesn't even have the most lethal magazine, soldier."

The man closest to him glanced at his gun, his arms relaxing a bit, giving Eli the opening he needed. With lightning-quick speed, he grabbed the rifle by the barrel, yanked it from the soldier's hands, and rammed the butt against his temple, sending his limp body to the ground. All his combat training came back in a flash as he aimed the gun at the remaining two soldiers.

"I used to fight ten men at a time," Eli said, confident and strong. "There's a reason I rose to prominence in the New Establishment. I'm a lethal killer and have no qualms about unleashing that skill on you. Now, you can lay down your weapons, or you can die today. Your choice. I assure you, if you surrender, no harm will come to you."

The two men glared at each other, wordlessly communicating. Defying Eli Hernandez was a dangerous decision in their world, which was probably the only reason he wasn't dead yet. Eli had worked hard to cultivate his reputation. Years of killing and torturing when needed, always for an audience, so tales of his malevolence would spread. Each action taken was a brick in the carefully built structure that defined him: hated, malicious dictator. Each instance was crafted so it would have enormous impact and disseminate across the barren planet. Fear was his commodity, and the world had consumed it voraciously.

And now, fear kept his enemies' fingers frozen. "Well?" he asked, his tone impatient. "I'm not going to stand here all day."

He could tell who the leader was: the man closest to him, for sure. His broad shoulders carried a confidence and bravado the other younger soldier didn't yet possess.

The older man lifted his rifle, aiming it at Eli.

The next series of events happened so quickly, Eli would barely be able to recall them afterward. Alora emerged from the forest and yelled, "Shoot him!" Heeding her words, he shot the man in the chest as Alora lodged two bullets in the shoulder and knee of the younger soldier. Both dropped to the ground, but the leader regained his wits and opened fire on the clearing.

"Run to the woods!" Eli yelled to Zach and Elle.

Zach nodded, grabbing her hand as they both darted toward the forest. Alora stood at his side, aimed his Glock, and shot the leader between the eyes. Walking over to his lifeless body, she spat on it. The original soldier Eli had wounded groaned below her. Pointing the gun at him, she shot him in the upper arm.

"Aaaaargh!" he screamed, clutching the bleeding would. "You bitch!"

"Careful, *viejo*," she said, glaring down at him. "Or you will end up like your friend here. You can still walk and will need to carry the young one to Terrum for medical treatment since I blew out his knee. Consider yourself lucky I'm leaving you alive."

"Tanner will kill us for our failure," he moaned, writhing on the ground.

"Tanner is a false leader," Eli said, crouching beside the man. "Do yourself a favor and join the Insurgency once you make it to Terrum. Break the prisoners free and help lead a revolution. It's the only hope of creating a better life for those you hold dear. Now, get up."

The soldier struggled to stand while Alora collected their rifles. With great effort, he lifted the younger soldier, threw the man over his arm, and slowly carried him from the riverbank.

"The second they get to Terrum, they'll send soldiers to kill us."

"Yes," Eli said, facing her. "We need to get back to the hub as soon as possible."

Nodding, she stared down at the dead soldier. "Should we bury him?"

"It's probably better if we cremate the body," Zach said behind them.

Alora's face contorted with joy as she turned and threw her arms around him. "Zach!" She hugged him so tight Eli could see the air *whoosh* from the man's lungs.

"Hey, Alora," he said, twisting back and forth as they embraced. "Man, I'm so glad you're okay. Thanks for saving our asses. Elle and I were thirsty, so we came to drink from the river. *Really* bad idea," he said, making a derisive face.

"Thank you, Alora. And Eli," Elle said, craning her head to look between both of them. "That was pretty awesome timing."

"Where are the others?" Alora asked, drawing back from Zach's embrace. "Are they okay?"

"Sara and Marie are both fine. We're camping in a clearing about fifty yards that way. Come on."

Eli held out his hand, offering to carry the rifles Alora held. She handed him one but kept a close grip on the other.

"I think I'll keep this one, just in case. You can't be too careful."

Her eyebrow arched above those cinnamon-colored eyes, making Eli grow stiff in his tactical gear. Adrenaline buzzed through his body, and he could still taste her on his lips. The combination was intoxicating.

"Let's go," he muttered to Zach, although his gaze was fixed on his wife's. "I'll come back with you to take care of the body once we reconvene with the others."

Solemn and resolved, they followed Zach to the campsite.

* * * *

Once the soldier's body had been disposed of, with prayers murmured by Alora, the team sat around the campfire regaling stories of their past days. Everyone was shocked to find Eli and Alora married, but they understood the circumstances that led to the union. Alora made it very clear the marriage was in name only, although she didn't outright profess her hatred for Eli. Perhaps they were making progress.

Under the blanket of stars, they discussed their next moves. Since they were only a day's journey from the safe house, they decided it was best to navigate there and collect supplies. Once that task was complete and they were fully armed and stocked, they could begin the trek back to the hub to repair the Sphere and travel to 2035.

"I'm still not sure we can trust this one," Marie muttered with an angry tilt of her head toward Eli. "You're the one that got us here, boy."

Eli grinned, wishing his soldiers had half her gumption. "I did, although it wasn't my choice. Tanner showed up at the headquarters with Nelson, and I had to think on my feet. I have every confidence Zach can repair the Sphere and will do my best to ensure you all make it to 2035 safely."

"You're not planning to come with us?" Sara asked.

Eli shook his head. "It's best I stay here and destroy the Sphere after you've traveled. Tanner needs to be eliminated, and I'm the best person to do it."

"If you stay behind, you're cementing your death too," Marie said.

"Yes," he said, arm dangling over his upturned knee as he leaned back against a log. "I'll go out on my terms. It's a choice I can be proud of. I've made so many choices that were lined with complexities and harmed so many. At least this one will do some good."

"A choice your mother would be proud of," Alora chimed in softly.

Eli nodded. "I'd like to think so."

The circle grew quiet as the embers of the fire faded, and eventually, they slept. Now that Tanner's men were onto them, they decided someone should keep watch while they slumbered. Alora volunteered, and Eli tried to get some sleep. Difficult, because he felt her gaze on him as he stared at the sky, head resting on his palms beneath his head.

"You're staring at me, dear wife," he chided softly, not wanting to wake the others.

"I don't understand you," she said, her voice quiet as it stretched over them. "And I am deeply disconcerted by things I don't understand."

Turning his head, he gazed into her cavernous eyes. "I think it makes me happy to hear you say that."

"You think?"

He gave a slight shrug. "Happiness isn't really an emotion I understand, so I'm not one hundred percent sure."

Long black lashes seemed to shimmer in the dimness as she slowly blinked. "That's very sad. Even though I have seen much tragedy in my life, I have also felt much happiness. Although you are quite deplorable, I find myself wishing you'd experienced the same." Full red lips curved, relaying her teasing.

"Perhaps in another timeline."

"Perhaps."

There, under the canopy of distant galaxies and overhanging trees, Eli fell asleep beside his wife, wondering if the warmth that spread through his chest was indeed happiness. If not, then at least contentment that the stunning, enigmatic woman was keeping watch over his deplorable soul.

Chapter 10

The group made it to the safe house before dark. The bunker had been well stocked by Lewis over the years and was situated far belowground so it was inconspicuous to anyone who passed by in the dense forest. There were modest sleeping arrangements—mostly cots, sleeping bags, and blankets—and there was enough food to feed ten people for several years.

Most importantly, there were weapons. Rifles, handguns, machetes, and even crossbows, all purchased by Lewis during his biannual trips to Solera and Terrum. Assessing the arsenal, Eli felt confident they could defend themselves against an attack on their trek back to the hub.

That night's sleep was the best they would have for the foreseeable future due to the massive locks on the bunker door, and they all slumbered peacefully, not needing a lookout. The women had taken the cots, although Eli wasn't sure if that was truly chivalrous since the rickety beds had seen better days. But they all seemed to appreciate the gesture, even if it was mostly for show.

Eli's lids slid open first in the morning, his gaze immediately landing on Alora where she lay above him, cheek resting on the back of her hand as it bracketed the pillow. The pink tip of her tongue peeked between her open lips as she breathed softly, in and out, her chest rising with each inhale. Ever so slowly, she seemed to sense his stare, and her eyes opened, soft and unsure.

"Hello, dear husband," she whispered. "Are you watching me sleep?"

Eli had no idea when he'd lost complete control of his body, but nothing else could explain the action his arm took on its own free will. Reaching toward her, he tried to tuck a strand of her silky hair behind her ear. Sucking in a breath, she flinched before he could touch her.

Mortified at the loss of restraint as well as her obvious revulsion, he forced his features into the emotionless mask he'd perfected over so many years. "I'm sorry," he murmured, slight anger in his tone. "That won't happen again."

Something flashed in her eyes. "I don't let men touch me without my permission. Perhaps I haven't made that clear, so let me do so now."

"Understood," he said, rising so he didn't drown in those endless eyes. "I'm going to unlock the safe house and go take care of business. Keep an eye on the others." Without waiting for a response, he all but fled the bunker, annoyed he couldn't seem to keep his hands off his gorgeous wife.

Alora noticed Eli's mood while the team packed the supplies that would get them through the several-day journey back to the hub. Recalcitrant and stone-faced, he appeared more like the man she'd always imagined instead of the one she'd caught glimpses of in the past few days.

She'd crossed paths with Eli several times over the years. Their first encounter had been her family's bloody demise, and she would always remember him as the teenager who wasn't quite a man who stood by, stoic, as her world collapsed.

The next time she'd seen him was years later, once she'd connected with Lainey and pledged herself to the cause. She was on a reconnaissance mission, eager to uncover secrets from drunk New Establishment soldiers who were celebrating their victory after a particularly bloody battle with the Old Rebellion. They'd set up camp in a large meadow forty miles south of Terrum, and Alora heard their drunken revelry as she approached. Tying her horse to a nearby tree, she'd reached into her bag for lipstick and pinched her cheeks, reddening them to increase her attractiveness. Many women from the surrounding compounds lived on the tossed coins and valuable trinkets thrown to them by New Establishment soldiers in exchange for a quick blow job or tumble. Alora could pass for a prostitute but was confident in her abilities to protect herself.

She'd been situated over a particularly sloppy soldier's knee, caressing his cheek with her long fingernail, coaxing information out of him, when Eli appeared. "We need you sober, Charles," he'd barked. "The Rebellion heard about the defeat and is sending reinforcements. Get up."

"Yes, sir."

Alora had been quickly dumped on her ass and swiped her hair out of her eyes to look fully upon the man who'd given the order. Recognition washed over both of them—hers materializing as a bucket ice thrown over her heart, and his evident as his broad shoulders stiffened. No longer a boy but a man stood in front of her.

"Hello, Alora," he said softly.

She rose, knees shaking so violently she was sure to collapse, but somehow, she stood tall. The crack against his cheek from her open palm was drowned out by the sound of soldiers milling about. Wanting to slap him again, she reared back, gasping when he caught her wrist.

"Enough," he said, drawing her against his body so he could whisper in her ear. "Strike me again, and I'll have to murder you in front of them. Get out while you can."

"Let me go!" Wrenching from his grasp, she rubbed her wrist and spat, the saliva landing on his shoe.

A slight flare of his nostrils was his only reaction. "You're lucky that didn't land on my face. It would've cemented your death. I'm cultivating something here you can't understand, Alora. Get the fuck out. *Now.*"

Something in his tone had forced her into action. She'd wanted to tell him she understood more than his pea-sized brain could begin to comprehend but knew she was in serious jeopardy of being outed as a spy. Although she hated following his directive, she heeded his words and left the soldiers behind.

Several years later, their paths had crossed when she visited what was once Florida. Some South American rebels had wanted to pass along intel, and they'd agreed to meet. They'd also passed through what was previously Colombia to check on Rosa, at Alora's request, since the woman was now in the twilight of her life, living on one of the safer compounds. Alora had sent her money and trinkets through various channels over the years, hoping to help her survive their barren world. Somehow, Eli had intercepted intel of her clandestine encounter. When she arrived at the designated meeting point, he stood blocking the entrance to the abandoned cemetery where they'd planned to meet.

"They're not coming, Alora," he said, impassive and cryptic. "There are two soldiers with me whom I ordered to canvas the area, but that will only take minutes. I suggest you disappear before they realize you are the traitor Javier and Cristobal were coming to meet."

"What did you do to them?" she asked, reaching for the gun at her belt.

"*Don't* pull it. If the soldiers see, they'll murder you," he ordered through clenched teeth. "I mean it, Alora."

Something in his tone caused her to halt. "I swear," she said, spine straightening as she drew closer, "next time I see you, I will kill you."

"You're not a vengeance killer, Alora," he said, staring into her as if he could see her very soul. "You only kill to protect and in self-defense, so your threat is moot."

"A murderer like you would know!" she hissed, cursing her erratic heartbeat.

He looked off into the distance at the soldiers. "They're returning. If you're ready to die, stay here and argue with me. You've got about thirty seconds before I have to order one of them to shoot you."

Alora spared him one last glare and jogged back to her horse, which was tied against a tree in the overgrown clearing that bordered the cemetery. Curious, she watched from her hidden spot as he spoke to the soldiers. They both gave a nod and exited, leaving him behind.

Slipping his hands into the pockets of his black pants, Eli strode to one of the headstones. Kneeling before it, he stroked it reverently, shoulders set in a solemn hunch.

Knowing what she did now, Alora would bet the gravestone was Ingrid's, and the deep emotion he'd betrayed was grief. How strange to remember that interaction now. That day, she'd been so convinced he was a monster. Today, she understood he was a secret spy, alone in the world, who intensely grieved for his mother. It shifted something inside of her, the feeling strange and unidentifiable in her gut.

She'd snapped at him this morning. It had been a knee-jerk reaction, borne from so many years of hatred. But also spurred by something else: the intense realization that she longed for his touch. This man who'd stood by as her family was murdered...and who had also urged her toward safety...and who grieved for his dead mother. The identities were so incongruent, she struggled to amalgamate them into one personality.

"Who the hell are you, Eli Hernandez?" she whispered to herself.

"Who you talkin' to over here, girl?" Marie asked, startling her from her thoughts as she approached. "Less woolgathering, more packing."

"Yes, ma'am," she said, smiling at the woman. She was all bark and no bite, and Alora loved her harmless brashness. "I think we have enough supplies to defeat the entire New Establishment. I like our chances."

"Me too, my dear," Marie said, softly patting Alora's face. "Since I've got you cornered, you want to tell me how you feel about being hitched to the man whose father killed your family?"

Alora pursed her lips. "Not really."

"Fair enough. It's written all over your face anyway."

"Is it?" Alora asked, arching a brow. "Are you a mind reader now, Marie?"

"Nope. Doesn't take a brain like Lainey's to comprehend human emotion. You've figured out he's not the devil, and you're not quite sure what to do about it."

"Demons come in many forms," Alora said, making the sign of the cross to ward off any bad effects of invoking devils and demons.

"And the ones that live inside your heart are the worst," Marie said, poking her chest.

"Ouch!"

"Oh, stuff it, Lora." The maddening woman was the only one who ever called her that, and it spurred a smile from her lips. "It's time you let those demons go. Fate is a strange force. It's possible you two were destined to meet all those years ago in Colombia. Destined to be tethered together by a shared, incomprehensible tragedy. Keep that in mind and ask yourself why you two always end up on the same path even though you're determined to navigate very different roads."

"I've cursed fate for so long, Marie. I make my own destiny."

"I know, sweetheart," she said, her tone sincere. "I can't wait for you to *breathe*. To truly let the weight of the world go. It will be magnificent to see. If not with my own eyes, then with my soul, wherever it ends up. I'm still betting I have a fighting chance with Heaven, if only because Hell won't take me."

Alora laughed, pulling the woman into a loving embrace. "They couldn't handle you, Marie. Only God can save your soul."

"Damn straight." Drawing back, she cackled. "I bet Eli's a tiger in the sack. All growly and determined to make a woman scream. I'd take advantage of that every day and twice on Sunday."

"Never going to happen," Alora said, giving her an acerbic glare.

Turning, Marie waved a flippant hand in the air. "I've never seen a bull shit, but whatever comes out must be the nonsense that just spewed from your mouth, girl." Giving a huff, she trailed to the other side of the room, effectively dismissing Alora.

Lord, but that woman uttered the strangest nonsense sometimes.

Resuming packing essentials into her bag, Alora assessed the contents and strung it closed. Eli stomped down the stairs into the bunker, the scowl she hadn't seen for days now present and immobile.

"We need to roll out within the next fifteen minutes. Is everyone ready?"

The team all uttered spattered affirmations as they loaded up with their bags and ammunition. Striding toward him, Alora felt her eyebrows lift.

"You're quite confident leading the team."

He shrugged. "Old habits die hard. My gear is already outside. Don't let them linger. We need to go." Pivoting, he ascended the stairs.

It was as if the man she'd spent the past several days with was gone, the old Eli now firmly in his place. Alora didn't like it one bit. Somehow, she'd become used to his compassion and kindness...his teasing and gentle smiles. His *friendship*. Somewhere along the way, they'd become friends.

She'd fucked it up with her rebuff this morning, but she doubted it was beyond repair. The question was: Did she *want* to repair it?

Not wanting to contemplate the answer, she focused on the task at hand, pushing aside the inner debate for another time when she didn't feel so unsettled. Gathering her team, they locked the safe house and began the hike back to the hub.

Chapter 11

It didn't take long to realize they weren't alone. Eli halted and lifted his fist in the air, causing the group to freeze behind him. Turning to face them, his eyes narrowed as he listened.

"I heard a gunshot," he said softly.

"Me too," Elle said.

"How close do you think they are?" Alora asked.

"It's possible it's a skirmish between New Establishment troops and one of the militias. Hunter's men were left behind and almost all escaped when the hub was raided. It could be one of their guns that discharged."

Alora saw Zach shiver and stepped closer, rubbing his back in a comforting gesture while the others discussed. Of everyone in their group, he was the least equipped to handle combat situations but had done quite well so far. Proud of him, she smiled.

"You holding up okay?"

"Yeah," he said, placing his arm around her shoulders. "I just wish I could help you guys more with this stuff. I'll come in handy when we reach the hub though."

"You're doing fine. Don't forget I'm here. If you want to talk, just ask me, *parce*."

"Will do," he said, giving her a salute.

"Let's continue on, but through the woods instead of beside the river," Eli said. "It will make the journey a day longer overall, but it will give us some much-needed shielding."

"I know this terrain like the back of my hand," Marie said, banging her walking stick against the ground. "Come on."

Taking the lead, she forged ahead, everyone lining up behind. The hike was tough but not impossible, each of them helping to navigate over downed trees and jagged stumps.

Many hours later, they were all laden with exhaustion.

"We'll camp here," Marie said, tossing down her stick and sliding her hands under the straps of her bag. Shrugging it off, she rolled her shoulders. "I don't need a rest, but Elle over there looks like she's about to pass out."

"I'm fine," Elle said, chin lifting defiantly.

"You ever learned to take a damn joke, girlie?" Marie chided. "I'm picking on you because you still look like you could win Miss America while I'm sweating like a racehorse over here."

"Miss America?"

"*Psst*," Marie scoffed, waving her hand. "I forgot you're all of twelve years old. It was an old beauty contest. They liked pretty little things like you, all blue-eyed and blond-haired."

"I am twenty-four years old and don't like being patronized," Elle said, chin thrust high. "I learned long ago what men will do to a woman they find pretty and hope to do my best to avoid that classification at all costs."

The group fell silent as the weight of her words washed over them. Stepping closer, Marie lifted her arm to soothe her, but Elle drew back.

"Sounds like someone hurt you. I'm sorry, Elle. I've got a big mouth and use it way too much."

"I don't need your pity," Elle said, spine so straight Alora thought it might never bend again. "I'm resilient and learned how to manipulate men and their stupid minds."

Interesting. The quiet young woman who'd helped carry Luke's letter through time had a hidden indomitable strength. It impressed Alora, who bore the brunt of her own dangerous and frightening encounters with men. Hoping to alleviate the heavy moment, Alora shrugged her pack off her shoulders and approached Elle.

"Sounds like we could trade war stories," Alora said.

"I would like that very much," Elle replied, her shoulders relaxing a bit under the straps of her pack.

"As would I. For now, I need to rest, regardless whether the rest of you do or not. Who's going to keep watch?"

"I will," Marie said, raising her hand. "Won't be able to sleep since I feel like an ass anyway. Go on and lay out your sleeping bags."

"I'll relieve you whenever you need, Marie," Zach said. "Just wake me up."

"Thank you, sweet boy," she said with a nod.

Letting go of the tense exchange, they prepared their bedding and drifted into slumber while Marie kept watch.

* * * *

Gunfire rattled through Zach's brain as he awoke with a gasp. Lurching up, he took in the surroundings as his heart threatened to pound out of his chest. Alora, Eli, and Elle had already jumped to attention, brandishing rifles as they fired into the darkness. Marie had crawled toward the banked fire and huddled with Sara, her arms around the woman as they shielded their ears. Crawling toward them, Zach put his body in between theirs and the forest, hoping to at least offer some protection.

"Stay here," he said to them as he spotted Marie's bag. "You've got a gun in there, right?"

"Yes, but do you know how to use it?"

"Nope. But I think it's time to learn." Rising, he scampered over to the bag and slid the rifle toward Marie. "Keep this, just in case." Reaching into her bag, he pulled out the handgun. It felt heavy in his hand, but the functionality seemed self-explanatory. Unlocking the safety, he scurried to stand behind Eli and Elle as they fired, protecting the camp. Alora was on the other side, shooting into the distance at the unseen soldiers who fired back.

A man walked into the clearing, and Eli shot him down only for two more to appear. He and Elle continued to fire, while Zach noticed something out of the corner of his eye. Jerking his head, he saw the soldier approach Eli with a menacing look upon his face.

Zach froze, losing control of his limbs as ice flowed through his terrified body. *Get it together, Bishop. He'll kill you without a thought.* The inner pep talk revved something inside his wiry frame, and he lifted the gun, aiming it at the man. Before he could command his finger to move, the bullet exited his gun. The man inhaled a shocked gasp and collapsed to the ground.

Alora shot two more men behind him, although the gunfire was muffled inside his ringing ears. In fact, he was pretty sure he was going to pass the fuck out. Closing his eyes, he tried to follow the yellow dots that appeared in the darkness.

Someone was chanting his name as a force pulled at his arm. Tugging it away, he turned to see who was shaking him.

"Zach?" Elle said, her thin fingers clenched so tightly on his bicep he thought the blood might drain away. "You with me?"

"Hey, buddy," Eli said, craning his neck to look Zach in the eyes. "You all right? We got them all—well, all in that battalion at least. You shot the bastard right in the neck. Not pretty, but it did the job."

His swollen tongue licked the roof of his mouth, dry as sandpaper, as he lifted the weapon still in his hand. It seemed to weigh a hundred pounds.

"I've never shot a gun before," he rasped.

"Oh, Zach," Elle said, releasing his arm and rubbing it in a soothing gesture, up and down. Her fingers felt like ice against his burning skin. "Well, you saved Eli. Pretty good outcome for a first-timer."

"Holy shit. Thank god. I saw the soldier approach, and the adrenaline just took over." Zach swallowed, feeling shaky as his hand trembled.

"I'll take that, son," Marie said, gently removing the gun from Zach's hand. "That was a lot of action. I think we all need to take a deep breath."

They stood silent, and Zach noticed Alora examining Eli's upper arm, which seemed to have been grazed in the skirmish. Their heads were bent together as they spoke low and soft. Zach took in Alora's body language as she stared at Eli. It was open and trusting—something he'd never imagined seeing between them. It seemed as if she'd accepted him as part of the team.

"I'll clean and bandage your wound, Eli," Sara said. "I have the first aid kit from the safe house."

"Quickly though," Eli said. "Tanner will send another battalion behind that one. Even though it's still dark, we need to keep moving."

"Fine with me," Sara said, rummaging inside the kit. "I couldn't sleep now anyway if I tried."

The others murmured their agreement, and after Eli's wound was dressed, bags were packed before they set off into the night. Elle fell into step beside Zach, sliding her hand into his and squeezing.

"How you doing?" she asked softly, so the others wouldn't hear.

"Okay," he said, gently smiling. "I don't think it's hit me yet."

Her expression was serious as she nodded. "I killed my first man when I was seventeen."

His forehead furrowed, and curiosity spiked, but he didn't want to pry.

"I don't mind telling you. I'm not ashamed. I learned a long time ago that this world is kill or be killed. Evil men tend to prey upon the weak, and I was determined not to become the prey. A drifter tried to put his hands on me when I said 'no,' and that was the last decision he ever made."

"Wow," Zach said, impressed at her ability to protect herself while saddened she'd had such a terrible encounter. "I'd never peg you as weak, Elle," he said, his palm on fire where it rested against her smooth skin. "You're tough as hell. I probably seem like a total dork to someone like you, who's seen so much."

"I've never really met a science dork," she said, biting her lip as her eyes shined in the moonlight. "It's hella cool."

"Yeah?" he asked, swinging their joined hands.

"Yeah." Shifting their hands, she threaded their fingers together.

Blood surged to Zach's crotch, and he hoped like hell she couldn't see his straining erection in the dimness. Although it was extremely embarrassing, he relished the opportunity to hold her hand.

Linked together, they marched onward, gaining strength from their clenched fingers. Eventually, when the sun was high in the afternoon sky, they camped again, vowing to only rest for a few hours. It was only a matter of time before another platoon arrived, and they had to balance staying sharp and not collapsing from exhaustion. Marie volunteered to keep watch, and Elle laid out her sleeping bag beside Zach's.

As his eyelids grew heavy, he reflected upon his actions. He'd killed a man only hours ago. Did he have a family? Children? The questions swirled inside his mind as he struggled to process them.

"Take some deep breaths," Elle said, face resting on her hand upon the pillow, "and try to find your center. You'll never find the answers you seek. They're too ambiguous. You just have to remind yourself that it was in self-defense and saved Eli's life. I know it sucks. Believe me."

Heeding her words, he crossed his hands under his head and closed his eyes. Inhaling the warm air, he acknowledged the feelings of pain, grief, anger, and sadness that weighed down his chest. In minutes, he gave in to unconsciousness, comforted by her proximity and her soft breaths.

Chapter 12

The next day, they hiked well past sunset and set up camp, hoping the darkness would give them some protection. Their stomachs grumbled, and they decided to heat up some of the beans they'd procured from the safe house.

Marie Elders observed the group as they ate, silent and thoughtful, and she realized something very important: she was freaking *tired*. It was something she'd never admit to the others because she'd learned long ago that complaining was futile. It made you a victim, and that was unacceptable. Victims believed others controlled their fate; that they had no choice. What a bunch of hogwash poppycock. A person always had control over their inner thoughts, which propelled one down the various pathways of life.

Now, with her "eighty-something-ish" birthday approaching, she was ready to make what was, perhaps, the most important choice of her life. Marie had been "approaching eighty" for so long, no one knew her actual age. In truth, she was almost eighty-three, but people had stopped asking her exact age years ago, which suited her just fine. Her bones were brittle, creaking and popping with sounds she'd rarely heard, even from the stragglers who'd shown up with broken appendages at her mom's clinic all those decades ago. Marie had enough common sense to know the shell that comprised her body was well past the need for a tune-up. It was ready to be sent to the junkyard.

That might have sounded cold to someone else, but she was a straight-shooter, and there was no point in lying about what was so evidently clear: it was her time.

She'd seen her mother through her time, and when her darling son George had hugged her before he rushed off to war, she'd known it was his time too. Mara's ending had been sad; Lewis's had been inevitable. Hot damn, she'd outlived them all.

Giving herself a silent pat on the back, she stood, ready to claim her destiny. If it was her time, she'd go out swinging until her damn arms fell off if that was what it took.

"Marie?" Sara asked, gazing up at her from her perch beside the fire. "You okay?"

"I have a plan," Marie said, making sure she made eye contact with each person so they didn't doubt her resolve.

"A plan for what?" Zach asked.

"To save your hides, boy," she said, her tone both teasing and firm. "I'm going to lead Tanner's men back to the safe house."

A moment of silence dropped over the clearing before Alora said, "No way, Marie. You're staying with us. We'll outrun them if we keep going."

Marie scoffed. "Outrun who knows how many armed men when this one's injured?" she asked, gesturing with her head toward Eli. "I don't think so."

"I'm fine," Eli gritted through clenched teeth, holding pressure to the bandage that covered his upper arm. "The bullet only grazed me."

"You're not that good of a liar, Mr. Super-Spy, so just shut it," Marie said, her firm gaze daring him to argue.

Eli muttered something under his breath but remained relatively quiet.

"Now, I don't believe in long goodbyes. Although I'm not a religious woman, I do believe this all has meaning. And I believe there's a place out there in a timeline not even Lainey's brain can fathom where we all meet up again, free from the restraints of our bodies and full of every ounce of our souls. I expect to see you all there once you've accomplished your mission and lived full, happy lives. Until then, here's my plan on how I'm going to die, so you all can get on with saving the damn world."

"Marie," Alora implored softly.

"Are you going to let me tell you my plan, or am I going to have to just leave while you all are sleeping? Because I'll do it, girl, believe me. I'm wily as hell and will be gone so fast, you'll forget I was even here."

"We could never forget you, Marie," Sara said, standing to walk to her side and place her arm around the woman's shoulders. "Tell us your plan. We're all ears."

Without reservation or fear, Marie informed them she was going to head back to the safe house. She would mark the path well so Tanner's men would believe the team had turned back to the bunker. In the meantime, the others would head to the hub.

"They'll eventually find me and realize I'm solo, but that will give you all time to get your butts back to 2035. I'm counting on you to fix that Sphere, young man," Marie said to Zach.

"Yes, ma'am," he said with a respectful tilt of his head.

"Then it's done. I'll need a gun to take with me. I'll be damned if I let those bastards murder me without putting up a fight."

Using his good arm, Eli propped himself to stand and walked over to her. Pulling his Glock from his belt, he handed it to her.

"Take mine. It's fully loaded and the best of the best since it's New Establishment property. Something makes me think you'll put it to better use than I ever could."

Marie slid her hand over the cold metal, testing the heaviness as she held it.

"You just remove the safety like this," Eli said, showing her, "and then aim it between Tanner's eyes. I mean, why not go for the gold?"

Her cackle filtered over the fire. "Indeed. You know, Eli, I think I might have underestimated you for a cold, unyielding asshole. You're actually quite funny."

A laugh escaped his throat. "I've never really had the opportunity to show my comedic side," he said, lifting a sardonic brow.

Surprising herself, she raised a hand to palm his cheek. "You've only had one opportunity. One choice you made so long ago. Brave and terrible, all in the same breath. It must be crushing."

His lips twitched as he shrugged. "You get used to it."

Marie's eyelids narrowed as she studied him. "Doubtful."

He stepped back, breaking their contact, and Marie realized he was uncomfortable being touched in a caring way. Interesting. What did one have to do to open him up enough for him to let them inside? Glancing toward Alora, Marie understood her considerate, passionate nature was perfect to tear down his carefully built walls.

"I wish to speak to Eli alone before I depart," Marie said, addressing the group. "I'll hang here with you all for a bit, then grab a few hours' sleep, and I'll head out two hours before sunrise. That will give me the jump on them and give you all time to start on your journey."

"I feel like I should stop you," Sara said, the nearby fire exacerbating the glow of her glistening eyes. "How can I let you head straight into your own death?"

"You know you must, my dear," Marie said, struggling to keep her own tears at bay. "Not only for you, but for the baby you carry. You must find Luke, and this is the best solution. If we stay together, they'll surely find us."

Alora shot to her feet. "You're pregnant?" She inched toward Sara, her stunning face full of love and hope.

"I'm pregnant," Sara said, nodding as she swiped a tear from her cheek. "Luke and I used protection, I swear, but it happened anyway. How mad do you think Lainey will be?"

"You'll only know if you go to 2035 and ask her, girl," Marie said. "I'm so happy for you."

The next several minutes were consumed with hugs and congratulations as the team celebrated some much-needed good news. Then they sat by the fire, Marie recounting stories from her long life. Everyone seemed to enjoy the tales about her vivacious mother, who'd healed so many who were underserved. Eventually, everyone fell into a light slumber except for Eli and Elle, who kept watch.

Marie woke and gathered her belongings. Slinging her pack on over her shoulders, she asked Elle, "You'll be okay keeping watch until Eli returns?"

"Yes," the young woman said, the set of her shoulders and uplifted chin showcasing her strength.

"When do you plan to tell them who your father is?" Marie asked her in a hushed tone.

To her credit, Elle barely flinched, but Marie noticed the almost imperceptible twitch.

"I don't know what you're referring to. My father was Jeffrey Cannon. I told Lainey that when I showed up at the hub."

And pigs might fly out of my ass, Marie thought. When you'd lived as long as Marie, you noticed things. Being that Elle was new and therefore needed to be vetted, Marie had paid special attention to the girl, noticing simple things that would otherwise seem irrelevant if they weren't trying to save the world. Like the birthmark on her inner arm, below the bicep but above the elbow crease. It was the exact shape and color, and in the exact same spot, as one Marie had observed on someone else years ago. Or the fact a girl with an Anglo-Saxon surname had such almond shaped eyes, set below hair that wasn't as blond as it appeared, judging by the roots that were now growing in. Many women had figured out how to dye their hair in the post-apocalyptic world, Claire being one of the most eager, and Marie had no doubt Elle was cunning enough to discern how to use lemon and honey to do the same.

"You have your own reasons for your lies, and I'll leave you with them. If I thought it would harm my friends, I'd out you in a second, but I believe your deception might actually have some purpose."

Elle's nose turned up as her body stiffened. "I have no idea what you're talking about, Marie."

Marie waved a dismissive hand at her. "Take care of Zach, girl. He's got the googly eyes for you. If you break his heart, I'll come back from the grave and strangle you."

Elle's gaze drifted to Zach, her face contorting with reverence, and the knowledge she returned Zach's feelings washed over Marie. "I'll take care of him," Elle said softly.

"Good," Marie said. "I can tell you've had hard times, Elle. Zach is the perfect man to build a new life with. He'll make a good partner. I wish you both happiness."

Elle lifted her gaze to the older woman, her blue orbs shining with wetness. "Goodbye, Marie."

"Goodbye, sweet girl. See you on the other side." Looking at Eli, she motioned her head. "Come on, son. I haven't got all day." Pivoting, she dug her walking stick into the ground and trudged away from the only family she'd known for the past several decades of her life. Her old heart ached to say one last goodbye, and she pushed the sentiment back down to the pit of her stomach, holding it deep inside so it wouldn't choke her.

Her life had been magnificent, full of so much laughter and so many important lessons about heartache and pain. Each one had caused her to pull herself up by her bootstraps and try again, knowing there would be more failure ahead, and that was okay. But this time was different. This time, she wouldn't fail. Her death would create the ultimate victory so her young friends could accomplish their mission and save so many. Damn, but there was a nobility in that. Pride swelled inside her withered body as she stomped ahead.

"You're amazing, Marie," Eli said softly, trailing alongside her. "The New Establishment made a grave mistake not recruiting you. I think you would've won the war ages ago."

Marie damn near giggled, the freedom of her decision making her feel lighter than she had in years. "You're goddamned right I would have, son."

As far as long walks into eternity went, Marie trudged along, admitting that this one was pretty spectacular.

* * * *

Eli reached the edge of the woods and halted when Marie came to a stop. The woman closed her eyes and lifted her face to the still-darkened sky. She possessed a deep resolve, spurring a jolt of profound respect in his solar plexus. Opening her eyes, she gazed up at him.

"I'd like to hear why you think you can't go back with the others."

Sighing, Eli placed his hands in the pockets of his black pants. "There's no future in 2035 for someone like me."

"Someone evil?" she asked, arching a brow.

"Yes," he muttered, feeling a muscle in his jaw tick.

One eye squinted as she studied him. "Hogwash," she muttered, slapping him on his upper arm above his injury. Eli somehow knew the location of the strike was intentional. Rubbing his throbbing arm, he scowled at her. "You need to go back and help Lainey and the others stop President Randolph. Then you need to tell Alora you love her and do your damnedest to convince her to make your sham marriage real. It's time for her to have some babies, and I think you're the one to give them to her and help her raise them."

A burst of laughter leaped from his throat. "Are you insane? The woman detests me."

"She needed someone to blame after Victor slaughtered her family. You were an easy scapegoat, although you tried your best to suppress the carnage that day. Deep inside, she understands that."

"I will always be the son of the man who killed her family. She could never love a child with my blood."

"Alora is remarkable and needs a strong man as her partner. Someone who challenges her and brings out her passion. You are an excellent match. I've never seen her as off-balance with anyone as she is with you."

He shrugged. "Like I said, it's because she wants to murder me."

Marie smiled. "Desire is a funny thing, son. I think she carries it for you even though it drives her mad. Can you imagine how fiery and passionate sex would be between you? Holy lord in heaven, you two would probably set the damn bed on fire." She fanned herself, causing Eli to chuckle.

"I think I'm getting embarrassed, Marie," he said, grinning. "Is this why you wanted to speak to me alone?"

"Yes," she said, swaying the stick back and forth as she spoke. "I don't think it's your time yet, Eli. You've done some terrible things in order to do what you thought was right, but I see more for you than the years you've spent in this timeline. I won't ask for your word, because who am I to ask that? But I will ask you to consider going back and helping the others. They're a family, which is something you've never really had, and I believe you might actually deserve one."

"I had a mother," he said wistfully, remembering Ingrid. "She was such a beautiful, caring woman. I wish I could've been the son she raised me to be."

"You still *can*," Marie said, cupping his cheek as her hazel eyes bore into his. "There's still hope for you, Eli. I firmly believe that. Now." She gave him two firm raps on the cheek—harder than they needed to be, but he expected no less. Damn, she was a firecracker. He hated that her light would soon be extinguished. "Don't mourn me, son. I won't have it. There are other things to expend your energy on." Lowering her hand, she gave him a nod. "Good luck, Eli. Take care of my family. I'm counting on you." Gripping the walking staff tight, she turned and began walking across the open meadow.

Eli watched her, spine straight and head held high, as she strode head-on toward the last events of her long life. Never had he felt such admiration for another human being.

He watched her after she'd crossed the field, her image long gone as he stood still and contemplative. Then he turned and said a silent prayer for her, although he hadn't practiced religion in so long. Not since he left his precious mother to forge the path of his ill-begotten life.

Determined to heed her parting words, he trailed back to camp, vowing to protect the team until they made it safely to 2035. And as for her other words? The ones about redemption and his ability to continue on and travel back with the others? He wasn't ready to hear them yet. Most likely, he never would be. The nefarious Eli Hernandez didn't deserve a future when he'd robbed so many others of one. Even if he secretly longed for it with every ounce of the soul he claimed to not possess.

Chapter 13

The group trudged on, a pall cast over them at the loss of Marie. Alora still carried hope in her heart that the woman would somehow survive—after all, Marie was the toughest of them all. But deep inside, she knew it was likely impossible. Sending her a silent prayer, Alora made the sign of the cross over her chest.

She sensed Eli watching her. He tended to do that quite often when he thought she wouldn't notice. They'd slipped into an amicable relationship, although it was devoid of the comradery they'd begun to build. Sighing softly, Alora admitted she missed it. The teasing quirk of his lips when she was chiding him. The softness in his dark eyes when he studied her. The way he'd begun to touch her although she claimed she didn't want to feel his skin upon hers. *Lies.* Alora detested liars and vowed not to become one. She'd developed some strange and complex feelings for her enigmatic husband and denying that was futile. Could she really have feelings for the man who'd hurt so many? Who'd hurt her family?

As the trek wore on, she studied his actions. He always offered to keep watch first so the others could rest. He had a keen eye for knowing when Sara needed help with opening the beans, or when Elle needed a lookout so she could take a bathroom break away from the group. He and Zach seemed to be developing a rapport, and they had many hushed conversations when they thought the others were sleeping. Alora was curious what they discussed since, even though she strained to listen, she could never quite discern the topics.

As they set up camp the last night before they would approach the hub, Alora lay on her side, attempting to listen to yet another one of their conversations. Furious that she even cared at all, she grumbled and punched the makeshift pillow of piled clothes, determined to sleep so she would be fresh—for if all went well, she'd be spending tomorrow night in 2035.

* * * *

Eli observed Alora thump her pillow and huff as she muttered something unintelligible from her spot on the other side of the fire. Lips quirking, he wondered if she was pissed at him for something. It was always a possibility, and he hoped she was in fact annoyed at him. At least that meant she was thinking about him. Since he couldn't seem to get the woman off his mind, the thought that she would be even partly consumed with him brought him immense joy.

Zach smiled. "Wonder what she's pissed about. Maybe she had a bad dream."

"Not likely," Eli muttered.

"So, um, thanks again for talking about this stuff with me. I feel like such an idiot but also want to be prepared...just in case...you know..." Trailing off, he rubbed his hand over his face, his gaze landing on Elle where she slept beside Alora. "I mean, I don't want to presume anything."

"Happy to help, man," Eli said, patting him on the back. "Women are complex creatures, and they're hard to read. Being prepared is a wise move."

Two nights ago, Zach had approached him, looking sheepish as his cheeks enflamed. In a whispered hush, he'd asked if he could speak to him while the others slept. Under the bright stars, he'd quietly informed Eli that he was a virgin who'd never even kissed a woman. It had shifted something in Eli's stoic heart, and he'd found himself wanting to help.

Zach had been full of questions, as most scientists were. How much tongue to use? Where should he put his hands? What if they actually made it to third base? How did he put on a condom? How did he ensure his partner felt pleasure?

Eli had tried his best to answer honestly, wanting to help the young man who'd been rather sheltered. Elle was a sweet girl and quite pretty, even if she had secrets. Hell, they all had secrets. Who was he to judge?

"I'm so afraid I'll blow it. Scientifically, the clitoris seems easy enough to navigate. The confluence of nerve endings needs to be stimulated repetitively for the woman to reach orgasm."

Eli breathed a laugh. "Yes, *scientifically*, that is correct. But in the heat of the moment, it's really hard to think scientifically. Trust me."

He glanced wistfully at Elle. "I'm scared of making a move, but I'm also scared not to. I don't want her to forget about me when we reach 2035."

"Then make a move," Eli said, giving a nod. "I think she would be open. Things are only going to get more dangerous as you all strive to stop President Randolph. You should at least tell her how you feel before you enter the ultimate fight."

"I'm going to." Zach traced a branch through the dirt as he pondered. "I really hope you change your mind and come back with us, Eli. Yes, the Sphere needs to be destroyed, but I can detonate the bombs we set up years ago for that. You don't need to sacrifice yourself."

Eli's foot shook atop his stretched-out legs, crossed at the ankles as he contemplated. "I need to kill Tanner."

"If we prevent the past, Tanner will never rise to prominence."

"If you all fail, he will still exist in this timeline. As much as I hope you stop Randolph, we can't count on it."

"What about Alora?"

Eli sighed. "What about her?"

"Don't you want to, uh, explore that?"

"That's a lion's den I have no desire to navigate."

Zach's expression relayed his disbelief.

"We have too much history. Terrible history. Wishing I could change it is futile. She'll always hate me."

"I don't think she hates you," Zach said softly.

"Severe distaste then," Eli said, grinning.

"Yeah, that's probably more spot-on."

Damn, Eli really liked this kid. He was surprised to realize he would miss him once they were gone.

"Thanks for all the advice, Eli. I've never had anyone to talk to about this. Probably would've asked Cyrus, but, well, you know…"

"I'm sure they're okay," Eli said, patting his shoulder again. "You should try to get some rest. We're going to book it back to the hub tomorrow."

Nodding, Zach maneuvered into his sleeping bag and pulled it tight over his chest. "Night," he mumbled.

"Good night, Zach."

Like clockwork, his gaze drifted back to Alora. Not watching her was impossible, which probably made him a huge creep, but at this point, he'd given up fighting it. Comforted by having her near—by having all of them near—he let himself enjoy being surrounded by people who seemed to accept him. Perhaps even care for him.

The powerful Eli Hernandez hadn't experienced true friendship in so long. His tentative bond with this ragtag team of time travelers was the closest he'd come to true human emotion since Ingrid. She would've liked them, each and every one. Especially Alora. His mother would've loved her passionate spirit, caring heart, and whip-smart intelligence. Eli was glad he'd gifted her the ring and felt she would keep it safe in 2035. He wanted it returned to a world in which he'd still been a good man, worthy of his mother's love. Thankful the treasured adornment had found a new home with his stunning wife, his heart thrummed in his chest, hopeful for the future he would never see.

Chapter 14

Alora crept softly upon the grass, familiar with the sparse woods they now navigated near the hub. Halting, she lifted her hand, fist tight, and turned to face the group.

"We're here."

They gazed back, determined and strong. Sara, unwavering in her desire to reconnect with Luke and tell him about the baby. Zach, their only hope of repairing the Sphere, appearing ready to try like hell. Elle, armed with a rifle about as big as her. Although slight, she projected a firm, resolved calm. And Eli, the man she'd recently married—although it was a sham—ready to help them and then meet his own death. The idea didn't sit well with her for some reason, and she'd contemplate it as they reclaimed the hub. In the end, she wasn't sure if she was ready to let him die. Time would tell.

"They will have increased the number of soldiers," Eli said. "We're heavily armed, which at least means we have a chance of not being slaughtered." Making eye contact with each person, he reiterated the plan. "Alora and I will approach and shoot as many as we can before they realize we're here. The silencers Lewis stored at the safe house will ensure the soldiers don't hear the initial gunshots. As soon as they discover us, Elle and Zach need to come in, guns blazing."

"I can wield a rifle too," Sara said, her voice clear and steady.

"You're pregnant, Sara—"

"I don't give a damn, Alora," she said, holding up a hand. "My husband is on the other side of that time machine, and I want to do everything in my power to get to him. I'll be on the line with Elle and Zach, rifle in hand. Don't try to stop me. I'm just as stubborn as you are."

Alora admired her gumption. "Well, rifle up then," she said, eyebrow arching. "Let's give these bastards hell."

Sara smiled and slung a rifle over her shoulder. "Hell yes. Let's do this, guys. I'm ready to blow this joint. 2035, here we come!"

Hands thrust into the center of their circle, and they gave a collective, "Hell yes!" in a whispered chant before Eli and Alora strapped down.

Gazing up at him, she asked, "Ready?"

"Ready."

They strode forward, hiding behind a tree as they observed the soldiers outside the hub.

"Three by the main entrance, and several flanking the side."

"Confirmed," he said, breath warm against her ear.

Turning to stare up at him, something lodged in her throat. Grasping the front of his shirt, she drew him toward her until they were almost nose-to-nose.

"Don't fucking die. You hear me?"

Dark eyes darted between hers. "Why?" he whispered, his breath exhaling in soft pants.

"Because I fucking said so. Be a good husband and listen to your wife."

Labored breaths exited his lungs as he surrounded her neck with his palm. Running his thumb across her lips, he whispered her name.

"I mean it, Eli," she said softly. Her tongue darted out to bathe her lips, and desire flared in his eyes.

"I'll do my best," he growled.

Nodding, she tugged him forward and planted a kiss on his lips. God, they were so full. She hoped like hell it wouldn't be the last time she felt them against hers.

Pushing him away, she pivoted and lifted her gun, aiming it at the man in front of the hub door. Making the sign of the cross, she whispered, "Lord, help us all."

She pulled the trigger, watching the bullet lodge in the man's forehead. He slumped to the ground immediately, and she instantly shot the other two guards dead. Eli was to her left, wreaking his own carnage on the guards at the side of the hub. Suddenly, what seemed like a multitude of soldiers charged from the far side of the building, and Alora sheathed her gun and slung the rifle across her shoulders. Aiming it at the men, she began to shoot.

Gunfire popped and spewed as the five weary travelers attacked their foes. One by one, they went down until Alora realized they were winning. Holy shit, they were winning! Eli shot two more soldiers, and the gunfire ceased as they assessed the surroundings.

"They're all down," Alora said. "Let's get inside and repair the Sphere. Now!"

The team ran toward the front door, pushing it open and trailing inside. Alora yelled to Eli to assess whether anyone was inside, and he did a quick scan of the premises.

"It's empty."

"Go!" Alora called to Zach, closing the massive front door and clicking the menagerie of locks. "They're sure to send reinforcements."

Zach trailed to the back of the hub, clicking the nonfunctioning keypad before realizing it was smashed.

"Yeah, that was me," Eli said, rubbing the back of his neck. "Can you still get inside?"

"I think we need to blow the hatch open. Give me a sec." He jogged down the hallway and returned with a small block. "From the lab. It's TNT. Stand back and hold your ears."

They all followed his direction, jerking from the sound as the explosives detonated. Reaching down, he tried to pull open the hatch door.

"Here," Eli said, tugging along with Zach. "Give it all you've got."

The door creaked open, and Zach tracked down the ladder, jumping onto the dirt-covered ground. The others followed, observing him as he looked over the Sphere and then the console that controlled it.

"I need a few minutes," he said, standing over the console. "The damage is pretty severe."

Alora shot Eli a look. "What?" he asked, lifting his hands in a frustrated gesture. "I tried my best not to ruin it."

"I can fix it," Zach said, heading back to examine the fuel rod and lasers. "Give me twenty minutes. I'll need Elle and Sara here so I can send them up to the lab when I need something. Alora and Eli, you should probably keep watch outside."

Alora noticed Elle's soft smile at Zach's authoritative tone. He was certainly in his element near his precious Sphere, and an intelligent, confident man was always quite sexy. Elle seemed to think so, at least.

"I'm ready for orders, sir," she said, giving him a teasing salute.

"Me too," Sara chimed in.

Alora gave him a nod and headed up the ladder, Eli close behind. As they moved toward the entrance, Eli's expression was pensive.

"What is it?"

"It was too easy," he said, shaking his head. "They know we're here. I don't know what Tanner has up his sleeve, but something's up."

"We'll just have to stay on high alert."

"Definitely."

They approached the foyer, and Alora realized the security cameras were still working. "Let's watch from here," she said, pointing to the monitor Cyrus had installed years ago. "If they come, we're better off being secured inside."

"They'll come," Eli said, lowering to the chair and rubbing his forehead. "It's only a matter of time."

Shivering, Alora sat beside him. "Then we'll be ready."

A muscle ticked in his jaw. "I fucking hope so."

Thick silence surrounded them as they waited, each tick of the second hand a step closer to their uncertain future.

* * * *

Elle watched Zach tinker with the Sphere, overcome by how confident and assured he seemed. Desire curled in her gut as he directed them to do different tasks, and she strove to help in the ways she could. When she located the toolbox he'd sent her to find, her fingers sparked with fire as she handed it to him. His skin brushed against hers, and he flashed a quick smile.

"Thanks."

Nodding, she asked, "How's it coming along?"

"Good." Setting down the tools, he began to repair what looked to be lasers along the right side. "Once I fix these, I'm going to start on the console. Shouldn't be long until we can fire her up."

The muscles of his arms flexed as he maneuvered the wrench, and Elle had the urge to fan herself. When had screwing in lasers become hot? Clearing her throat, she backed away and accidentally bumped Sara.

"Sorry," she murmured.

"Something about a man with tools," Sara whispered so Zach wouldn't hear. "It's so damn hot."

"Right?" Elle asked. "I've never really been that kind of girl, but yeah..."

Sara chuckled. "And what kind of girl is that?"

She shrugged. "One who gets all starry-eyed around men. I haven't had the best experiences around men in my life. But he's...different," she said, gazing at Zach.

"That he is. He's such a sweetheart. And really smart. It's a potent combination."

"Tell me about Luke," Elle said. "My Grandpa Will said he was a great man. He admired him immensely."

Sara told her about Luke and how they'd fallen in love even though she hadn't been searching. "Sometimes, love finds you whether you're ready or not. I'm so blessed he found me."

Before she could respond, Zach called them over. "I'm going to attempt to start the arms. I want you all to stand against the wall, just in case something malfunctions."

They followed his direction, backs against the rocky wall as he depressed buttons on the console. The circular metal arms creaked and began to move, accelerating until they were rotating so quickly they appeared as one continuous circle. Hitting several buttons, Zach tested the lasers, each of them seeming to fire correctly. Flipping open a clear cover, he gave a quick tap, and the fuel rod sent a jolt of electricity to the center of the Sphere. Replacing the cover, he clicked several buttons, effectively halting the machine.

Turning to face them, he said, "Honestly, I could tinker for hours, but it's functional. I don't postulate a significant variation in the degree of safety if we try to transport now. Whoever transports first will take the biggest risk."

"I'll do it," Elle said, realizing this was an opportunity to prove her worth in the group. "I'm the youngest and healthiest, with the least to risk. Let me go first."

Concern drenched his light green gaze, causing her heart to swell. "I can't promise you'll make it safely, Elle. I'll try my best but can't guarantee it."

"I'll take the chance," she said, straightening her spine. "What do I need to do to prepare?"

"We need to get everyone in the protective suits and gear up."

"Okay," she said, shoulders set. "Let's do it."

"I'll go get Eli and Alora," Sara said, trailing up the ladder and disappearing from view.

"Elle," Zach said, walking toward her. "Are you sure?"

"Hey," she said, lifting her hands in a shrug. "We all have to go back in that thing. I'm happy to be the first one. If I croak, at least I did some good, and you'll know you have to tweak it more."

He licked his lips, looking so nervous as he stood before her. Taking pity on him, she slid her palm over his cheek, loving how the scant, prickly hairs tickled her skin.

"Do you want to kiss me, Zach? Before I go?"

His throat bobbed. "Yes. But I..."

Her brow furrowed. "What?"

"I've never done it before," he whispered.

Her heart cracked into a million pieces at the genuine and embarrassed admission. How hard it must've been for him to tell her that.

"That's okay," she said, drawing him toward her with firm pressure. "Come here."

He breathed her name upon her lips, the air warm and composed of everything Zach. Touching her lips to his, she opened them, searching inside his mouth with her tongue. He groaned, sliding his hands around her waist, drawing her to fit into the curve of his tall frame. Tentatively, his tongue licked her bottom lip, then her own wet tongue, and she flushed throughout her entire body. Threading both hands in his hair, she twirled her tongue around his, sliding, licking...wanting to suck that small part of him inside herself and never let go.

He ground his erection into her stomach, firm and proud as he moved his mouth over hers. Oh, how she wished they had more time to explore the budding desire that burned between them. She'd never been with a man who was gentle... Would it be different? Would Zach teach her what it felt like to make love, rather than the crushing experiences she'd had so far?

He released her tongue, placing soft butterfly kisses over her top lip and then the bottom one. With one last sweet kiss, he rested his forehead against hers.

"Elle," he whispered.

Smiling, she caressed his face as she gazed into him, feeling so connected to a man—a first for her. "Yes?"

"I don't want that to be the last time we kiss."

"Neither do I," she said, placing a soft peck on his wet lips. "So make sure you send me back in one piece, okay?"

"Okay," he said, squeezing her.

"Okay, kids," Eli said, charging down the ladder. "There's plenty of time in 2035 to finish what you started here."

Alora and Sara followed close behind, stocked with radiation suits. Elle drew away, unable to control her smile.

"I hear you're going first," Eli said, handing her the suit.

"I am. I hope you choose to join us, Eli. I'd very much like to get to know you. There are things I'd like to tell you one day."

His eyebrow lifted. "More secrets, Elle?"

The corner of her lip curved as she began to don the suit. "Always. But you understand that better than anyone."

His soft smile affirmed her statement. Elle studied him, inwardly contemplating. It was impossible to live on the Eastern Isle without hearing tales of the nefarious dictator. Stories of his cruelty and disregard for anyone who didn't accept the regime were vast. She understood the energy it must've taken to develop such a reputation—especially now that she'd met him and realized he was anything but evil. It required intense dedication, which was something she inherently comprehended. Knowing they shared the same ability to forge ahead for the cause comforted her since she also had a cause that required her utmost determination.

Once they all had donned the suits, Elle turned to Zach.

"What do I need to do?"

He explained that he was going to set the time machine to transport Elle to May 25, 2035. "I've thought about it a lot, and Lainey would've most likely contacted Nelson and solicited his help to rebuild the Sphere in 2035. She would've needed some time to navigate things, and having you arrive in late May will mean Nelson is already on board. Once you land in the park, you'll want to head to Nelson's home. He and Lorna can then help you connect with Lainey. Understood?"

"Yes," she said, nodding. "Will you all transport back to that date as well? Should I wait for you?"

"Wait for an hour. If we don't arrive, then go ahead and find Nelson. But I'll do my best to get everyone to the same point. His address in 2035 was 2121 2nd Street North West. Repeat it back to me."

Inhaling a deep breath, she repeated it, and Zach nodded.

"Got it. Good luck, guys." After a furious round of hugs, she stepped inside the Sphere, clutching her hands together to ward off the shaking. Zach gave her a huge smile and blew her a kiss, proving he was probably the sweetest man on the planet.

Closing her eyes, Elle listened to the arms whirl above her head. Moments later, she felt a tugging behind her back and tried not to fight it, although that went against every instinct in her terrified body. Opening her mouth to scream inside the plastic head covering, nothing escaped as she was dragged into darkness. Unable to open her eyes as intense forces of gravity tugged on every cell of her body, she lost her battle with unconsciousness and relented to the dense obscurity.

* * * *

Alora watched Elle disappear through the wormhole before Zach shut down the Sphere. Once the arms had stopped whirling, Zach's fingers sped over the laptop keyboard as he computed. Almost sixty tense seconds ticked by as they waited. Lifting his head, he said, "According to my calculations, she should've made it safely to May 25, 2035."

"You and Sara will go next," Alora said to Zach. "The New Establishment could show up any minute, and I'm not leaving before everyone has traveled safely. Show us how to operate the thing."

She and Eli walked around the console while Zach gave them the most important tutorial of their lives. After he was finished, she nodded.

"I've got it. Clear button sets the arms in motion. Red button lights the lasers. Flip the plastic cover and push the black button, which will shoot the nuclear jolt needed to create the wormhole."

Zach smiled. "You're officially a scientist now, Alora. Well done."

She shot him a droll look. "Not sure about that."

Zach programmed some strange symbols into the console's keypad. "Okay, I've set it so that once we travel back, you just hit the 'Enter' key, and it will reset the equations to send you and Eli to 2035."

"Just Alora," Eli said. "I'll destroy it after you're all gone. How do I detonate the dynamite you all have set up?"

"Cyrus and Lewis built the destruction system into the wall of the cave years ago in case we were ever raided and needed to destroy the Sphere," Zach said, walking to a panel on the wall. Pulling it open, he pointed to the red button in the center. "Push it and then haul ass out of the bunker. It has a twenty-second timer, and then everything within thirty feet of the bunker will be toast. Also, since we have a nuclear fuel rod here, things could get messy fast. If it goes into meltdown, the entire area will experience radiation poisoning for several decades."

Eli nodded. "Understood. Let's get you two into the Sphere."

Once they were suited up, Alora stood behind the console, attempting to remain calm while blood pounded in her veins.

"You ready?" Eli asked, coming to stand beside her.

Nodding, she depressed the first button, and the metal circles began to spin. Zach and Sara clenched hands inside the contraption as Alora ignited the lasers. Finally, she flipped open the shield and pushed the black button. The wormhole appeared behind her two friends, growing wide until it sucked them into its void. Gasping with wonder, she watched them disappear.

"Holy shit," she whispered.

"Never gets old," Eli muttered. "That's for sure."

Staring down at the console, Alora tapped the "Enter" key. As Zach had stated, several equations flashed on the monitor until the numbers froze, ready to send her back. Facing Eli, she opened her mouth to tell him that he was coming with her no matter what the hell he had to say about it. They'd figure out a way.

Unfortunately, the words never left her mouth. Instead, she coughed droplets of blood upon his shirt and chin as the air was forced from her lungs. A look of intense horror crossed his handsome features as she clutched her side. As if in slow motion, she glanced down to find blood gushing from the fresh wound.

"No!" Eli screamed, encircling her with his arms.

The ringing in her ears was so loud she barely heard the soldiers as they barreled down the ladder. Tanner Cross followed the five armed men, two of them clutching a struggling Dr. Nelson Longwood and Marie Elders.

"It's over, Eli," Tanner said, gesturing to the men who held her friends. "Alora is bleeding out, and these two are as good as dead. We're claiming the Sphere once and for all and will use it to further our cause. Hand over your gun."

Alora leaned against the console, gasping for air as her knees wobbled. Unable to stand, she slid down the side, crouching in the dirt as she leaned against the cool metal. The pain was intense but not unbearable, either due to adrenaline or to the fact she was closer to dead than alive.

Eli pulled his gun from his belt and shot two of the men, but he was overpowered quickly. Writhing in their grip, he called to her.

"Try to crawl into the Sphere! I can still try to send you back!"

"It's over," she tried to yell, the words lodged in her throat along with the blood that would soon drown her. "Detonate the bombs. We can at least kill Tanner too." She had no idea if her words were intelligible as she fought to retain consciousness.

As she watched him struggle along with Marie and Nelson, Alora had the strange feeling they'd done this all before. A weird sort of déjà vu settled over her body, and she wondered how many timelines they'd experienced in which they made it this far, only to die. Despair at their inability to vanquish evil wracked her broken body, and she closed her eyes, unable to fight any longer.

The bright light called to her. It was everywhere...surrounding her...sure and strong like Luke's strong arms... Luke? Why was he here on her journey to heaven? How strange. Was he an angel? No, that couldn't be right...

"Come on, Alora," Luke's voice said in her ear as he dragged her to the light. "Stay with me."

Shots fired as she heard Hunter's voice in tandem with Eli's. The light grew brighter, but she forced her lids open to see Hunter and Eli overpowering the men, freeing Marie and Nelson and pushing them toward the light too.

"Go!" Eli said, urging Hunter toward the glow. "I'll destroy the bunker."

"No!" Alora yelled, her voice hoarse as Luke dragged her. "We're not leaving you, Eli."

Her husband's gaze met hers, resolved and filled with sadness. "Goodbye, Alora," he said. Lifting the gun, he shot Tanner once more for good measure.

The bodies of the New Establishment soldiers lay dead upon the ground, reminiscent of how her family had lain so long ago. Would she ever cease having moments filled with Eli's tall frame standing over slain corpses? Praying to God this was the last time, she grunted and extricated herself from Luke's grasp. Crawling away from the blinding light, she inched toward Eli where he stood by the panel.

"Damn it, Alora," he cursed, coming to kneel beside her. "You're bleeding out. You've got to get to the other side and get treatment."

"Not going without you," she rasped. "So fuck you, Eli. Push the damn button, and let's go."

"Come on, guys!" Lainey's voice screamed from so very far away. How was she here too? Alora collapsed on the ground, control slipping with every second.

Eli gave her a stern glare and cursed. Rising, he depressed the button that would set off the dynamite. Rushing toward her, he scooped her into his arms. Then he carried her into the blinding light as she clutched onto his shirt, coughing up blood as he whispered in her ear.

"I've got you, *querida*."

The words filtered through her bleary mind as his warm body bracketed hers. And then she gave in to the forces pulling her toward the other side, hoping God would welcome her home. Ready to see her family once more, she wasn't afraid. Perhaps her only regret would be not living long enough to ask Eli Hernandez why he'd called her his beloved...or why it had spurred such intense longing in her rapidly dying heart.

<h1 style="text-align:center">Chapter 15</h1>

Alora swirled her tongue around her mouth, the roof covered with some god-awful substance that tasted terrible. Grimacing, she licked her cracked lips, wishing like hell for some water.

"There she is," a soothing voice said, a soft hand clenching hers as it lay limp on the comforter. "See? I told you she was going to be okay."

The familiar sound of Marie's *harrumph* filled her ears, and Alora wanted to weep with laughter. She was alive? Forcing her lids open, she rapidly closed them against the bright light.

"Close the blinds, Marie," Lainey said, her thumb making gentle circles over Alora's skin. "It's too bright."

"She's been asleep for damn near twenty hours. Could use some sunlight, if you ask me."

Once the light was dimmed, Alora cracked open her lids. Attempting to speak, she looked upon the face of her dearest friend.

"She's just worried about you," Lainey whispered, giving a wink. "You know Marie. Her love language is gruff."

"Love language, my ass," Marie said, sitting back down on the other side of Alora. "You all should've let me die in 2075. This hellhole isn't ready for two of me."

Elation swam through Alora's veins. "We made it?" she croaked.

"We made it," Lainey said, beaming. "Elle showed up and told us everything. Zach and Sara arrived seconds later. Zach is a damn genius and arrived two days before we were going to put the mini-Sphere in motion and come get you."

"Mini-Sphere?" Alora asked.

"Technology in 2035 is unbelievable, my friend. Nelson and I figured out we needed to make the time machine portable if we were going to have any chance of success. So we created the mini-Sphere. It's housed in a case that carries the entire contraption, mini-fuel-rod and all. We did it."

Alora shook her head on the pillow. "You're amazing."

"Me? You survived being abducted by the New Establishment—with a little help from Eli. Seems we have you to thank for getting him here."

Alora sighed. "I begged him to come, didn't I?"

Chuckling, Lainey nodded. "You sure did."

"*Mierda.*" Alora slapped her hand to her forehead.

"Ain't no shame in asking a man as mysterious and handsome as Eli Hernandez to travel through time with you, especially since he has a propensity to save your damn hide. He might come in handy. And maybe you can give him a reason to stop brooding all the time," Marie said, circling her hand over her face.

Feeling drained, Alora pushed her head back into the soft pillow. "How bad are my injuries?"

"Pretty nasty gunshot wound, but Sara removed the bullet and sewed you up. You should be back to normal in a few weeks. But it's important you rest."

Looking at Marie, Alora slid her hand across the bed and grasped the woman's weathered fingers. "What happened after you left us?"

"Tanner's men found me, but they decided I was better kept as a hostage. I did manage to throw them off for a day, which is why you all were able to infiltrate the hub so easily, I imagine. When Lainey showed up with her fancy new time machine, Hunter appeared from the damn thing and took the soldiers by surprise."

"That was the bright light I saw," Alora said with wonder. "I thought I was crossing into heaven."

"Not yet, girl," Marie said, disentangling their hands and standing. "We've got a lot to do, and I need to cook us some dinner. We've got nine mouths to feed in this two-bedroom townhouse, and I aim to do it. I'll make something special for you since you probably can't swallow. Tomato soup will do. Yes," she said, talking to herself as she trotted out of the room, "tomato soup today, and cream of mushroom tomorrow..."

Alora laughed once she'd disappeared down the stairs. "I'm pretty sure she's going to outlive us all."

"Truer words," Lainey said with a grin. "We popped you full of ibuprofen, but if the pain is really bad, I can get my hands on something stronger."

"No," Alora said, shaking her head. "I want to keep my wits about me. I'm fine. Just a bit groggy and woozy. I'd love some water."

"I'll get some for you and leave the door cracked. Just call me if you need me. Eli has been checking on you too. Is it okay if I send him in?"

Alora's eyes narrowed. "Give me a day to recover. I need all my strength to spar with him. Can't let him have the advantage."

"Wow," Lainey said, eyebrows lifting. "I never thought—"

"It's nothing. I mean it, Lainey. Now that we've made it here, I've got one goal, and that's my focus."

Lainey chewed her bottom lip as she contemplated. "Man, you're good. I think you've almost convinced yourself you don't care for him."

"I don't," Alora lied.

With one last knowing smile, Lainey stood. "Okay. I'll concede for now because you're injured." Leaning down, she placed a sweet kiss on Alora's forehead.

Once she had some water, Alora drank several huge gulps and collapsed back on the bed. Running her fingers over the bandages, she realized how lucky she was to be alive. God must still see some purpose for her, and she aimed to complete it.

Knowing she needed to heal if she was going to accomplish anything, she forced herself to nap, wondering why she could somehow still sense Eli's presence even when she was dreaming.

* * * *

Eli refilled the empty glass and headed upstairs, setting it on the table before glancing down at Alora. She breathed deeply, those full red lips slightly parted, and he ached to hold her. Coming so close to losing her had shifted something in him, and he wasn't sure he could ever go back. Somewhere along the way, his infatuation had turned to reverence, lust had turned to complete surrender, and admiration had turned to...*love*?

Was it possible he loved this woman who turned his soul on its side and challenged him more than anyone he'd ever known? If he had to fall for anyone, of course it would be her. The gloriously magnificent woman who was his match in every way...except for her absence of evil. No, she would never share the darkest parts of his soul. Could she even begin to love him back? Improbable. His disastrous actions on the day they met would forever cloud their relationship.

As they should, he thought, understanding he didn't deserve forgiveness. He'd stopped hoping for that from her—or from anyone—long ago. Desperate to touch her but knowing she'd asked Lainey to tell him to stay away, he forced his hand into a fist and left the room before he trailed a finger over her soft cheek.

The team was downstairs in the living room catching up on the past weeks—or months, in some cases, thanks to differing timelines—and Eli sat in the empty leather chair feeling like an interloper in the close-knit group.

"I'm so thankful we all made it," Lainey said, grasping Sara's hand as she sat beside Luke on the couch. "And you're pregnant! I'm so happy for you guys."

"I was worried you'd chew me out," Sara said, "but his swimmers are too strong, I guess."

"Damn right, woman," Luke murmured, nuzzling her hair. Their affection was obvious, and Eli wondered how thin the walls of the townhome were. By the look of it, those two were having trouble keeping their hands off each other as it was.

"As great as this place is, I don't think it's really meant for nine people."

"You're right about that, Eli," Lainey said. "We need to form a solid plan. First of all, we need to surveil my grandfather and figure out how to infiltrate the White House. It's going to be extremely difficult, but we knew that going in. It's the end of May, so we have approximately three months to form a rock-solid plan. In the meantime, we have enough money in our stockpile to rent the four-bedroom apartment two blocks away on Juniper Street. I was thinking Elle, Marie, Alora, Eli, and Zach could stay there. Zach, you'll have to sleep on the living room couch, and you'll all have to share the two bathrooms. Hope that's okay."

"No problem, boss," Zach said, giving her a salute.

"Nelson can stay here with Luke, Hunter, Sara, and me. We'll figure out the sleeping arrangements, guys. It's not ideal, but we'll make it work."

Marie buzzed in from the kitchen, mitts covering both her hands as she waved to the group. "Well, come on, kids. It's getting cold. The table's set for four, and the rest of you will have to eat out here. Soup, salad, and lasagna from the stockpile Lainey had in the fridge. Forgot how much food we had in this decade. It's going to make me lazy to have it at my fingertips."

"You could never be considered lazy, Marie," Lainey said, rising and sliding her arm over the woman's shoulders. "Thank you for cooking. Let's dig in, everyone."

As they ate, Eli noticed how quiet Dr. Longwood was. There was something on the man's mind, and he felt in his gut that he was biding his time until he could speak to Lainey.

Sure enough, once the dinner was finished and the red wine had been opened, the scientist quietly asked Lainey to speak on the front porch. As they trailed outside, Eli headed up the stairs to check on Alora. She was softly snoring, but the cup on the bedside table was empty. Picking it up, he refilled it with tap water from the downstairs kitchen sink since it had some sort of fancy filter on it. Carrying it back upstairs, he set it on the table.

This time, he couldn't subdue the need to touch her—to verify that she was alive. Ever so softly, he stroked his fingers over her silky hair. Her lips smacked together as she craned toward his touch. Knowing he was playing with fire, he trailed down the stairs to join the others.

* * * *

Dr. Elaine Randolph sat in the rocking chair next to Dr. Nelson Longwood, marveling at the fact she'd just seen his younger self yesterday.

"You look really good, Nelson."

"Thanks, little brainy," he said, but the smile didn't reach his eyes. "It's been hard surviving without Lorna."

Inhaling a contemplative breath, Lainey leaned her head back on the chair. "It's suicide, Nelson. How can I send you back there?"

A breathy laugh escaped his lips. "You already knew I was going to ask."

"I understand your need to get back to her, but you're safe here. I'm terrified to transport you right back into danger."

"Right back to *her*, Lainey. To the other half of my heart. You'd do the same in a second if Hunter was stuck in 2075. Wouldn't you?"

Sighing, she nodded. "A few months ago, I would've said 'no fucking way' because I'd convinced myself it wasn't going to happen. Now, he's become such a part of me, I feel like he's another limb or something. I have absolutely no idea how that happened, and it's quite disconcerting."

Chuckling, Nelson slipped his hand into hers. "It's called love, Lainey. Happy to see you join the rest of us and experience it. Lewis would be so thrilled."

She squeezed his hand. "He would, wouldn't he?"

"Absolutely." Their hands swung slowly between the rocking chairs as they sipped the wine. Finally, Nelson said, "If you don't send me back, I'll just track down my younger self and convince him to do it since he helped you build the mini-Sphere. He's got the technology now, but contacting that version of myself could have so many disastrous consequences." Looking deep into her eyes, he said, "Please, Lainey. She's all alone. I have to go back."

"Okay," she said, hating to lose him when she'd just found him again. "Do you want to say goodbye to everyone?"

His features drew together. "No. Not in this timeline. I think it will shift focus from your mission. Let's transport tonight, once everyone's asleep. You all can say your goodbyes to the younger versions of myself and Lorna once you all grow old in the new timeline. I like that ending better."

"You'll probably die when we stop my grandfather and reset the timeline," she said softly.

"As long as I'm with Lorna, I don't really give a damn, Lainey."

Lainey took a slow sip of wine. "Okay. Tonight, at two o'clock. We'll transport from the back yard. We'll do it as quickly as possible, and hopefully, we won't wake the neighbors. The mini-Sphere is bright and loud as hell."

"With all the noise in this decade, it will be a blip on the radar." As if to prove his point, a low-flying plane sounded overhead, drowning out their voices for several seconds.

Chuckling, she nodded. "This decade is noisy, for sure. Can't wait to settle down on a quiet winery in the middle of nowhere once I save the world."

"Is that what you have planned once you succeed?"

She nodded and caught him up on the plans she'd discussed with Hunter. They'd both decided they wanted a quiet life surrounded by lots of land and lots of wine for Lainey. Oh, how she still longed to drink her expensive Malbec one day. She would savor that damn glass until the last full-bodied drop.

"Your future sounds bright, Lainey. I'm so happy for you."

"I'm still trying to navigate the best I can. I still plan on appearing to Eli when he's seven years old in 2039. By that time, we'll know more about the New Establishment. I understand that even if I stop my grandfather, there will be others who will rise to prominence. I'll do my best to prep Eli and sow the seeds that will hopefully ensure a peaceful future. After that, I'm going to travel to 2063 to warn Kara of her death date. It may be inevitable in every timeline, but I'll give her the basic information I can without upending the space-time continuum."

"Did Hunter ask you to do that?"

She shook her head. "He doesn't know. I don't want to give him false hope."

"That's dangerous, Lainey. You should tell him, so he can protect you."

"I'll most likely tell him right before I go, just to be safe. If I tell him before that, he'll try to stop me."

"But you're intent on going."

"Yes," she said, staring off into the distance as she drank another sip of wine.

"Why?"

"Because I love him. And if I can save him from experiencing the pain of her death, I'll do it. She dies in every cycle on April 9, 2063. Hopefully, this cycle will be different—for her and for all of us."

"If you save her, there will be no chance of you two getting together in the new timeline."

"Nope," she said, shrugging. "We only get one shot at it, Hunter and I. These two souls in these two bodies in this moment in time...as long as we both shall live. I figure love has about a one-in-a-million chance of working out anyway. Somehow, he and I found it in this incarnation of ourselves. Who knows how many others there have been?" Tracing her finger on the glass, she grew pensive. "Honestly, I don't even care. I love him so much that I'm immensely grateful to have him in this one speck of time. If we're lucky, we'll live out the rest of our lives together. I'll leave the other infinite possibilities to chance because I've already won the prize."

"Said like a woman deep in love. Lorna used talk about me like that. Now, she says I snore too much and I steal all the covers."

Lainey swatted him as she snickered. "That woman loves you to the point of insanity."

"She does. I can't wait to see her again."

They spoke for another hour, saying goodbye even though they didn't utter that specific word, and eventually, the house stilled as night descended upon it. At 2:00 a.m., Lainey walked outside, the case that contained the mini-Sphere clutched in her hand. Setting it on the grass, she unlatched it and pried it open.

The inner workings of the time machine all glinted inside the small case. The shiny buttons, tiny lasers, and small mechanical arms that were still capable of bending gravity. A small nuclear fuel rod housed a miniscule uranium pellet that the younger version of Nelson had gotten his hands on by way of some backdoor deal with a Russian scientist. Lainey had worried for his safety if he were to ever get caught, but he'd dismissed her arguments, telling her that preventing the apocalypse was more important than one man's safety.

"What's that look for?" Nelson asked.

"Younger You did a shady deal to get the uranium for me," she said, pointing to the mini-fuel-rod. "It was kind of badass."

Nelson ran his fingernails back and forth over his chest. "Glad to be of service, ma'am."

Laughing, she punched the small keypad, typing in the date she wanted to transport Nelson to: September 20, 2075.

"You don't have to enter any equations?" Nelson asked.

"Not with this high-tech little dream. Younger You and I took the working equations and configured them all into the keypad. I mean, this is really cool stuff, Nelson. I'm expecting you to tell me how brilliant I am."

Pulling her close, he drew her into a smothering embrace. "You're a genius, little brainy, and like a daughter to me and Lorna. I love you."

Tears welled in her eyes as she squeezed him. "I love you too."

Stepping back, she swiped the tears from her cheeks. "Ready?"

"Ready."

She clicked the buttons, setting the metal arms, about shin-high, into motion. Next, the button for the lasers was depressed, and then the one for the fuel rod jolt. A small wormhole appeared, black and ominous, and eventually grew to roughly their height.

"We just step into it," she said, grasping his hand. "No radiation suits needed."

Nodding, he let her lead him through the wormhole.

Lainey closed her eyes as she felt the now-familiar sucking sensation on every inch of her skin. Exiting the other side, she lifted her lids to observe the Australian hub.

"The transport is so smooth," Nelson yelled above the noise.

Lainey nodded. "Much smoother than the original Sphere. We tweaked everything with 2035 technology." Although the wormhole itself was dark, the light that swirled around it was bright and glowing. "I've got to go—it's too bright," she yelled, her hair flying in the wind produced by the machine. "Tell Lorna I love her."

Observing Nelson's broad back as he walked toward the hub, she entered the wormhole and transported through. Reappearing in 2035, she stepped from the device and began the shutdown sequence. As she pressed the buttons and closed the case, she imagined Nelson and Lorna's reunion. Smiling, she carried the mini-Sphere inside and set it on the floor beside the bed.

Removing the jeans and light sweater she'd thrown on, she slipped on one of Hunter's T-shirts and climbed into bed. Snuggling up to his side, she sighed as he stroked her hair.

"He made it?"

"Mm-hmm," she said into his chest.

"You okay, sweetheart?"

"Yeah," she said, nuzzling him. "It's just so strange. Everything's coming together, but I feel off-balance. There are so many timelines and so many mistakes to be made. How do I ensure I don't fuck up? Lord knows, we've failed at this before. I've already figured that out."

"Not this time, duchess," he said, kissing her hair. "This time, we're going to win. And then I'm going to find that damn Malbec you rave about so you can drink it and move the hell on."

They softly stroked each other as they contemplated the gravity of their mission. After a few moments, Hunter said, "You know, you already made one mistake tonight."

Lainey felt her eyebrows draw together. "What was it?"

Hunter's fingers delved beneath the waistline of her underwear. "You wore panties to bed."

Planting her elbows on his chest, she plopped her head on her fist. "Oh, yeah? What are you going to do about it?" She ran her leg over his hairy one, seductive and slow.

Quick as lightning, he flipped her, lacing his fingers with hers and drawing them to lie beside her head on the pillow. "I can think of a few things," he said, the gravel in his voice sending shivers through her rapidly heating body.

"Well, soldier," she said, arching a brow. "I'm all ears—"

Her words were swallowed whole by his talented mouth and searching tongue. Pushing away her doubts and fears—for the time being at least—she proceeded to be thoroughly ravished by the man she loved with her entire soul.

Chapter 16

The next morning was filled with quite a few groans as well as pops and creaks from the majority of the household who had slept on the floor. They'd all volunteered to do it—after all, the living room was large, and they'd been sleeping in the woods for weeks—but for some reason, the carpeted floor was extremely uncomfortable.

"I'm too damn old for this," Eli said, rubbing his neck. "We need to rent that apartment ASAP."

"We made the appointment with the realtor for eleven o'clock," Luke said as he came down the stairs. Even though he had a limp from a long-ago injury, he looked like a man who'd slept in a comfortable bed. Bastard.

"Great. I'll go with you to see it. Can we rent it today?"

"The realtor said as long as we pay six months' rent up front, they don't need to do a credit check."

"Perfect," Eli said. "How likely is it that it's already being surveilled?"

"Pretty likely," Hunter said, striding into the living room. "The New Establishment has had eyes on us since we arrived here, but so far, they haven't made contact. I still see their agents from time to time and wonder what they're waiting for. When we saw your father in the alley, he said they'd decided it was in Lainey's best interests to rebuild the time machine. I'm not sure if they've also discerned it's best for her to confront Randolph. We just have no idea."

The unknowns worried Eli. He understood they'd traveled these roads before, and they'd failed to stop Randolph in previous timelines. Perhaps the New Establishment wanted Lainey and her team to confront Randolph because that was the moment she failed in every timeline. If so, they would need to switch up the playbook and institute some surprises for the bastards.

As the team rose, Nelson's absence was noted, and Lainey explained that she'd sent him back to reconnect with Lorna in 2075. "Let's do the best we can to ensure we're successful, so his efforts for all these years weren't in vain. We'll secure the apartment and then we'll get to work, guys," she said as they all sat in the living room eating the breakfast Marie had prepared.

The eleven o'clock appointment was smooth and uneventful, and they walked away with a shiny new four-bedroom apartment. The members of the team began moving in, and Eli pulled Lainey to the side as everyone was consumed with the flurry of the move.

"I'd like a breakdown of the surveillance equipment and how to use it. I haven't used technology since I was young and need a refresher."

"Sure," she said, studying him. "Where are you at, Eli? I know you weren't set on coming here. Are you committed to this? It's going to be extremely difficult, especially since it's inevitable we'll run into your father."

"I'm committed," he said, rubbing his hand over his chin. "I'm glad Tanner was killed. If we fail, it makes me feel better about that timeline. But I'm wondering…"

"Yes?"

"Your team is extremely close. I understand that. I'm not sure I fit cohesively into the group."

"You fit just fine," she said, giving his arm a pat as he winced. "Did I hurt you?"

"I got grazed a few days ago," he said, rubbing the muscles around his wound. "Sara treated it, but it's still a bit sore."

"Yikes! Sorry. Really bad aim," she said, wincing. "I was just trying to say that you're a part of this team, Eli. Your knowledge of the history of the New Establishment will come in extremely handy as we figure out how to infiltrate Randolph's circle. Don't doubt your value and know that we're a pretty easygoing group. Just be nice, and we'll pretty much accept you. See, Elle's got it down pat already."

She pointed to Elle, who was standing in the back yard excitedly talking to Zach as he detailed her on the mini-Sphere. They both seemed enthralled by the device.

"Just talk to Zach about science, throw some wine my way, don't antagonize Alora, and you'll be all set."

"Alora is antagonized if I'm within fifty feet of her," he muttered.

Lainey's brows lifted. "Good. That means she cares. Lucky you."

Lucky him. Sure. Wanting to help the others, he perused the living room, seeing if there were any straggling items that needed to be transported to the new apartment. Alora appeared, gingerly walking down the stairs, and he rushed to her side like a damn sap.

"Here," he said, offering her his hand. "Lean on me."

"I'm fine," she said, waving it away. "Thank you though."

A rebuff with an acknowledgement of thanks. Not so terrible in the grand scheme of things. Eli decided he'd take it. Small steps were better than no steps.

Eli headed to the new place along with Alora, Elle, Marie, and Zach, and they settled in, each picking their rooms. Eli offered to sleep on the couch, but Zach was adamant he didn't mind. And perhaps it would give him the opportunity to hang with Elle each night before she went upstairs to bed. *Sly dog*, Eli thought. The young man was learning.

The rest of the day was spent at the thrift shop and the dollar store, ensuring they had functional clothes and basic toiletries to survive for the next few months. And then they got down to business. Lainey held tutorials in her private rented townhome's back yard, showing everyone how to use technology in 2035. They all were fastidious students, except Marie, who told them she'd already lived through the decade once and actually thought the planet was better off without technology. She fell back into her old pattern of cooking meals and doing the laundry, which was actually a godsend for two housefuls of people intent on saving the world.

Once they were well versed in the technology of 2035, Lainey addressed the group as they sat around the large back yard, which would be their strategic operations center, even if quite an informal setting. It was surrounded by a ten-foot-tall wooden fence and offered much-needed privacy as they planned the intricate operation.

"Okay, guys, we're not going to rewrite history here. The White House was infiltrated by two separate parties on November 24, 2009, and we're going to replicate those steps."

"How did the intruders gain access?" Eli asked.

"The Obamas held a state dinner that night to honor the Indian Prime Minister and his wife. Tareq and Michaele Salahi were a married couple who, despite not having an invite or being vetted by the staff or Secret Service, made it through multiple checkpoints. They were formally announced as they entered the gala and shook hands with Obama, Biden, and Colin Powell, among others. They just showed their IDs, claimed they had an invitation, and the Secret Service waved them through, instructing them to just keep showing their IDs along the way."

"Wow," Alora said. "That takes balls."

"No kidding," Lainey said with a chuckle. "That same night, another man named Carlos Allen also snuck into the dinner. He didn't know the Salahis and infiltrated separately on his own. He walked right in along with the Indian Prime Minister's procession."

"Well, I guess it shows the White House security is fallible," Eli said, leaning on the wooden picnic table, eyes narrowed in contemplation. "Did either party suffer prosecution?"

"Not really. Both parties were eventually questioned by authorities but deemed harmless. But let's be clear," Lainey said, holding up a finger, "if they can do it, we can. It will require intense and meticulous planning, but I have faith in our team."

"This is probably a stupid question," Eli said, rubbing the back of his neck, "but why can't you just transport us there in the time machine?"

"Not a stupid question at all," Lainey said. "First of all, the machine requires a time jump of at least twenty-four hours to function properly. It's designed to travel through time, not distance, so I couldn't stand outside the White House at five o'clock and transport inside to the same moment. I'd need to jump at least twenty-four hours ahead. Does that make sense?"

The group murmured their assent.

"Secondly, the time machine relies on nuclear energy. The bunker is lined with zirconium, tungsten, and concrete, with a density of three hundred pounds per cubic foot. The time machine won't function properly inside the bunker, so we can't use it there."

"Sounds like poppycock to me," Marie muttered as she watered the small garden she'd planted against the fence. "But what do I know? I'm just here for shits and giggles."

"Thank you for your commentary, Marie," Lainey said, shooting her a good-natured glare. "The mini-Sphere will also draw too much attention if we use it to access the hallway leading to the bunker. It's loud and extremely bright and will alert every guard and agent we're there. That's why we have to access the bunker the old-fashioned way."

"But we can use the mini-Sphere to transport out?"

"Yes," Lainey said, nodding to Alora. "Once we've stopped Randolph, I don't care how loud we are as long as we escape quickly. We'll head to the hallway and use it there to transport to the rental home we've secured in Boonsboro, Maryland, exactly twenty-four hours later. It's remote but still close enough to D.C. that we can monitor things. Cyrus has agreed to call me as soon as we jump ahead in time and confirm that we succeeded."

"Are you going to carry the time machine inside?" Alora asked. "Surely, they'll scan you. They'll scan us all. How are we going to get access while carrying our weapons?"

"Nelson and I are developing asbestos sheets to place around our guns as well as an asbestos lining for my purse that will house the mini-Sphere. Asbestos shouldn't be inhaled over long periods of time, but for these purposes, it's fine, and asbestos shields metal from detection."

"Science wins again!" Zach said, holding his finger in the air.

"Always," Lainey said, giving him a wink. "Still, it's not going to be easy. We need to identify a few Secret Service agents we can sway to our side. The best way to do that is some good ol'-fashioned blackmail."

Alora sighed. "My favorite."

That spurred a chuckle from the group before Lainey continued.

"We'll need one inside conspirator in the security detail at the metal detector since my purse will probably be flagged for additional screening. After all, it will be quite large since I have the mini-Sphere inside. We also need to recruit agents to help us gain access to the hallways that lead to the bunker and look the other way when we breach. Alora, Eli, and Hunter will be in charge of the surveillance and for digging up dirt on several of the agents. As for everyone else, I'd like to define your roles moving forward."

They spent the next several minutes firming up details. Zach and Elle were responsible for cataloging the surveillance intel so they could look for patterns. Lainey would continue to lead the team, with Luke and Sara mostly providing moral support. With his pronounced limp, it was tough for Luke to do too much surveillance, and since she was pregnant, Lainey wanted Sara as far from danger as possible. With the plan set, the team got down to business.

* * * *

Two weeks into the surveillance, Eli, Hunter, and Alora decided to take a White House civilian tour. It would grant them a certain comfortability with the interior and help them gain intel. Although highly guarded, the plan was for one of them to hopefully sneak away and take pictures of closed-off portions of the mansion—most specifically, the hallway that led to the bunker. If they got caught, they would be imprisoned without hope of rescue since no one else on Lainey's team could take the chance of showing up to bail them out. Knowing this, they forged ahead, preparing for the dangerous mission.

The night before the tour was scheduled, Eli headed to the shared bathroom, noticing Alora through the crack as she examined her wound. Clothed in only a bra and thin shorts, his heart immediately went into overdrive.

"You might as well come in," she said, her eyes never leaving the reflection as she tentatively pushed the slightly swollen tissue. "If you're going to gawk, go ahead and get an eyeful."

Pushing the door open, he stepped inside, annoyed she didn't even bother to look at him. Shutting the door, he clicked the lock, causing her eyes to snap to his in the reflection. Thrilled he'd elicited a reaction, he closed the distance between them, aligning his front with her back until they brushed softly against each other.

Ever so gently, he ran the backs of his fingers over the purple skin that surrounded her wound. It was healing nicely, but he still worried she was taking on too much activity too quickly.

"How does it feel?" he asked, his lips brushing her ear.

"Better every day," was her breathy response as she gazed at him in the mirror.

Drowning in her melted chocolate eyes, he continued the feather-soft caress. She stayed still, the movements of her luscious body consisting of the rise and fall of her chest and the pulsing vein in her neck.

"I've missed you," he whispered, nuzzling her hair.

"I've been right here."

His free hand moved to her waist, palm sliding over the smooth skin as it quivered underneath. "In a house full of too many people," he said sardonically. "I didn't realize how good I had it when it was just you and me, alone in the woods."

She breathed a choppy laugh. "And what would you do if you could go back and have me all to yourself?"

Eyes cemented to hers, he slid his hand to the band of her shorts. Giving her ample opportunity to say "no," he fingered the soft fabric. When she only stared back, he glided his fingers underneath, reveling in her quick inhale. Sliding them down, under her panties, he brushed the soft curls.

"*Dios mio,*" she panted.

"God isn't here, *querida.* Just you and me. Are you wet?" He splayed his fingers over her soft folds, dying to delve between them.

She arched a brow, seductive as a damn sex goddess, and said, "There's only one way to find out."

Grateful for the consent, he pushed between her folds, searching for her essence. When he found her opening, wet and slick, she hissed and closed her eyes, throwing her head back on his shoulder.

"Do you know how many times I've imagined you just like this?" Circling her opening with his finger, he gently began to nudge inside. Slick with her juices, he filled her with his finger, hooking it as she writhed against him. Her swollen walls clenched him, and he gritted his teeth. Lifting his hand, he cupped her face, turning her head to capture her gaze.

"Do you want me to make you come?" he asked, his lips brushing hers.

"Yes," she moaned, pliant and limp in his arms. He'd longed to see her like this for ages, open and willing in his embrace, and it shattered something inside his soul.

"I don't have enough lifetimes to do everything I've fantasized about doing to you, Alora." He slipped another finger inside, thrusting into her tight channel as she writhed. "Doing *with* you. Do you know how much I think about you? It drives me fucking insane."

"I don't think about you at all," she whimpered, mouth open in a gasp as he jutted his fingers relentlessly inside her.

"You're a terrible liar, sweetheart. You always have been. Let's put that tongue to better use than spouting lies."

Her lids slid open to reveal eyes blazing with arousal. "Screw you, dear husband." Extending her tongue, she bathed her lips, seductive and slow, setting his body on fire.

Lowering his mouth, he captured her lips, pillaging them as if he were the last man on Earth and the fate of the world depended on devouring her mouth. And, god, what a mouth it was. Deep...wet...hot... Her tongue surrounded his, slick and strong, as she battled with him. It was a furious kiss, filled with all the things they longed to say to each other but hadn't found the strength to utter. Gathering her honey on his fingers, he slid them up her folds, finding the sensitized bud that pulsed between them. Pulling her apart, he began to circle it, causing her to mewl into his mouth.

He caught it as he caught her other purrs and groans, his tongue searching her warm depths as his fingers lifted her higher toward the ultimate reward. Wanting nothing more than to give it to her, he sucked her bottom lip between his teeth.

"You're melting for me, sweetheart. So goddamn sexy."

She panted rapidly, clutching his hair. "I'm going to come," she said, her tone a high-pitched wail he'd never heard.

Thrilled he could make her lose control, he nodded. "Fuck yes, you are. You're going to come all over my fingers, aren't you, *querida*?" Feeling something roar within, he captured her lips again, needing to claim as much of her trembling body as possible.

She kissed him back so passionately, so wantonly, he knew this was only the beginning. He needed more, so much more from his beautiful Alora. He wanted to take his time with her and lay her open so he could worship her in all the ways she deserved. He wanted to cherish her and, when the time was right, tell her he'd somehow fallen under her spell and never wanted to be released.

A ragged cry escaped her throat, and her body began to convulse. Pressing his face against hers, they shared the same breath as she fell apart in his arms.

Anxious to prove she could trust him, he held her close, needing her to understand he'd never let her fall. Her head jerked upon his shoulder, thrown back as her long lashes fluttered, and then she burrowed into his neck. Clutching him there, she spurred her nails into the soft skin, causing him to hiss.

"Sheathe your claws, woman," he teased, placing soft kisses along her temple as resounding shudders rocked her frame.

"How am I still standing?" she mumbled into his pec.

"Because I've got you." Drawing his fingers from her core, he lifted them to gently touch her chin. "I've always got you." Overcome with desire, he spread her own wetness over her swollen bottom lip as she stared at him through slitted eyes. Gaze locked with hers, he closed in and slowly licked her essence from her mouth. Needing more, he drew her lip between his own and sucked her dry.

After a while, she began to kiss him back, soft and lazy, as they gazed into each other. Content to hold her and kiss her forever, he didn't give a damn that his arm was straining or there was a slight hitch in his back from the awkward angle. After all, he wasn't twenty-five anymore. But with her in his arms, he might as well have been immortal, for she gave him a superhuman strength he'd never felt before.

Placing his forehead against hers, he kissed her nose, causing her to scrunch her features.

"Damn," she said softly, caressing his cheek. "You're actually sweet. How am I going to resume hating you?"

His lips quirked. "I'm certainly not sweet. But I'm pretty damn lucky to finally be holding you like this, Alora."

"Ugh," she said, rolling her eyes. "Sappy sweet. I'd be grossed out if you hadn't just made me come in my damn dollar-store panties."

His chuckle enveloped them both. "They're pretty soft for bargain basement prices."

Smiling, she ran her thumb over his lips. He'd never seen her so relaxed and understood she rarely let her guard down. Humbled by her trust, he kissed her roving thumb.

"Your turn," she whispered, arching a brow.

Inhaling deeply, he straightened, lifting them both in the process. "Not tonight. I don't want the first time you touch me to be rushed or muted."

Her eyebrows lifted as if she couldn't believe he was turning down her offer.

"I'm honored you want to, believe me," he said, sifting his fingers through her hair. "But we have a shit ton of other people in this house, many of whom are probably already wondering what the hell we've been doing in here. When you finally touch me in all the ways I've imagined, I want you all to myself, without the gang around," he finished, gesturing with his head toward the door.

"How positively idealistic," she said, her grin adorable as she leaned against the counter. "You're a romantic."

"Honestly, I probably always have been," he said, feeling his cheeks warm, which further caused him to feel off-balance. "My mother was a hopeless romantic who filled my head with stories of true love and soul mates. I was doomed from the start."

"The evil Eli Hernandez, our own Prince Charming. Who knew?"

Laughing, he gently grasped her waist. "Who knew?" Leaning down, he murmured against her lips. "Once the White House tour is complete, I'd like to find time to spend a night with you."

Her dark eyebrow arched. "Only one night?"

"We'll see how it goes," he said, giving a good-natured eye roll. "I want to see if there's any way we could possibly try to make this marriage real."

Her shoulders tensed, sending a jolt of raw pain through his heart. Although he'd come to accept the depth of his feelings for her, she obviously hadn't done the same. It was very possible she only felt desire toward him and was looking to scratch an itch. But she had begged him not to stay in 2075, and that was something at least. Determined to latch onto whatever kernel of emotion had urged her not to leave without him, he lifted her chin.

"Real in that we're two consenting adults who are very attracted to each other, Alora. I want to explore that and see where it takes us."

She seemed to relax at that, if only slightly, and he waited for her response.

"All right. We'll find some time to be alone. Perhaps rent a hotel room. As much as I love the team, I don't want them in my business."

"Fair enough." Straightening, he dropped his hands, immediately mourning the loss of her soft skin against his.

"You must have to...relieve yourself," she said, gingerly running a finger over his fly, which now covered a semi hard-on. Witch.

"You're an evil woman," he said, grinning as she patted his cheek.

"Good night, Eli. I'll leave behind something to ease your ache." Drawing a plastic container from her tiny bag, she placed it on the counter. Standing on her tiptoes, she whispered in his ear. "It's for sensitive skin. You'll be fine." Placing a chaste kiss on his jaw, she exited, closing the door behind her.

Picking up the bottle, he couldn't control the laugh that escaped his throat. The little she-devil had left a bottle of lotion behind. Deciding not to turn away a kind gesture from the woman whose table scraps of affection he coveted, he ended up putting the lotion to very good use as he remembered her falling apart in his arms.

Chapter 17

Alora secured her hair in the soft band so it fell in a long tail down her back. It was almost to her waist now, and she'd need to remedy that when she had time to worry about things like haircuts and self-care. For now, she tugged the silky blouse over her hips, tucking it into the black dress pants she'd found at the thrift store. It was important she appear as any other tourist on this morning's tour. Stepping into the wedges she'd also procured in her bargain shopping binge with Sara, she looked at her reflection in the mirror.

Her face remained makeup free, although she'd used the moisturizer she'd found on the counter this morning. Had Eli pleasured himself with it last night after she left? And why was the thought so damn arousing?

She'd let down her walls with the man she carried so many complex feelings for. Control had been her only constant for so long—it was strange to release it, if only for a moment. His skillful fingers had brought her such pleasure. What would happen if they had an entire night to themselves for him to use those magnificent hands? Shivering in anticipation, she realized she couldn't wait to find out. Screw deluding herself. She wanted Eli, and as soon as there was an opportunity for them to explore their intense attraction, she'd damn well take advantage.

As always, when she thought of her murky feelings for Eli, the maddening doubts circled in her brain. Was she betraying her parents and sisters by wanting the man who'd abetted in their murders? Did his efforts as a spy to help Lainey's cause redeem him from the evil deeds of his past? Unfortunately, she didn't have the answers and feared she never would. Her relationship with Eli would always be laced with multifarious questions and reservations. Alora would need to rely on her gut, which hadn't steered her wrong in four long decades. For now, it told her Eli's intentions were pure, and she would choose to believe that. Heaven help her.

Descending the stairs, she found Hunter and Eli at the bottom. His dark eyes roved over her as Hunter smiled. Annoyed by his inspection, she lifted her hands.

"Do I pass muster?" she asked, arching her brows.

"Sorry," Eli said, shaking his head. "I've just never seen you dressed up. You look pretty."

Gulp. Alora almost swallowed her tongue. This sweet seduction thing he had going on was intensely sexy for some reason, and she was falling for it like a damn sucker.

"Thank you," she said softly, unable to form one of her usually clever retorts.

"He's right," Hunter said, stepping toward her and clasping her hand. It was a reassuring gesture, reminding Alora how much she liked the man her dear friend had fallen in love with. "You look stunning as always, Alora. Are you feeling okay?" Concern swam in his gray eyes as he wondered about her injury.

"I feel fine," she said, clenching his hand before letting it go. "Let's infiltrate these bastards. I haven't done surveillance in a while, and I'm ready to kick some ass."

"Let's do it," Hunter said, flashing his brilliant smile.

After the taxi dropped them off a few blocks from the White House, Hunter pulled the tickets Zach had secured, each one matching the names on the fake IDs he'd created for them.

"There are cameras everywhere, so it's unlikely we'll be able to break away from the group for any reasonable amount of time. Still, let's familiarize ourselves with the layout. We know the hallway that leads to the door that opens to the stairs to the bunker. If you can get a clear shot of the hallway with your phone, do it."

Eli and Alora nodded, and they walked to the large mansion to file in with their designated group. After showing their tickets, they were led inside by the tour manager, a young woman named Catherine.

Catherine was thorough and detailed during the tour, and Alora listened out of one ear, interested in the history. Many of the portraits that lined the walls were white men, visibly showcasing the country's history of systemic white privilege at the highest level of government.

"Interesting to see the height of humanity before the fall," Eli murmured beside her.

Alora scoffed. "If this is the height of humanity, we were always doomed. Once we reset the timeline, they'd better put some women in here—brown, Black, and all shades in between. Otherwise, our efforts might be in vain."

"Maybe you could run. I wouldn't mind calling you 'President Castillo.'" He slightly waggled his brows.

"Keep your weird role-playing fantasies to yourself, Hernandez," she muttered, noticing they were moving toward the room with the bunker hallway off to the side. They were in the back of the group, and she had to stand on her toes to see Catherine.

"Ah, what a treat," Catherine said to the group, gesturing to a light-brown-skinned woman who appeared at her side. "This is Aiysha Gaynor, President Randolph's Press Secretary. It's always a pleasure when we encounter staff on the tour."

"Hello," Aiysha said, waving. "President Randolph would like to bestow his thanks upon all of you for taking the tour. You'll all be getting Randolph 2036 hats upon your exit. We hope we have your vote in the upcoming election."

Alora grimaced. "Yeah, I don't think that's happening."

Hunter expelled a breath behind her. "Not likely."

There were guards flanking every closed-off area of the room, and Alora realized her best chance of getting any sort of intel was *now*. Reaching into her purse, she pulled out the circular tube of ChapStick. Flicking her hand, she ensured it rolled forcefully down the hallway that led to the bunker door. Grasping her smartphone in her hand, she lifted the cloth divider and ran after the tube, hoping she appeared to be a frazzled tourist.

The tiny vial rolled down the slick floor at a fast pace, aiding her efforts. Jogging after it, she lifted her phone and surreptitiously took as many pictures of the hallway as possible. The wound at her side pulsed, but she pushed through. The mission was important, and Alora was an expert at performing through pain.

After several moments, a hand clamped around her arm.

"Ma'am," the hulking guard said, halting her. "You can't be in this area."

"Oh," Alora said, running her hand over her ponytail. "How stupid. I lost my ChapStick and was trying to retrieve it," she said, gesturing toward the tube that now lay against the far wall.

The man glowered and walked toward the vial, picking it up and returning it to her.

"Thank you," Alora said, stuffing it into her purse along with her phone. She certainly didn't want them confiscated. "I'm terribly sorry."

"Come with me." Placing a hand on her upper back, he directed her to the group. Speaking into his comm device, he said, "Breach in the East Wing. Confirm if we should question the offender."

Alora's heart leapt into her throat. "There's no need to question me, sir. I'll just rejoin the group now that I've retrieved the ChapStick."

The man glared down at her as he waited for his commander's response.

"What do we have here?" a kind voice asked. "Hello, Arnold," a woman said, reading the guard's name tag. "Is everything okay?"

"Yes, Ms. Gaynor," Arnold said, addressing President Randolph's Press Secretary. "The civilian was trespassing in a closed-off section of the White House."

Alora reached for the tube and held it high, hoping her instincts were right about the woman as her expression was kind and curious. "ChapStick malfunction. I ran to get it. It was a really stupid move."

Smiling, Aiysha reached into her own bag and pulled out a vial of lip gloss. "Can't live without the stuff, so I certainly understand. Perhaps Arnold doesn't quite grasp how important these little necessities are to us. I'm glad you retrieved it. Please enjoy the rest of the tour."

"It's protocol to question anyone who breaches the secure areas, ma'am," Arnold said gruffly to Aiysha.

Her features drew together. "For chasing down ChapStick? Seems a bit excessive."

Arnold's gaze trailed between the two women as he contemplated. Lifting the comm wire to his face, he said, "Threat level assessed and dismissed. No further action required."

"Thank you, Arnold," Aiysha said with a nod. "I'll make sure to inform President Randolph of your diligence. He'll most likely want to meet you."

The man's spine straightened with pride. "Thank you, ma'am."

"Come on," she said, waving to Alora. "I'll lead you back to the group."

Alora trailed beside her, taken with her kindness. "Thank you, Ms. Gaynor."

"Aiysha, please," she said, extending her elbow. Alora looked at it, unsure what to do. "It's a habit," she said, shrugging. "Ever since the coronavirus outbreak when I was thirteen, my parents instilled in me that I should always give the elbow instead of shake."

"Pleasure," Alora said, bumping her elbow. "Thank you for understanding. I'm such an idiot sometimes."

Aiysha's lips curved. "You don't seem like one to me. Have fun on the rest of the tour."

As Alora stared into her brownish-green eyes, a strange feeling seeped into her pores. Recognition? There was something so familiar about the woman even though they'd obviously never met. The shade of her irises was one Alora had never seen before, dark yet translucent, and they were stunning.

"Thank you. I truly appreciate your kindness." With a nod, she rejoined Hunter and Eli.

Once the tour was finished, they sat outside at a local restaurant dissecting the pictures on Alora's phone.

"Great work, Alora," Hunter said, staring at one of the blown-up images, expanded by his two fingers. "You got a shot of both men guarding the door at the end of the hallway. I think Zach can magnify the picture enough to discern their names from the badges. Then we'll surveil them. Any men guarding the door to the bunker will be Secret Service. Hopefully, we can infiltrate the regime that way, among others."

Alora puffed her cheeks, expelling a breath. "I thought I was going to be taken for questioning at one point. The Press Secretary saved my hide."

"That was nice of her," Hunter said, his brows drawing together. "And no one's 'nice' just for fun in this world, especially not a member of Randolph's staff. What was her angle?"

"I have absolutely no idea," Alora said, baffled. "She seemed to want to help me evade questioning by the guards."

"What advantage would that create for her?"

They pondered, unable to come up with any logical explanation.

"It was so strange," Alora said, shaking her head as she remembered the encounter. "She seemed familiar to me in a way. Like I've met her before, but I know I haven't. Lainey's convinced we've done this all before and ultimately failed, so perhaps it's some sort of weird déjà vu or something."

"We'll have Zach run a trace on her, just to be sure. Let's get back to the apartment. I want to get these pictures in his hands this afternoon."

They all reconvened at Lainey's backyard home base, sitting at the large tables they'd procured from the local WalMart. Elle worked on magnifying the pictures while Zach did a background check on Aiysha.

"Um, wow," Zach said, eyes narrowing as he stared at the screen. "You guys aren't going to believe what I found on Aiysha."

"Is she part of the New Establishment?" Alora asked.

"No way in hell," Lainey said, trailing down the stairs with a strange grin on her face. "Aiysha hates those bastards as much as we do."

"How do you know this?" Eli asked.

"Because Cyrus told me," Lainey said, lifting her arms in a slight shrug. "Aiysha is his daughter."

They all stared at Lainey, wide-eyed, as comprehension washed over them. "I thought her name was Elaine," Alora said.

"It is. Elaine Aiysha Montgomery. She started going by her middle name in college, and it stuck."

"No wonder she seemed so familiar to me," Alora said, shaking her head. "She's a perfect amalgamation of them both. Her eyes... Wow, I'm slacking. I totally should've known."

"Don't beat yourself up," Lainey said, placing her arm over Alora's shoulders. "Nothing is blatantly obvious when you're a time traveler. The nuances are vast, and I'm convinced we miss so many as we putter along."

"Aiysha's background is pretty awesome," Zach said, clicking through the various reports he'd generated. "Twenty-eight, married. Went to Yale, was President of the Minority Political Club, and continued to rise to prominence from there. It seems she was extremely helpful to securing the minority vote for President Randolph in his 2032 victory. In return, he hired her as Press Secretary."

"Are we sure she has no ties to President Randolph's more nefarious causes?" Eli asked. When the group bristled at his question, he held his palms high. "Just asking as someone who understands how easy it is to develop a backstory that isn't real."

"She doesn't seem to be related to the Knights of Washington or any of the other secret societies President Randolph frequents," Zach said. "Those societies don't really accept many members who are Black or female."

Alora scowled. "Better for her, but it shows their ignorance."

"She's legit, guys," Lainey said, "and firmly supports our efforts."

"Awesome," Zach said. "I can't wait to meet her. So strange to think Cyrus and Claire have a daughter older than me. Mind blown." He held his hands to his temples and stretched his fingers wide, mimicking the statement.

Standing, Alora stretched, feeling the tug from her wound. "I'm going to head back to the townhouse. My side is killing me, and I need some of the magnificent Advil that seems to be so abundant here."

"Do you need me to come with you?" Eli asked, standing as worry crossed his features.

You wish, buster, was her first thought. Although she'd let her guard down last night, their next sexual encounter would be on her terms, when she was good and ready.

"No, thank you. Stay and have some of Marie's fantastic dinner. I hear she's making a pot roast. I'll eat what's left in the refrigerator at home. My cell will be on if you need me."

Feeling exhausted, she left them behind to get some rest.

Chapter 18

Later that evening, Zach sat outside the rented four-bedroom townhome, rocking in the wooden swing that had been installed by the previous tenants. Extremely grateful to them, it had become the zenith of his entire source of happiness. He and Elle had fallen into a pattern where they swung lazily every night it didn't rain, always engaging in engrossing conversations about life and science and dreams... Every word uttered from her pink lips was one he cherished as he fell deeper down the chasm of love.

She never got too personal, which was fine. There was time for that. For now, he was content to tell her everything about his own life, although there wasn't much to tell. He'd left his home at sixteen when he realized his exceptional aptitude. Understanding it could possibly help his mother feed his five younger siblings, he sought a way to monetize it. Rumors of the eccentric scientist who lived in the foothills of Virginia had always circulated around his small compound in what was formerly upper Vermont. After much pleading, he convinced his mother to travel to find it. Since his father had long passed, his fourteen-year-old sister, Constance, looked after the rest of the brood while they were gone. When he'd hugged her goodbye, he hadn't known it would be the last time.

He thought of them often, his mother and siblings, and hoped they were all well. The generous portions of food, gas for their lamps, and other recompences Lewis had bestowed upon his mother in exchange for him staying at the hub should've vastly increased their chances of survival.

"What are you thinking?" Elle asked, her expression wistful.

"That I miss my sister. My whole family, actually."

"The decision to stay at the hub when you were still so young is really brave." Red flushed across her cheeks, so charming under the moonlight. "A true sacrifice."

"It wasn't so bad," he said, stroking her hair, his arm across her shoulders. "Everyone at the hub is amazing. I loved Lewis like a father. It was heartbreaking when he and Mara died." Seeing the question in her eyes, he elaborated. "We're pretty sure he had lung cancer, although we don't know for sure. Mara died several years earlier. She was pretty healthy, so it was probably a virus of some sort, perhaps brought back by Lewis when he returned from one of his excursions. I think he always blamed himself for her death."

"They couldn't have known for sure."

"No, but it's the most likely explanation. Regardless, he was devastated. Lainey pulled him through, but eventually, he left us too. I was really worried for Lainey for a while—they were really close—but she focused on her purpose and forged ahead. What she's found with Hunter is awesome. Lewis would be happy."

"Love is pretty awesome," she said, relaxing back into the swing.

He almost blurted it to her then. Those three words that would probably send her running for the hills. Instead, he pushed his lips together and told himself to stay quiet.

"You know," she said, lifting those doe eyes to his, "I really enjoy coming out here and making out with you every night. But do you think you might ever make a move that's a bit more..."—she circled her hand, searching for the word— "forward?"

Zach almost swallowed his tongue. Clearing his throat, he said, "I don't want to disrespect you, Elle."

Sighing, she slid her hand over his cheek. "God, who are you, and why didn't I find you years ago?"

"I'm so glad we've found each other now," he said, caressing her soft hair.

Her chest expanded as she inhaled a deep breath. "I bought some condoms when I went to the drugstore the other day. We need to use them if we have sex, which I really hope we do. But I want to tell you something first."

Zach could barely concentrate on her words since his brain had turned to mush at the whole "I hope we have sex" statement, but he tried to concentrate. "Okay."

Licking her lips, she seemed so hesitant that he tried to soothe her. "You can tell me anything."

"I know." Her eyes darted between his. "Unfortunately, I wasn't lucky enough to possess the mind of a genius and granted the opportunity to live on a fancy hub. My life hasn't been a cakewalk."

Hating that she'd ever experienced any pain, he grimaced. "I don't ever want you to hurt again. I'll try my best to protect you, Elle."

Closing her eyes, she breathed a gentle laugh. "I can protect myself," she said, reclaiming his gaze, "but would really like to build something with you, Zach. I thought once I came here and accomplished my goal, I'd ride off into the sunset. I didn't really think too far past that. But now I've realized I want more with you. God, it feels so weird to say it."

Extreme elation coursed through him as she continued.

"I'm not saying you have to marry me and give me a hundred kids—lord knows, this is still so new. But I'm saying you matter enough to me to make me want more."

Tamping down the urge to tell her he'd marry her tomorrow and give her a thousand babies, he told himself to be cool. "I want more with you too," he whispered. There. That was chill, right? Could she tell that he was two seconds away from doing cartwheels in the back yard? Apparently not, since she just stared up at him with that sweet face.

With a ragged breath, she said, "I'm not a virgin, Zach. Far from it. I'm telling you that because I'm pretty sure you are."

A plethora of emotions threatened to drown him. He was terribly embarrassed that he was so inexperienced.

"I am. But I'll do my best to make you feel good—"

She covered his lips with her fingers. "I'm dying for you to touch me. Everywhere. I know you'll make me feel good."

Wondering where she was going with the conversation, he nodded against her fingers.

"We need to use the condoms because I can't guarantee I don't have something." Removing her hand, she harshly rubbed her forehead. "Fuck, this is so hard. I'm a survivor, Zach. I had to be. I realized when I was fourteen that I was attractive enough to use my looks to manipulate men. Soldiers and merchants used to pass by our home on the way to Terrum. We lived outside the compound because my mother didn't trust the man who ran it. She wasn't mentally stable."

Zach tightened his arm around her shoulders, urging her to continue.

"Being outside the compound made us vulnerable. Men were always sniffing around, looking for a place to stay and for things to steal. My mother would...offer herself." She glanced toward the ground. "You know, so they wouldn't hurt us. But eventually, she became ill and a bit deranged, and she was no longer the one they wanted."

Rage scorched his gut, growing as she forged ahead. "I understood that I could manipulate them if I offered them sex. Most men are stupid creatures and easily swayed by a woman offering sexual favors. I gave myself to two men who passed by when I was fourteen. That was the first time. I just turned off my brain and did it. When we were finished, they left behind a huge bag of coins. It got us through the next year, and then we needed more money."

Tears burned his eyes as he imagined her losing her virginity to two strangers because she felt she had no other choice. Visions filtered through his mind of stealing the mini-Sphere and traveling back to that specific point in time just so he could save her and strangle the two men who could treat a young girl so carelessly.

"Eventually, I began offering favors to several of the men who passed by. We had a stable off to the side of our small cabin, and that's where I would take them. I'm not telling you this so you pity me or to make any sort of excuses. I chose my own path. It was the only choice I could see at the time, and I'm not ashamed. I truly hope you can understand why I made those decisions. If you can't accept it, I understand. I needed you to know my past so you realize who I really am."

A tear slid down his cheek, and he would've been mortified, but he was so focused on her that he didn't have space for any other feelings.

"I'm so sorry," she said, wiping the tear with her thumb. "You probably deserve someone better than a half-baked prostitute from a dystopian future. If you want to cut this off right now, I don't blame you."

"Why are you apologizing?" he asked, his voice gruff with hurt—not for himself, but for her. "You did what you had to do to survive. I just hate that men would take advantage of you like that."

"I don't see it that way, but I recognize why you do," she said, stroking his cheek. "You would never even consider exchanging sex for money. The act isn't transactional for you. It's emotional. Sadly, the world is harsh, and most people don't have the same mindset."

"I want to make love to you," he said, cupping her face, "and you're damn right it's emotional. You don't have to give me anything in return. That's what love really means."

"I don't think I've ever truly known anyone who comprehends that word. But you really do, and our team does too. I've never been with a man who hasn't leered at me and treated me like property."

Placing his forehead against hers, he held her face in his hands. "I'll treat you like a queen. I promise."

"I know," she whispered before capturing his lips with her own. It was a sweet kiss, full of hope and innocence. Drawing back, she said, "I told Marie a few days ago. Since she lived in this decade and her mom was a doctor, I figured she could help me find a physician who would see me without insurance. I made an appointment to go to a clinic on Friday morning."

"We'll use a condom, sweetheart," he said against her lips.

"Yes, we'll definitely do that. But I want to get tested too. It might not uncover everything, especially since they won't have tests for any viruses that appeared or mutated after 2035, but it's a start. Just know that I'll never be one hundred percent sure. I don't want to lie to you about anything."

"Thank you," he whispered, placing a feather-soft kiss on her lips. "For trusting me. If you can trust me with this, I guess I can tell you that I'm terrified to make love to you. I'm so afraid I'm going to be terrible at it."

She laughed, causing him to frown. "Damn, you're adorable," she said, shaking her head. "You're going to be fine. I'm so attracted to you, Zach."

"You are?"

"Yes," she said, nuzzling his nose. "Can't you tell? I never dreamed I'd find someone like you. I might become a stalker if you ever leave me. I'm trying really hard not to scare you off."

Chuckling, he nodded. "I was just telling myself to be cool so you wouldn't run away. I'm pretty sure I'm obsessed with you. In a good way, not a creepy way. I think."

They snickered in the darkness as an owl hooted from a nearby tree. Eventually, they strolled inside, Zach taking his usual position on the couch.

"Good night," she called, waving before she walked upstairs to her room.

"Night," he said, not even trying to control his smile.

Lacing his fingers behind his head, he realized he couldn't sleep if he tried, for he was pretty sure Elle had told him tonight that she loved him even if she hadn't said the exact words.

Hell yeah, Bishop. Rolling over, his photographic brain began recalling all the tips and tricks Eli had given him so he'd be prepared when he finally made love to the woman of his dreams.

* * * *

The team uncovered a plethora of information on President Randolph's Secret Service detail, especially the two men Alora had captured guarding the entrance to the bunker. Within several days, they knew each man's life story, down to their second and third cousins and any illicit dealings in their past that could be manipulated.

"You're a genius, Zach," Lainey said as the team sat outside her townhome. "I think we have a shot of blackmailing these guys to gain access during the state dinner."

"Thank Elle too," Zach said, giving his girlfriend a wink as she sat beside him. He'd started calling her that after the night they poured their hearts out to each other, and she hadn't told him to fuck off, so he figured they were a full-fledged couple. "She's a whiz at this stuff. For someone who grew up without technology, she's a natural."

"Thank you," she said, giving him a cheeky grin. "I want to pull my weight."

"Since Claire's not here, it's nice to find a new partner in crime."

From Zach's intel, a plan was formed where Hunter, Eli, and Alora would make contact with the Secret Service agents they felt were most vulnerable to blackmail. Through careful and systematic steps, they would piece together a way to gain access to the bunker and ultimately confront Randolph.

With the plan in place, Zach closed his laptop as the others dispersed, ready for one of Marie's hearty dinners. Elle remained beside him, leaning her elbow on the table and resting her chin on her fist.

"I got the results back," she said, hair blowing in the breeze as she gave him a tender smile.

"Yeah?" he asked, tucking a strand behind her ear.

Nodding, she said, "I was positive for a few strains of HPV, but not the ones that cause cancer. The doctor said they'll most likely clear my body and I should be okay. Otherwise, I was fine."

"Okay," he said, rubbing his hand over her upper arm. "Do we need to take any extra precautions?"

She shook her head. "If the strains were cancer-causing, you'd have to worry about possibly contracting it from kissing me there," she said, eyes darting to her lap, "since it could lead to the virus causing throat cancer down the road. Thankfully, they're not. I need to go in every year for checkups and go to the doctor immediately if I develop a UTI or notice anything abnormal. But otherwise, we should be fine." Her cheeks reddened as her teeth toyed with her bottom lip. "This is so embarrassing, but I care about you too much not to discuss this. Tell me if you want to run for the hills."

"No way," he said, softly pecking her lips. "I'm a scientist, Elle. All of this is just mutated cells and biology to me. But I'm glad you're okay, and I really appreciate you getting tested and being so honest. I'm not too familiar with how relationships work, but I would bet this stuff isn't discussed by some couples because they're too embarrassed. I'm glad we're open with each other."

"Me too," she whispered, love shining in her cobalt eyes. Yep, she loved him. Zach didn't need the words; he felt it in every inch of his soul. It was magnificent.

"So I guess that means we need to, uh, take the next step."

Her eyebrows lifted. "I think it does."

"I can sneak into your room and ravish you," he teased, waggling his eyebrows, "but we have to be quiet. The walls are super-thin."

Chuckling, she nodded. "They sure are. Should we wait until we have the place to ourselves? Maybe Marie's next group dinner at Lainey's apartment? We can say we're bowing out to spend some time together."

Zach's eyes darted between hers. "They'll know in a second what we're doing."

"So? I'm pretty sure they already know we're together. You have called me your girlfriend a few times."

"Yeah," he said, rubbing the back of his neck. "I should've asked you first..."

"I'm honored to be your girlfriend, Zach. There was no need to ask me."

"Okay," he whispered, cupping her face as his body threatened to melt into a puddle at her words. "We'll wait for Marie's next dinner."

"Can't wait. Let's see how many condoms we can plow through."

A joyful laugh sprang from his throat. "That sounds like a fantastic numerical experiment." Wrapping her in his arms, he buried his face in her neck and whispered words of love he wasn't quite bold enough to say against her lips. That day would come soon enough. For now, he was content to revel in her embrace.

Chapter 19

Alora tossed another picture onto the pile she'd already shown the furious man sitting across from her. Arching a brow, she asked, "Do you need more? I have plenty. Perhaps your wife would like to see?"

The man struggled, attempting to dislodge his wrists from the zip tie Eli had placed around them, identical to the one that also constricted his ankles. When the man attempted to stand, Eli cupped his shoulder and pushed him back down onto the bench. They sat at a picnic table on the man's backyard patio, having waited until his wife and children left the house to make contact. Hunter and Eli had made quick work of subduing him, and here they now sat, attempting to secure his compliance.

"I'm not helping any of you," he said through clenched teeth. "I don't care how many pictures you have."

Alora made a *tsk, tsk, tsk* sound as she drew some more glossy pictures from her bag. "Now, Gordon, let's not be hasty. I like this one in particular," she said, sliding the picture across the table and tapping it with her red nail, courtesy of the fantastic nail polish selection she'd discovered at the drugstore. "*She's* fucking you, while you're fucking *her*. Christine will be happy to know you've got enough energy for two prostitutes. Well done."

"My wife has had three children and doesn't care about sex anymore. The prostitutes are just an outlet."

Alora rolled her eyes and leaned forward, capturing his chin in a firm grip. "You listen to me, *malparido*. Your wife deserves a damn medal for spawning three children with your worthless genes. Once we're done with you, take some time to consider what a selfish prick you are and stop sticking your dick in other women. In the meantime, you have a choice. Do you want us to show these to her?"

Releasing an angry sigh, he shook his head. "No."

"Okay," she said, releasing him and giving a firm nod. "Here are your instructions for the night of September fourth. One of your fellow agents, Liam Downey, has already agreed to ensure the cameras are on a spool so they don't show us tracking down the hallway. Liam will also be the one to inspect Lainey's bag at the security check and send her through. Eventually, we'll approach you, and you'll grant us access to the door that leads to the bunker. Your associate Ronald has

97

already agreed to meet us at the bottom of the stairs and grant access to the metal doors that lead inside."

"What did you uncover on Ronald and Liam? I thought they were both boy scouts."

Alora shot him a sardonic glare. "Ronald came here illegally from the UK, forged passport, social security number, and all. Apparently, he created a new identity to escape paying child support over there. His forgery skills are second to none, but what a bastard. I hope you'll report him once our mission is complete."

Gordon expelled a breath. "Wow. He told me he had a slight accent because his mother was British."

"Yeah, so are his abandoned kids. Liam just has some good 'ol-fashioned gambling debts the Irish mafia wants to recoup, either with his life or with a lump sum payment. We're going to pay the lump sum once he helps us." Alora didn't divulge that Cyrus and Claire were the ones who were funding that pay-off. Apparently, they'd done quite well with their investments over the years—a fortunate turn of events resulting from their relocating from a dystopian future in which they'd possessed knowledge that companies such as Apple, Uber, and Netflix, among others, would do quite well.

"All in all, you guys are a bastion of upright citizens in the Secret Service," Alora said sardonically.

"Says the woman holding me hostage with two thugs," he muttered.

"Oh, we're thugs?" Hunter asked Eli. "Good to know. I think that's a compliment coming from this asshole."

"Every single picture is backed up on multiple servers and ready to send to your wife and the media if anything goes awry, Gordon," Alora said, tapping the pictures. "The second any of us is harmed, they will be distributed immediately. Do you understand?"

"Yes," he said, nostrils flaring.

"Good." She slid a prepaid phone across the table. "It's untraceable, so don't even try. If you get a call, answer it. If you get a text, respond to it." Standing, she trailed to his side and patted his cheek. "Don't let us down, Gordon."

"Fuck you."

Alora scoffed. "Not even in your wildest dreams. We'll be in touch."

The three of them began trailing from the yard while Gordon struggled. Turning back, Hunter approached and threw a pair of clippers on the table. "Good luck. You should be able to figure out how to extricate yourself before Christine gets home." He walked toward Alora and Eli before turning back. "It's a waste of time to run prints on those clippers, by the way. None of us are in the database. Just saving you the effort." With one last mocking smile, they exited the yard and climbed into the rental car parked a few blocks away.

As they drove, Alora did the mental calculations in her head from the passenger seat. "We've got three men on board now," she said, pensively staring out the window. "That should be enough."

"Agreed," Eli said from the back seat.

"I think so too," Hunter said, steering onto the highway that would take them back to D.C. "If one of them breaks and tells one of the clean Secret Service agents, we're in deep shit."

"I think they're all scared enough of being exposed that we'll keep their silence. But only time will tell," Alora said, fingers clenching on the door handle.

"Time," Eli said, his tone contemplative. "Our never-ending foe."

"Or friend," Alora said, "if we ultimately succeed."

"Why, Alora, how refreshingly optimistic of you."

She rolled her eyes. "Quiet, dear husband, before I use Hunter's extra pair of clippers to extricate your tongue."

His warm chuckle washed over her as they drove down the busy highway. Alora smiled softly as she gazed out the window, catching Eli's gaze as he watched her in the reflection. His resulting grin threatened to melt her panties. Bastard. Why was he so fucking sexy? She wished for him to have one physical flaw, perhaps a large mole on his nose with tiny white hairs that sprung haphazardly from the center. Alas, he was a damn Adonis.

They hadn't shared any more encounters since the tryst in the bathroom. Alora had been so consumed with the task at hand, her attraction for her husband had taken a back seat. Squirming, the slickness that now coated her core indicated she needed to move him to the front sooner rather than later. After all, she was still a woman, and even women who were saving the world needed to experience pleasure once in a while. Needed to feel *alive* so they were reminded what they were fighting for.

Yes, she thought, tracing her finger over the juncture where the window disappeared into the car's frame. She was going to seduce her husband soon. Shivering at the thought, she half-listened to Hunter and Eli's conversation as she silently plotted.

* * * *

Victor Hernandez waited patiently for Edward James Randolph to formulate his thoughts. The president faced the window in the oval office, looking out onto the lawn as he contemplated. Finally, he turned and sat behind the large mahogany desk.

"It's settled then," Edward said with a firm nod. "We'll detonate the nukes on September fourth, before the state dinner."

Victor stifled his grin, pleased that Edward was towing the line. Everything was falling into place, and he could all but *feel* the newfound power blazing within. "A wise choice," Victor said from the leather chair facing Randolph's desk. "Everything we've coveted for decades will be achieved, Edward."

The president's expression showed his disdain that Victor had addressed him by his name instead of "sir." Victor didn't give a damn. The man had begun to question their plans the closer they came to implementing them, which was worrisome. Moreover, he had no idea his granddaughter had invented a time machine and was now working against him.

Victor had tried to warn Edward and his associates about Lainey and her team when he discovered Puss in Boots. The cat was the first subject to successfully travel through time, and Victor had discovered him in an alley while strolling through Washington D.C. It was quite fortuitous, really, although he'd realized they thought him insane as he detailed them on time travel and the dystopian future. Edward was steeped in the notion that setting off the nukes would ultimately end Russia's ever-growing world dominance and would allow America to spread systematic democracy. *If he only knew*, Victor thought, inwardly scoffing.

Systematic democracy was an oxymoron. The world had evolved into a cesspool of lazy humans intent on saving the least among them. Those ideals didn't represent freedom or democracy to Victor—he thought they didn't to Edward either, but the man's slowly shifting outlook was cause for concern.

"Yes," Edward said, running a hand over his face as he gave a resigned sigh. "As far as you know, does anyone else outside our circle know of my plans to release the nukes?"

"No," Victor said, comfortable with the lie since Lainey's team were the only others who knew, and he planned to eliminate them once they confronted Edward in the bunker. Victor understood now that they all had to converge in that singular moment for the New Establishment to rise effectively. If not for that, he'd simply murder them all as they slept. God, how he wished to do so. *Patience, Victor*, he inwardly chided. Their time would come, as would his rise to prominence. Edward would die as well, by his own hand, and he couldn't say he'd miss the president.

No, losing Edward would pave Victor's way to becoming the head of the new organization he planned to build. One in which he could assume his rightful place as leader and fashion the world to his vision. It would be glorious.

"With that resolved, I'll leave you to focus on your busy schedule," Victor said, standing.

Edward gave a nod. "Aiysha should be outside. Please send her in."

With a tilt of his head, Victor strolled to the door, opening it to reveal Aiysha on the other side. "Ms. Gaynor," he said cordially.

"Hello, Mr. Hernandez," she said, determination in her steely greenish-brown eyes.

His own eyes narrowed as they shared a silent battle of wills. She'd always seemed suspicious of him, but she was young and idealistic, which, in his mind, made her extremely weak. If she thought she was a capable foe for his network of connected associates, she was vastly mistaken.

"If you'll excuse me, the president needs to see me." Dismissing him, she strode into the office, closing the door in his face.

"Bitch," he hissed under his breath, annoyed he had to put up with her. But he'd be able to eliminate her soon enough—to eliminate *all* of them. Basking in the surge of power those thoughts provoked, Victor left the White House, wanting to surveil the agents Lainey's team was blackmailing. They'd need to do their part and ensure her team converged upon the bunker. Stuffing his hands in his pockets, he slipped away, unnoticed by so many.

But not for long. Soon, he would be noticed by all. Lips curving in a sinister smile, Victor reveled in that singular fact.

Chapter 20

The team worked diligently, building a "practice run" in Lainey's back yard and performing extensive drills to mimic their infiltration of the bunker. Multiple scenarios were postulated and practiced in case the clean Secret Service agents caught on to their scheme. Schematics of the White House were spread all over the tables, and every possible escape route was plotted. One day, as they took a break to eat lunch, Lainey addressed the team.

"I'd like to discuss the final phase of the plan, guys. It's important we all understand each and every step." Once she had their undivided attention, she lifted her fingers, ticking them off as she listed the final items they would complete if they succeeded.

"One, we're going to ensure Speaker of the House Anita Rohan gets sworn in as president. I have no desire to kill my grandfather, grandmother, or the Vice President, so, hopefully, they will be taken into custody, and she will assume the office."

"But if we have to shoot to kill, we will," Hunter reminded them.

"Two," Lainey continued, "I need to travel to 2039 and make contact with Young Eli. Even if we prevent President Randolph from setting off the nukes, the seeds of the New Establishment have already been sowed. I'll gain his trust, inform him of the past and the future that we prevented. It will give us a future ally if a new threat emerges."

"I always played soccer on Tuesday and Thursday afternoons in the field by my house in Florida. We'd moved inland by that time due to the rising sea levels. Mom trusted my friends enough that she let us go without parental supervision. It's a good place to find me."

"Noted," Lainey said, smiling at Eli. "Let's sit down tomorrow so I can memorize all the details. Three," she continued, "Hunter and I will then reconvene with you all in 2035 and destroy the time machine. We'll all forge ahead and build new lives for ourselves. Hopefully, ones filled with happiness and exciting new beginnings. Zach has already begun establishing more extensive paper trails, functional social security numbers, and other documentation we need to establish ourselves and thrive."

"You can all see how fun it is to get *real* jobs," Marie muttered as she tugged weeds from the garden. "No more futzing around with fancy equations while ol' Marie cooks and cleans. No, siree."

Laughing, Lainey glanced at Marie. "Hunter and I would really like you to stay with us once we've determined where we're going, Marie. I'll leave that for you to decide."

She gave a *harrumph* and shrugged. "Might as well, for the time I have left."

Lainey grinned at Hunter, who winked back at her. Marie's grumbling couldn't mask the softening of her shoulders as Lainey spoke the words.

"Okay, I think that's it. Let's continue the practice runs. In the meantime, I'm going to head to the drugstore for supplies. We're almost out of shampoo in the upstairs bathroom...again."

"Guilty," Sara said, raising her hand. "I take so many baths now, and Luke massages my scalp while I'm in the tub. It helps with my morning sickness, which probably sounds weird. Sorry, guys."

"It's fine," Lainey said, grasping her hand. "The money Dad stockpiled will definitely get us through the next few weeks, and I anticipate we'll have about nine thousand left to divide among us once we purchase the tactical gear and weapons we need. Not a ton to start a new life with, but better than zero." Circling her hand, she commanded the team. "Let's get to work."

Alora, Eli, and Hunter resumed practicing the White House infiltration runs as Zach and Elle worked on expanding the documentation for everyone. Luke helped Marie cook while Sara napped. And Lainey...well, she did go to the drugstore, but not before she took care of another very important task.

* * * *

Lainey sat on the bench, observing the man as he strolled down the path. He'd told her so many times how he loved the trails on Roosevelt Island. One could see a number of D.C. monuments and sights from the trails, which had always enthralled him. Whistling, he shuffled along, wireless earbuds in his ears.

Standing, Lainey searched her surroundings, thankful the park wasn't full of people. Stepping into the path, she gazed into eyes so much like her own as the man halted. Removing the earbuds, he smiled.

"Can I help you?"

Tears welled in her eyes as she pursed her lips, struggling to speak. "You're Lewis Randolph," she said, her voice gravelly.

"One and the same. Are you a reporter? I don't really speak on behalf of my father and am far-removed from politics. If you're searching for a story, you won't find one here."

She breathed a laugh and shook her head. "Nope. I'm someone who just really needed to see you. Although, it's a complete violation of every paradox and space-time principle you taught me."

His eyebrows drew together. "Were you one of my students? I feel terrible, but I can't place you."

"In a manner of speaking, you could say I was your most prominent student. You taught me everything you knew for many years."

Hazel eyes searched hers as comprehension began to form.

"I told myself a thousand times I wouldn't approach you," she said, swiping away a tear. "But I had to. We're so close, and I needed to see you just one more time."

Lewis's eyes narrowed as he studied her. "You look so much like Mara," he whispered.

"Yes," she said, smiling, "but with your eyes. I know this is extremely shocking, and I'm sorry for that. But I need to ask you a question."

His breathing was labored as he nodded.

"If the world was destroyed and you were trying to save it, why would you set off simultaneous EMPs? I never quite understood that decision."

Contemplating, he rubbed the back of his neck. "I would possibly consider it the best course, to reset the world so any remaining nuclear arsenals couldn't be launched."

"I think I understand that reasoning, but it's faulty. It ends up sending the world into chaos, allowing a very dark regime to emerge."

He exhaled through puffed cheeks. "Once I realized that, I would've regretted it immensely and done everything in my power to go back and change things."

"You did," she said, aching to hold his hand but knowing she couldn't. "And we're so close, Dad. I promise."

"I feel it," he said, rubbing his hand over his heart. "Our connection. It's palpable."

"I loved you more than anyone. I was devastated when you left me. Your last words to me were, '*See you in 2035, my darling girl.*'"

"And here we are," he said, smiling so warmly she felt it in her toes.

"And here we are," she said with a tilt of her head.

"How can I help you?"

"You can't. I've already taken such a risk by coming this close to you, but I'm human, and what are we if not flawed?"

"So true," he said, lips curved as his eyes twinkled in the way she so fondly remembered.

"But if we fail, remember this conversation. I don't think setting off the EMPs is the best course of action. Perhaps we can at least change some outcomes even if we don't succeed."

"All right," he said, solemn. Silence stretched between them until he finally said, "I find myself wanting to hug you. Very badly."

"I want to hug you so much I feel it in my bones," she said, taking a step back. "But we both know we can't. Physical contact between direct family members in different timelines could set of the very apocalypse I'm trying to prevent."

His throat bobbed as he swallowed thickly, nodding in accord. "I wish you the best of luck, my darling girl," he said, his voice raspy with emotion.

"Thank you, Dad. I miss you so much."

Wetness swam in his eyes as he gazed at her with reverence.

"Goodbye," she whispered, giving him a slight wave. Pivoting, she walked away before she lost the will to do so. Thankful for that one final, brief moment with him, she headed home.

Chapter 21

With two weeks left until they would confront President Randolph, the pieces of Lainey's team's plans were falling into place. The three Secret Service agents were on board and compliant as far as they could tell, and Zach had hacked into the Social Security database to create functional numbers for them all. Those, along with the detailed paper trails he'd created for everyone, would ensure they could thrive in the world if they succeeded.

"Family dinner will be ready in a few minutes," Marie yelled from the kitchen as the late afternoon sun shone above.

"*Psst,*" Elle said beside Zach, poking his arm as she closed her laptop. "I think that's our cue."

Nervous as he'd ever been, he nodded. Standing, he trailed into the kitchen to find Marie buzzing around.

"Uh, Elle and I are going to skip family dinner and pick up something to have at home. But we'll definitely be here for next week's dinner since it will be our last before we confront Randolph."

Marie cackled as she pulled a pan from the oven with mitts over hands. "You finally gonna do the horizontal tango with your pretty little girlfriend?"

"None of your business," he said, frowning as she removed the mitts.

Stepping toward him, she patted his cheek. "Good for you. She'll take care of you, son. Have fun. I'll tell the others you won't be joining us."

"Thank you, Marie." Placing a soft kiss on her white head, he walked outside to find Elle ready to go. Extending his hand, she took it, squeezing even though his palm was wet. Man, he really hoped he didn't blow it. Literally. He wanted so badly for his first time—and their first time together—to be mind-blowing.

Their hands swayed as they walked down the sidewalk and arrived at their townhome. Elle led him up the stairs and into her room before closing the door behind them. Walking toward the nightstand, she opened the drawer, locating the box of condoms and setting it on top.

"Do you want to eat something first?" Zach asked, berating himself for the stupid question. But he also didn't want to deny her if she was hungry.

"No," she said, clutching the hem of her T-shirt and pulling it over her head before tossing it on the nearby chair. Zach sucked in a breath at the sight of all her smooth skin surrounding the pink bra. Stepping toward him, she lifted his hands, placing them over her breasts. "Touch me, Zach."

His hands squeezed her small breasts over the bra as he fought to breathe. Blood surged to his shaft, which was squished inside his jeans. Good lord, the friction was intense. *Don't come in your pants, Bishop,* he chided himself, realizing he would absolutely *die* if he blew his load too early. Gliding his hands behind her back, he fumbled with the clasp of her bra as she smiled at him.

"The clasp is tricky," she said, her expression so understanding as she stared up at him. "You'll get it. Slide it together, then unlatch it."

Biting his tongue and looking over her shoulder, he finally unfastened the damn thing and threw it to the floor. Sliding his hands back around, he cupped her breasts, loving how round and pert they were in his hands. Gently rubbing his thumbs over each nipple, he felt like a damn conquering Viking when she inhaled sharply.

"You like that?" he whispered.

"Yes," she said, biting her lip. "I love having my nipples played with. And kissed," she said, arching a seductive eyebrow.

Listening to his woman, he crouched and slid his arm behind her knees, lifting her and carrying her to the bed. Laying her down, he crawled over her and latched onto a puckered nipple, sucking it with his lips as she clutched his hair and bowed beneath him.

"Slow down, Zach," she cried, causing him to freeze.

Lifting his gaze to hers, he said, "Sorry. Shit. Did I blow it already?"

"No," she replied, sifting her fingers through his hair as she shook her head on the pillow. "But women need a buildup most of the time. It adds to the pleasure and makes the crash so much better."

"Okay," he said, determined to please her. "Like this?" Gaze cemented to hers, he extended his tongue and licked her nipple, slow and steady.

"Yes." The breathy word sent a shiver though his vibrating frame. "Just like that."

Locked onto her gaze, he licked her several times, varying the direction, before moving to the other nipple and doing the same. The little bud puckered against his tongue, so taut and sensitive, and his eyes almost crossed at the erotic image.

"Suck it," she commanded softly.

Opening his lips, he surrounded the tiny nub, sucking it gently as she writhed beneath him. He feasted on her like a starving man, only breaking contact when she tugged his shirt from his quaking frame. As he lathered her with his saliva, marking her with his scent and taste, she reached for his fly, unbuttoning his jeans and sliding her hand inside. Deft fingers delved between the folds of his boxer briefs until her soft skin brushed his straining cock. Groaning as he devoured her breast, her fingers encircled his shaft and gently tugged.

Zach lifted his head and sucked in a huge gulp of air—and then his body jerked as he came all over her hand.

* * * *

Elle's eyes widened as Zach's body began to lurch above her. He moaned her name, followed by a round of thick curses, as his wet release sprayed all over her hand. After convulsing atop her, he collapsed over her body, burying his face in her neck. His wiry frame trembled as he recovered from the orgasm.

"God fucking damn it!" he cursed into her neck. "Fuck!"

"Hey," she said, stroking his hair. "It's okay. Did it feel good?"

Expelling a frustrated breath against her skin, he pushed himself up and grabbed the tissues on the bedside table. Sitting back on the bed, he wiped her hand, looking terribly embarrassed and forlorn as he cleaned his release from her skin.

"Zach," she whispered, wanting so badly to comfort him. "It's okay—"

"No, it's fucking not," he said, not meeting her eyes as he wiped her hand. "What a loser. I can't believe I blew it like that. Fuck," he said, looking as if he was about to punch his fist through the wall.

Pulling her hand from his furious motions, she sat up and slid her fingers under his chin, forcing him to meet her gaze. His gorgeous green eyes swam with shame and remorse, and her heart broke for him.

"Why are you beating yourself up? I'm so happy you came and experienced pleasure. Now that you have, we can go again. It's not a big deal, Zach."

"It *is* a big deal," he said, running his fingers through his hair. "I've imagined this so many times—"

"So have I," she said, cupping his chin, "and I really hope you're not going to give up after one orgasm. I was really enjoying what you were doing to my breasts."

Concerned eyes searched hers. "Yeah?"

"Yeah," she said, leaning forward to kiss him. "I'd like it if we could get back to that. Now that you've taken the edge off, you can relax."

He licked his lips, the action sending a surge of desire to her core. Lying back down, she circled her nipples with her fingers. "Don't you want to keep licking them?" she asked, trying to sound seductive.

"Hell yes," he breathed, tossing the forgotten tissues to the floor. Gliding back over her, he resumed kissing her nipples until she was breathless.

Fisting her fingers in his hair, she tilted his head to stare into his eyes. "Take off my pants and touch my pussy, Zach."

His nostrils flared at the command, making him look sexy and raw. She noticed his hands were shaking as he unclasped her jeans and shucked them from her legs before removing her underwear. Situating on his knees, he ran his palms over her

108

abdomen as her skin quivered beneath. Reaching her core, he spread her open, examining her like the trained scientist he was.

"Where's your clitoris?" he asked, sliding his fingers up and down her slit.

"I love your eagerness," she said, thinking it so cute that he wanted to dive right in and make her come. "But you can just touch me, sweetheart. Everywhere and anywhere you want to. It will feel good. I promise." Spreading her legs further, she invited him to explore.

Heavy breaths exited his lungs as he traced his finger over every inch of her wet folds, spreading the moisture from her opening across the heated skin.

"Yes," she whimpered, loving how gentle and reverent his caresses were. "Make me wet all over. That makes it feel better."

Lowering his head, he licked her between the folds. "Like that?"

Tossing her head back on the pillow, she groaned, "God, yes, like that. Don't stop."

His lips assaulted her flushed skin, tiny grunts of pleasure escaping his throat as he pillaged her. "You taste to so good," he murmured, the words vibrating against her skin. It would take time for him to perfect the strokes of his tongue so he could make her come this way, but, oh, how thrilled she was to let him practice. He ate and nibbled and sucked her for several more minutes before she closed her thighs around his head.

"I need you inside me." Those eyes snapped to hers, full of anticipation and fear. "If you come right away, we'll just do it again when you recover," she said, shrugging against the pillow. "We have a whole box of condoms, Zach. Whatever happens, happens. I just need you inside me."

"Okay," he whispered, reaching for the condoms and pulling out a packet before shucking the rest of his clothes. His hands shook so badly as he opened it, she bit her lip to contain the smile, not wanting to further his embarrassment. In truth, his nervousness was so damn cute. She wished he could understand how attractive his eager yet hesitant anticipation was. The fact she was the first woman he would ever make love to was extremely meaningful to her.

Once he was sheathed, he crawled over her, resting on one elbow. With his other hand, he reached down and grasped his shaft, searching for her entrance. She opened her legs wide, gasping when the head of his cock touched her opening.

His gaze was so intense as he began to push inside her. Wanting to put him at ease, she slid her thumb over his lips.

"It feels so good," she whimpered, arching her hips toward him to aid his motions. "You can smile, you know?"

He breathed a laugh and shook his head. "I'm terrified to blow it again."

"Don't be," she said, surrounding him with her arms. "Keep going."

Eventually, he was fully enveloped by her slick walls and balanced on his arms as he loomed above her. Staring deep into her soul, he withdrew and slid back in as her heart swelled in her chest. When he increased the pace, she noticed the beads of sweat forming on his forehead as he concentrated.

"Faster," she said, digging her nails into his upper back.

"I'll come if I go faster."

"Then come," she said, gyrating her hips, meeting his thrusts as he groaned.

"It's too soon," he said through gritted teeth.

It was then she realized she needed to urge him along so he could lose his virginity once and for all. When that was done, Elle felt he would truly be able to relax and stop worrying about his performance. Drawing his head down, she touched her lips to his.

"Zach?" she called softly.

"*Urghnh*," he mumbled unintelligibly against her lips as he jutted between her thighs.

"I need to tell you something."

"Yeah?" he growled.

Staring into his hooded eyes, she said, "I love you."

Those eyes widened as he gasped. And then he shouted her name and came inside her pulsing body.

✳ ✳ ✳ ✳

Hours later, Zach lay sprawled across the bed, Elle strewn perpendicular across his stomach as they both gulped for air. Barely able to lift his arm, he swiped his hand over his sweat-soaked face.

"Holy shit."

"Still can't talk," Elle muffled into the sheets, haphazardly wrinkled and disheveled. "Might never recover."

Exhaling an elated sigh, Zach thanked every god above that she was sated. After she'd spoken the words that completed his still-pounding heart, spurring him to another embarrassing orgasm, he'd actually chilled out long enough to relax. Once he felt comfortable, he'd been able to truly enjoy the experience, spending time finding all the tiny spots that made her cry in ecstasy. They'd made love twice more, the last one being so exceptional they now lay destroyed upon the bed, unable to move and barely able to breathe.

"So damn good," he murmured, searching for her face with his still-tingling hand. Finding it, he brushed the hair away, caressing her cheek as she grinned back at him. The slaked arousal in her cobalt eyes made something inside him roar.

"You figured out sex," she teased, one side of her face still planted on the bed.

"Sure did," he said, so damn proud of himself as his finger traced her cheek. "Tell me again," he said, running his thumb over her bottom lip.

"I love you," she said, smiling as she kissed his thumb. "And if you love me, you'll move into this room and do that to me every damn night."

"You want me to move in here?"

She playfully rolled her eyes. "Duh. Of course I do. Unless you want to continue sleeping on the couch."

"I want to sleep wherever you are," he whispered.

She nodded, biting her lip.

"Elle?"

"Hmm?"

"I love you too."

"I know," she said, the corner of her lip curving. "But do you love me enough to walk to the Wendy's on the corner and get me a Frosty and some fries? I'm starving."

"Sweetheart," he said, willing his body to move so he could maneuver to kiss her. "I love you enough to even throw a burger on top of that."

Giggling against his lips, she softly kissed him back. "My hero."

With one last sweet peck, he headed to get them some food so they could replenish their energy, for now that he'd "figured out sex," there was no way in hell he was stopping anytime soon.

Chapter 22

Eli studied Alora as she fired the gun beside him. The curve of her jaw was set as she fired multiple rounds from the semi-automatic handgun. Emptying the chamber, she lowered the firearm and inspected her handiwork. Yanking off the protective glasses, she cleaned them on her shirt and replaced them before muttering, "You're not going to hit the target if you're staring at my ass, Eli."

Since he was busted, he let his gaze linger on the gorgeous globes beneath her black yoga pants. Fuck, they were perfect. Would the skin tremble under his teeth as he gently bit her there?

"You make it hard to concentrate when you wear those tight pants, sweetheart."

She shot him a droll look. "Careful. You're coming close to being an ass. We were making such good progress."

"Were we?" he murmured, turning to face the target. "I can't ever tell with you." Lifting his own gun, he proceeded to shoot several bullets through the silhouetted outline drawn on the target.

"Nice shooting," she said, cocking her gun. "Victor taught you well."

After she completed another flawless round of shooting, he said, "Yes. One of the greatest skills he taught me was how to kill effectively." Alora might have shivered, but he couldn't be sure. She didn't meet his eyes but seemed to be listening, so he continued. "Who taught you to shoot so well?"

She spared him an annoyed glance.

"What?" He lifted his hands, attempting to relay his genuineness. "I'm curious."

"After your father murdered my family, I traveled to many different settlements along the Isle, spreading the word about his evil regime. Many of the men respected my father and taught me how to defend myself."

"Seems they taught you more than that. You're fierce, Alora."

"Circumstances dictated I had to be," was her quick retort.

Sighing, he understood she still implicated him in those circumstances. "I guess so. Well, it's pretty damn attractive. Especially when you're wearing those tight pants." Turning back to the now replaced target, he unloaded another round, proud of his perfect aim.

"I like our chances against Randolph," she said, assessing his handiwork. "Although we're most likely insane to try, we are skilled enough to beat him if things go exactly as planned."

Eli arched a brow. "When was the last time things went exactly as planned for you?" he asked sardonically.

She huffed a humorless laugh. "When I was thirteen."

He nodded, rotating the Glock in his hand. "We're most likely going to fail. Or die. Or both."

"Yes," she said, swallowing as she stared back at the targets. "But we'll die with honor."

"Even me?"

She squinted, contemplating. "Maybe. Let's see how you perform under pressure."

"Why, Alora," he said, inching closer, "is that a euphemism for something else?"

"You wish, *amigo*," she said, rolling her eyes.

He slid his hand over her wrist, loving her quick inhale. She could pretend all she wished, but he was so in tune to her body's responses. Eli was a confident man and understood she wanted him as badly as he did her.

"I owe you a night on the town, away from the group."

Her dark eyes shifted between his as the wheels churned in her brain. Finally, she said, "Tuesday. That will be one week before we infiltrate the White House."

"Tuesday," he said with a tilt of his head. "I'll take care of everything. Do you have a dress?"

"Not in this timeline, except for the gown I'll wear to the state dinner. Dresses aren't practical for our purposes, but I did splurge on some dress shoes at the thrift shop and will make sure I look presentable," she teased.

"You could wear a damn paper bag and look presentable, Alora. I'm honored to spend some time with you."

She scowled. "Don't start that super-sweet crap again."

"Why?" he teased, leaning forward to whisper in her ear. "Afraid you might like it?"

She palmed his face, pushing him away as he chuckled. "Doubtful."

"I'm going to make you regret saying that, sweetheart."

The look she shot him sent his heart into overdrive. "We'll see."

Hunter chose that moment to appear, having finished with his own target practice. "You guys ready?"

"Yes," Alora said, lifting her chin and effectively dismissing Eli. Pivoting, she stalked from the room back to the main lobby.

"You two have some serious chemistry," Hunter said to Eli.

"No shit."

"Good luck, man. She's a hardened soul."

Eli blew a breath through his lips. "Tell me about it. I helped make her that way."

Patting him on the back, Hunter led him from the room as Eli reminded himself regrets were a waste of time. All he could do now was forge ahead, grateful for the fact the stunning, stubborn woman at least desired him back.

* * * *

Alora observed Eli, her finger drawing a pattern across the table, as he finished his steak. Setting down the fork and knife, he sat back and rested his hands over his abdomen, looking sated and satisfied.

"I assume it was good?" she asked, lifting the wine glass to her lips to swallow the last drop. His eyes darkened as he watched her, and she seductively licked her bottom lip, savoring the bold liquid.

"Witch," he said, shaking his head. "You're doing that to drive me insane."

She pressed her teeth into her lip, enjoying the way his nostrils flared in reaction. "Perhaps. You seem to think I'm a witch. I'm not sure how I feel about you calling me that."

Chuckling, he lifted a brow. "You are, and you know exactly what you do to me."

Circling the empty glass on the table, she said, "You've called me something else too. *Querida*. I wasn't sure you spoke Spanish."

"I speak very little, but my mother was fluent. She grew up in Mexico, and my father was from the Dominican Republic. I'm first-generation American on her side, and second-generation on his side. She raised me until I sought Victor out as a teenager. It was very important to her that I have an American accent and spoke English, so she didn't teach me Spanish."

Alora's brows drew together. "She should've been proud of your heritage."

"Yes, but her experience shaped her views. She encountered a lot of discrimination as a caterer for wealthy homeowners in Palm Beach. We lived in West Palm. The other side of the tracks, so to speak."

"How did she meet Victor?"

"He was a financial advisor for one of the wealthy men my mother worked for. From the stories she would recount, he was quite sweet when they first met. She got pregnant, and he married her. I think she was very much in love with him."

"I hope you don't mind me prying," she said, thanking the server as he removed their plates. "I'm just so interested in how the nefarious Victor Hernandez fell in love."

He huffed a breath. "I'm not sure he loved her, although he might have cared for her in the beginning. She was extremely sweet and caring and charming. I think he was besotted by her..."—he waved his hand, searching for the word—"*innocence* or something. Once she had me, it all went to shit. He became more prominent as he

114

gained more wealthy clients and wanted to be part of that world. He moved to D.C. and was determined to infiltrate Randolph's circle of powerful and connected men. My mother never cared about that and just wanted him. He left and never looked back."

"How sad." Splaying her fingers, she looked at the ring. "Did she ever fall in love again?"

He shook his head. "She wore that ring until I left to track him down. He'd had it engraved with her new initials on their wedding day. When I left, she asked me to take it, hoping I would give it to my wife one day. I didn't tell her all the details of what I was doing. I told her I wanted to live with my dad for a while and get to know him. I'm pretty sure it broke her heart, but there was no way to really tell her about my mission. So I left her alone and heartbroken." Sighing, he glanced at his crossed hands. "I really am a son of a bitch."

Alora hurt for him, overtaken by the waves of sorrow emanating from his muscular frame. "It's what you had to do. You made the right decision."

Shrugging, he lifted his glass and finished it. "We'll know in a week, once we confront Randolph, if I made the right decision. If we fail, I will have decimated her for nothing." Strong fingers toyed with the stem of his glass. "Hell, I will have decimated myself for nothing. All the death. All the war. All the screams and cries I hear in my nightmares. Every ounce of energy I spent crafting my nefarious image, demolished by one final failure. It's overwhelming to even contemplate."

Silence blanketed the table as she wondered what to say to comfort him. Coming up with zilch, she toyed with the ring on her finger.

"Well, I'm glad Ingrid taught you *some* Spanish at least," she said, trying to lighten the mood.

"I didn't realize *querida* meant 'beloved' until years after I left. I would always ask her what it meant, and she would say, 'It is an endearment for someone who carries your heart.'"

Alora gazed into his piercing eyes, unable to look away; powerless to dismiss what he was telling her. "Do I carry your heart, Eli?" she asked softly.

Before he could answer, the server arrived and dropped off the check.

"Saved by the bill," Eli said, lifting the black holder. Opening it, he whistled. "Thank goodness Lewis stockpiled so much currency after the apocalypse. This dinner cost a fortune. Lainey seemed happy to fork over the dough though. I think she wants you to be wined and dined."

"I hope I'm worth it," she teased.

"It's not my money, so I couldn't say," he said, playfully mocking her back.

She scrunched her features as he laid several bills inside the holder and closed it. "Ready?"

Standing, he extended his hand. Alora grasped it, understanding the next few hours would be important. Would it just be sex, or would she open her heart to more? Still unsure, she held tight as Eli led her from the restaurant.

The hotel a few blocks away was minimalistic. They'd paid cash for a room before dinner and strolled through the lobby in silence. The elevator lifted them to the third floor, and he held his hand over the door, gesturing for her to exit first. Giving a nod, she walked toward the room, wondering when in the hell things had turned so formal.

Her hand shook slightly as she dipped the plastic key in the slot—from anticipation more than nerves. Sex was something she'd done many times over in her life, and she rarely felt nervous before the act. Sex with someone who incited so many *feelings*? That was rather new, and she couldn't quite decide how she felt about it.

The room was dark, and Eli flipped on the lamp atop the desk by the window. It cast a dim glow across the room, adding to the atmosphere.

"I need to use the bathroom," she said, her voice gravelly. "I'll be right back."

He nodded, lifting his hands to unbutton his shirt as he kicked off his shoes. Presumptuous bastard. Quelling the inner thoughts, she realized they were a reflex from all the years she'd hated him. It was still a natural response to question his actions and deem them irreparable. But they'd come here to have sex, so why shouldn't he take off his shirt? That was all this was, right? A consensual night between two adults?

When she finished in the bathroom, she stared into her own eyes in the mirror. "Just sex, Alora. Save the world and see if you survive, and then you can examine the rest. For now, sex." With a firm nod, she exited the bathroom.

Eli stood at the window, hands in his pockets, torso and feet bare. Sucking in a breath, Alora's vow to stay indifferent vanished as if it had never existed. Scars— what looked to be at least fifty or more—splayed across his back in a mesh of weathered skin.

"*Virgen santisima,*" she breathed, approaching him and observing his back. "Who did this to you?"

"You were going to see them anyway," he said, the words toneless as he continued to stare through the window, "so I wanted to get it out of the way."

Lifting her hands, she gently touched her fingertips to his back as the muscles stiffened underneath. Slowly, she traced the scars as tears clouded her eyes.

"When did this happen?" she asked, the words barely escaping the lump in her throat.

"It was part of my initiation into the New Establishment. My father felt I was weak and would beat me with a strap until I cried. Eventually, I stopped crying, and the beatings ceased."

Unable to speak, she traced his back, wanting to soothe him although the wounds had healed long ago.

"The last day he beat me, I turned on him and grabbed the strap. I told him it was done and I would never cry again. And I haven't. Even when my mother died."

Images of seeing him kneel at Ingrid's grave all those years ago flashed in her mind. "How old were you when the beatings stopped?"

"Almost eighteen."

She closed her eyes, realization slamming into her as she calculated. "How bad was the beating after my family was killed?"

He gave a humorless laugh. "Pretty fucking bad. But worth it. All the batterings were worth it because they eventually made me into the hardened man I am today. They solidified my father's trust in me; therefore, they were necessary."

Alora shook her head as her palms traced over his back. How had he survived? Empathy swelled in her chest, and she leaned forward, touching her lips to one of the scars. He hissed, head falling forward, as she continued to kiss trails over the damaged skin. Eventually, she rested her forehead on his back and slipped her arms around his waist, holding him tight. They might have stood there for hours, breaths labored and pulses pounding, until he slowly circled in her embrace. Threading his fingers through the hair above her neck, he captured her lips with his own.

Her arms glided around his neck, Alora no longer deluding herself that she was emotionless. Mired in feelings she couldn't control, she kissed him back with ardor, sliding her tongue over his, tasting every crevice of his warm mouth. Uttering a sexy growl, he bent down and palmed her ass, lifting her so she crossed her legs behind his back. Never breaking their kiss, he carried her to the king-size bed, lowering so they crashed onto the mattress.

Her hands were everywhere, searching for a stronghold as he ravished her mouth. Finding his belt, she unlatched the clasp and tugged it free. Grasping the hem of her shirt, he pulled it over her head and tossed it to the floor before he claimed her mouth again. Slipping his hand under her back, he flicked her bra clasp and tore the garment from her body.

His hot mouth was on her breast immediately. Licking, sucking...driving her to the edge of madness as she clenched her fingers in his thick hair. He trailed to her other breast, pulling the nipple between his teeth before gently nipping it. The shock sent sparks of desire through her body, and she moaned his name, desperate for more.

As his mouth wreaked delicious havoc on her breast, he unfastened her pants and tugged the zipper down, all but yanking them off her legs while she still wore her cute inch-and-a-half heels. "Let me take off my shoes," she rasped.

"Leave them on," he said, rising above her to grasp her panties, which were now haphazardly strewn across her hips. Sliding them off her legs, he stepped between her thighs and slid his palms under her calves. "I want to fuck you while you wear them. You look so gorgeous like this."

Rising to her elbows, she tried to catch her breath. "Condom?"

"Back pocket," he said, gesturing with his head. Reaching around, she searched like hell for the foil packet, which wasn't easy since he still held her legs. Finding it, she placed it between her teeth, holding it there while she fully undid his pants and shucked them and his underwear to his knees. Ripping open the packet with her teeth, she slid the condom over his impressive cock, saliva pooling in her mouth in anticipation.

"I swear, I was going to take this slow," he said derisively, fists clenching around her legs.

"Next time," she said, falling to the bed. "Fuck me. Now."

Eyes cemented to hers, he touched the tip of his cock to her dripping core, searching before slightly slipping inside. Holding her legs high, he pushed inside, causing her back to bow upon the bed.

"Okay?" he grunted, panting as he assessed her reaction.

"Yes," she said, gazing up at him. "Don't hold back, or I'll fucking murder you."

A breathless laugh escaped his throat as his hands tightened on her legs. Lifting them high, he began to fuck her. His hips moved at a frenzied pace, back and forth, as she clutched the comforter, trying to hold her quivering body in place. Throwing her head back on the bed, she opened her body to him, welcoming him inside, mewling when the head of his cock jutted against the inner wall of sensitive nerves that could send her flying.

"Right there!" she cried, pushing her body into his, needing more. "Oh, god, yes!"

He pulsed in and out, the sound of slapping flesh reverberating through the room as he groaned above her. Just when she felt her orgasm on the horizon, he pulled out, causing her to moan.

Dropping her legs, his hands encircled her waist, flipping her over as if she were a feather. Grasping her hips, he drew her to her knees and thrust into her sopping wet core from behind.

"I have too many fantasies to only fuck you one way, Alora," he grumbled in her ear as his hips plowed into hers, over and over. "I need to make you scream so you remember." Bringing his fingers to her center, he delved between the swollen folds and began circling the pulsing nub.

She whimpered as her forehead fell to the bed, her head too heavy on her shoulders to hold high any longer. Sinking into the soft comforter, black hair slithered over her face as she struggled to breathe.

"Yes, *querida*," he rasped as his body aligned with hers. Rolling them slightly, he slid his palm under her knee, lifting it as he hammered her from behind. His other arm still snaked underneath her, stimulating her clit, while every inch of her body burned.

Burrowing his face into her neck, he murmured indecipherable words as his fingers and magnificent cock threatened to send her over the edge. "Damn it, Alora," he growled, "I'm going to come. Are you close?"

"Yes," she cried, pushing her hair out of her face and turning her head to gaze at him. Grasping her nipple, she tugged, the pleasure-pain inciting even more bliss as his eyes enflamed with desire.

"Yessss," he hissed, placing his forehead against hers. "Squeeze those tight little nipples while I fuck you."

"Oh, god," she cried, plucking the sensitive point as her eyes cemented closed. "I'm almost there."

His lips devoured hers as his hips battered her, the smooth skin of her ass soaked with his sweat. Suddenly, she snapped, a high-pitched wail escaping her throat as she began to come. He cursed into her mouth, licking her everywhere while her body spasmed against his. Screaming her name, he joined her over the edge, cupping her mound as his cock jerked inside her. His muscular frame bracketed hers as they came, both quaking and uncontrolled, their sweat-soaked bodies slippery and enflamed.

Eli shuddered as the remaining jolts of his release sputtered into the condom. Struggling to breathe, Alora pushed her face into the mattress, loving how he nuzzled the sensitive skin of her neck. Every nerve-ending was raw, and she let them buzz, reveling in the moment of pure pleasure. Pretty sure she might never move again, she emitted a low mewl when Eli cupped her mound tighter.

"Mine," he growled into her neck.

"*Mine*," she corrected, snuggling into him. "But you can borrow it from time to time."

Chuckling against her skin, he nipped her. "Witch."

Content and sated, they lay intertwined as their breath slowly returned to normal.

"Damn condom. Give me a minute." Easing out of her, Eli trailed to the bathroom, returning to gaze down at her.

Squinting, she asked, "When did you lose your pants? I don't remember that part."

His smile would've singed off her clothes if she'd been wearing any. Grasping her ankle, he undid the tiny clasp and removed her shoe. "I don't remember." Placing a kiss against her ankle, he returned it to the bed and removed her other shoe, giving that ankle a kiss as well. Extending his hand, he urged her to take it. "Get up so we can pull down the covers."

"No," she said, biting her finger as she shot him the most seductive gaze in her arsenal. "Can't move."

His chest swelled as he drew in a large breath. "It should be illegal to look the way you do right now. Fuck, Alora." Bending down, he lifted her over his shoulder. Holding her in place by clamping a hand on her butt, he turned down the bed and laid her atop the sheets.

Splaying her hair over the pillow, she stared up at him, sure his mouth was damn-near watering. "How long until you can go again?" she asked, rubbing one leg over the other.

"Fucking illegal," he muttered, lowering to one knee and then the other, stretching over her as he balanced on straight arms. "Ten minutes," he said, giving her a wet kiss. "But until then, I can make you come again."

She bit her lip. "That's a pretty stiff promise—"

He captured the words with his lips before trailing them down her neck and across her collarbone. "You're goddamn right it is. Shut up and let me love you, Alora."

"Hey—" she said before he cut her off by covering her mouth with his hand. Before she could bite the hell out of it, he sucked her nipple between those talented lips, bathing it with his tongue as she squirmed below him. Her cries of pleasure were muted by his palm until he slid it away from her mouth, over the valley between her breasts, while simultaneously kissing a path down her abdomen and to her mound.

Settling his palms over her inner thighs, he pushed them open. Staring at her through hooded lids, he lifted a finger over his lips.

"No talking, Alora. Unless you're screaming my name." Replacing his hand, he pushed her thighs farther apart and lowered his face to her wet core.

Giving in to the desire, she figured it wouldn't hurt to watch in silence as Eli made her come with that sexy-as-sin mouth. In fact, he made her come multiple times before he slipped on another condom and fucked her like his life depended on it. Hell, maybe it did. Too tired to care, Alora passed out before he'd even disposed of the condom.

Which might have been why she let him pull her into his arms and spoon her until they all but inhabited one connected body. Alora rarely cuddled, but exhaustion led to necessity as she gave in to sleep, his broad palm splayed over her heart.

* * * *

Eli's eyes fluttered open as the smell of Alora's skin permeated his nostrils. Inhaling it, he closed his lids again, unable to control his slight shudder. Waking with her in his arms was mesmerizing, and elation coursed through his veins. Forget not understanding happiness—he'd found it last night a thousand times over. Each time she whimpered his name, or clenched his hair between her strong fingers,

120

or opened herself to him so he could burrow inside her. Finally, he'd experienced what he'd craved for so very long, all thanks to the woman who now owned his soul.

She stirred against him, causing his shaft to twitch against her skin. Hard and ready, he pushed into her lower back, loving how she pushed right back. Gazing up at him, her lids were heavy.

"Good morning, dear husband," she said, that sultry voice driving him insane.

Gently urging her to lie on her back, he slid over her, threading his fingers in her hair as it fanned across the pillow. Her legs fell open, and he situated between her thighs as he loomed over her. His cock had a mind of its own, searching for her wetness like a beacon in a dark sea. Finding it, he slid the head over her opening, coating himself with her essence. Dying to feel her slick walls against his sensitive skin, he searched her stunning brown eyes.

"I need to grab a condom."

She was still for a moment before arching toward him, causing him to clench his teeth so hard he thought his jaw might break.

"Alora—"

"Pull out before you come," she said, covering his mouth with her fingers.

"Are you sure?" he whispered against them.

"Yes." Silky hair slid across the pillow as she nodded. "We might only have days to live. I want to feel you inside me—"

She gasped as he nudged inside, eyes widening as her lips parted in a silent cry. Armed with her consent, he pushed, inch by inch, until the tight walls of her channel threatened to choke him. Locked onto her, he began to move.

The undulation of his hips was slower this time as he concentrated on every point where his hardness met her soft folds. Sliding her palms over the globes of his ass, she attempted to pull him closer.

"Harder," she whispered.

"Not this time, sweetheart," he said, hating to deny her but needing more than a blinding fuck. He needed to love her; to slowly cherish the gift of being inside her gorgeous body.

Recognition washed over her face as she realized he was making love to her, the act emotional instead of purely physical. Fear entered her eyes, sending a jolt of pain through his heart.

"Eli..."

"Why did you beg me not to stay in 2075?" he rasped, maintaining the pace of his hips as he continued to love her. Anger flashed in her gaze, spurring a frustrated growl from deep in his throat. "Don't close up on me," he demanded, breath labored as his heartbeat grew more intense.

"I didn't beg you," she said, spearing her nails into his ass.

"Yes, you did, you little she-devil," he said, lowering his forehead to hers. "Why?"

"So I could kill you myself," she said, eyes closing as her head fell back on the pillow.

"No!" he said, the thrusts of his hips increasing as he shook her head in his hands. "Don't diminish this. Look at me." Her lids shot open, irises swimming with more emotion than he'd ever seen, filling him with hope. "Do you care for me, Alora?"

"No."

"Liar." Nipping her lips, he reveled in her shudder beneath him. "Tell me the truth."

"Fuck you," she gritted through clenched teeth.

"Damn it, woman. Tell me."

A cry escaped her lips, although he couldn't be sure if it was from desire or frustration.

"Do you care for me, *querida?*"

Tears formed in those angry eyes as her chin trembled. "No."

Feeling his orgasm on the horizon, he knew he would need to pull out soon, but also knew he might never get the opportunity to be this close to her again.

"I need to know you care for me, Alora. That this wasn't just a fluke."

A tear escaped her eye, trailing down her cheek and cracking his heart wide open. "Why?" she whispered.

"Because I love you," he said, unable to hold back the words. A whimper escaped her lips as she shook her head on the pillow. "Yes, sweetheart. With all my soul. I need to know if you could ever feel the same."

"I can't," she warbled, gasping as he thrust against her quivering inner walls, already understanding her body so well. "After everything that's happened between us, how can you ask that of me?"

Tears welled in his own eyes, which he'd thought impossible since his father beat the urge to cry out of him decades ago. "Please tell me there's still a chance," he pleaded one last time.

"I can't." The words seemed ripped from her throat as her body thrashed with pleasure below him. Cursing the day he'd ever joined his father in a secret quest to save the world, he jutted his cock against her sensitive spot until her body bowed beneath him. Pulling from her snug channel, he emptied himself on her stomach, dying inside from her refusal to even consider loving him back.

They recovered listlessly, both consumed with the knowledge things had drastically changed. Unlike last night, there were no lingering caresses; no loving nuzzles. Reclaiming their breath, their bodies cooled as he slid away. She got up to shower, the bathroom door making an ominous click behind her. He was already dressed when she emerged wrapped in a white towel. He used the toilet while she dressed, and then they exited the room, dropping the key at the front desk, never uttering a word.

Once they were back at the townhome, Eli headed toward his room, hands in his pockets, feeling utterly defeated. Before entering, he called to her.

"Yes?" Her expression was unreadable, although her knuckles were white as she clenched the doorframe to her own chamber.

"I'll grant you a divorce. Unless you don't think we need one since our marriage wasn't ever formalized in this timeline. Whatever you want to do."

The creamy skin of her throat bobbed as she swallowed. "I don't think we need a divorce. Like you said, the marriage is void now that we're here."

Ouch. How could small words strung together into one sentence hurt so damn much?

"All right," he said, nodding. "Consider it void. Good night, Alora."

Something flashed across her face, and she appeared to open her mouth to say something else. Her gaze fell to the floor before she lifted it again.

"Good night, Eli." Stepping into her room, she closed the door behind her.

Wishing he'd never made the irrevocable decision to travel back to 2035, he lay down on his bed wondering how the hell he was going to live without her if they succeeded.

Chapter 23

Alora gritted her teeth as she fiddled with the tiny clasps on the technical gear. They'd procured it from a local vendor since Lainey was adamant every person infiltrating the White House would need full bulletproof gear. The vendor had ensured them the gear was made from special polymers that would go undetected in the multiple security checks they would encounter. Unfortunately, the damn clasp wasn't fastening, and she was about to yank it off and shoot it, making it the first casualty of the day.

They'd come outside clad in tank tops, T-shirts, and thin shorts to strap on the light but effective gear before placing their formal clothes on top. Eli was next to her, fastening his vest as if he'd sewn the damn contraption himself. Perfect fluid motions clicked the snaps into place, and he was ready to go. Of course, he could see her struggling out of the corner of his eye—of this, she had no doubt. But offering to help her would mean he had to speak to her, and that certainly hadn't happened since their disastrous night together. No, except for a few mumbled words, he'd mostly avoided her, making her furious for some reason.

What did he expect? That he would give her the best sex of her life and tell her he loved her, and she'd forget that he stood by as her family was murdered? That he'd hurt so many along the way, even though it could be justified as part of the cause? And then he'd gone and shown her his scars. Bastard. Although the sight had softened her—hell, their interactions since she was captured at the hub had softened her—it was impossible for her to *love* him. Completely absurd. Muttering under her breath, she was about to tell Lainey she was foregoing the gear when Hunter appeared at her side.

"Here," he said, his broad hands snapping everything together in seconds. "Looked like you were struggling."

"Thank you."

His silver eyes roved over her face. "Are you good?"

Lifting her chin, she nodded. "Yes. I'm ready to finally beat these bastards."

He didn't look convinced as his gaze darted to her left hand. "You going to wear your ring during the attack?"

Alora splayed her fingers as she glanced down. "He asked me to keep it safe. Who knows what's going to happen? Maybe we'll get sucked through a wormhole and end up on another planet. I can't keep it safe if it isn't in my possession."

His eyebrows lifted, indicating he understood the ring held significance for her, even if she wouldn't admit it. "Okay."

Alora ran her hand over her face and sighed. "Let's go. I'm ready."

They returned to their rooms and donned the formal attire, although Alora left the heels at the front door, not wanting to put them on until they'd had their last meeting in the back yard. Her red dress, which she'd found at a local thrift store, was sequined, and it hugged her tight curves as it fell to the floor. Confident the vest underneath wouldn't be detected, she sighed at her reflection, her eyes wary underneath the fancy updo Sara had twisted her hair into.

When she walked down the stairs to the back yard, she noticed Eli and Hunter in their rented tuxedos, both so handsome. Eli looked regal, that magnificent profile striking against the midday sun, and anger flared that he didn't even react to her appearance. She knew she looked stunning in the dress, and his lack of regard...well, it hurt. Damn it, it hurt to the core of her soul. If his wish was to wound her as deeply as she'd clearly wounded him that disastrous night, he was valiantly succeeding. Frustrated their relationship had devolved to this point, she lined up beside him and Hunter, waiting for Lainey.

Lainey walked down the stairs clad in her own bulletproof vest under her black sequined dress. "Come on, guys," she said, waving the group toward her. "One last strategy session."

She addressed the group, going over the plans, confirming everyone knew their role. Alora, Eli, Hunter, and Lainey each had the invites Zach had forged. Although they weren't official, they would hopefully pass muster if one of the agents requested proof. Hopefully, it wouldn't come to that, as the intruders to the 2009 dinner had confidently stated they were on the list and had been allowed in by security.

Elle and Luke would pose as tourists and keep watch on the grounds outside the White House with the almost invisible comm devices that fit inside their ears. Once they confirmed Randolph had been taken into custody, they would return to the apartment where Zach, Sara, and Marie would have everyone's belongings packed into a rented van to transport to Boonsboro. The five of them would spend the night in the house Lainey had rented, awaiting the team's arrival through the Sphere exactly twenty-four hours from when they confronted Randolph.

It was an ambitious plan, and Alora glanced at Eli beside her. Flashes of their one night together filled her brain, spurring an intense desire to hold him and tell him how sorry she was. For what, she didn't know. It was unfair of him to ask her to love him—in that belief, she was firm. But she could've been more...gentle? Caring? Open? Inwardly sighing, she pushed the thoughts away, realizing it was too late to act upon them. Instead, she would do everything in her power to ensure they both survived the night, and then they could talk. Then, perhaps, she could find the will to budge, if only a little...

A muscle ticked in his jaw as he listened to Lainey, indicating he knew she was studying him. She'd rarely encountered someone so intent on ignoring her. It might've made her chuckle if it wasn't so damn infuriating. Annoyance flared, and she tamped down any remaining sentiment. Screw it. She had an extremely important mission to accomplish, and there was no space for lingering thoughts of love and feelings. All her work—so many decades of plotting and surveillance—had led them here, and she wouldn't waste time on someone who couldn't even look her in the damn eye.

They trailed to the front sidewalk, energy buzzing in the air from their hesitant anticipation and excitement. Alora strapped on her shoes before joining the team outside. Elle and Luke donned ballcaps, attempting to look more like D.C. tourists, and they called a rideshare.

"Please be safe," Zach said to Elle, cupping her face as he leaned down to kiss her. Their budding love was beautiful and sweet, so different from the complex dynamic between Alora and Eli. What if she'd met him in another time, when they were both young like Elle and Zach, before Victor had murdered her family? Would they have fallen into sweet, innocent love?

Scoffing, Alora admitted that she hadn't been sweet for a very long time and most likely never would be again. Eli seemed to admire that about her—perhaps one of the people who truly appreciated her grit and difficult nature. He seemed to thrive when they sparred, and the bouts were thrilling for her as well. Sadness pervaded her veins as she realized they might never engage in a battle of wits again. That was rather hard to do when one of the people involved refused to acknowledge the other.

The rideshares arrived, Elle and Luke jumping into one as Lainey, Hunter, Eli, and Alora filtered into the luxury ride they'd procured. It would help solidify their status as invited guests to the state dinner. Sara, Zach, and Marie waved them off, looking pensive but hopeful. Lord knew, they'd need all the hope they could get.

They arrived at the White House and pulled up to the first checkpoint. Alora noted Elle and Luke's rideshare had stopped following them two blocks ago, so they must have disembarked in front of the White House.

"Are you both in place?" Alora spoke into the small device in her ear.

"Confirmed," Luke's voice crackled. "Good luck, soldiers."

The guard at the first checkpoint had an expression so austere Alora felt the first tremor of fear in her gut. Steeling herself, she handed him her ID along with the others'. The man spoke into the device with a black cord that led to his ear, his words mumbled.

"Ma'am," he said to Lainey, "we can't locate any of your names on the invite list."

"That's impossible," Lainey replied, firm and calm. "Please check again. I was personally invited by the Vancouver U.S. Consulate General."

The man spoke into the comm before glancing toward the line of cars that was building. "Go ahead and scan the car for weapons," the guard said to another nearby officer as he waited for a response.

The officer trailed a detector under the car and around the bumper before reporting back. "The car is clear, sir."

Several horns began to blare in the background, and the guard scowled. "Please move forward and have your IDs ready for the next checkpoint, ma'am," he said to Lainey.

"Will do," she said, giving a firm nod.

He waved them on, and they proceeded to the next checkpoint.

"Close call," Eli muttered.

"There are more to come," Lainey replied. "Stay sharp."

After traversing another gate, they encountered a second checkpoint, repeating the same process. Addressing the guard, Lainey feigned indignation so well that Alora decided she'd missed her calling as an actress. If they succeeded, her friend might make it in Hollywood if the whole science thing didn't pan out.

"I understand, ma'am," the guard said, still holding her ID. "But you're not on the list—" Lifting his hand to the device at his ear, he barked, "Repeat!"

His eyes were focused as he listened. Nodding, he handed Lainey back her ID. "Continue forward," he said, turning to explain his actions to the guard beside him. "Press Secretary Gaynor approved their entrance. Apparently, there was a mistake from the consulate's office, and that's why their names are missing."

Rolling up her window, Lainey looked to the ceiling. "Thank you, Aiysha," she whispered.

Eventually, they pulled up to the White House and exited, Alora taking Eli's offered hand as she stepped from the vehicle.

"Thank you," she said, finally making eye contact with him.

"Sure," he said, releasing her hand as if it made his skin burn. Still, he offered her his arm, Hunter doing the same for Lainey, and they headed up the stairs.

Lainey placed her purse on the conveyor belt, the interior lined with asbestos. The small handguns Alora, Eli, and Hunter carried were wrapped in asbestos sheets and secured to their bodies. Slowly, they all walked through the metal detector, each passing through without tripping the alarm.

"I need to search your bag, ma'am," one of the agents said, and Alora recognized him as Liam Downing, the agent they'd recruited in exchange for paying off his gambling debts.

"Oh, sure. Just to prepare you, I was Science Teacher of the Year in Vancouver. It's why the Consulate General invited me to the dinner. I brought some of my gadgets to show the other attendees."

The man peeked inside, opening the briefcase that held the mini-Sphere and shining his flashlight inside. "Congratulations on the honor. Please step ahead." He held out the bag, his expression unreadable.

"Thank you." Slinging the bag over her shoulder, she trailed ahead, Alora, Eli, and Hunter all following behind.

"We'll announce your names as you enter," a woman said, walking forward. "Ms....?"

"Mrs. Elaine Rhodes and Mr. Hunter Rhodes," Lainey said.

"Eli Hernandez and Alora Castillo," Eli said to the woman.

"Perfect." The lady appeared frazzled, and Alora wondered if she was new. Thankfully, her inexperience seemed to place her focus on the function and not the guests. She relayed their names to the announcer, who formally introduced them as they walked into the foyer.

After shaking hands with several diplomats who comprised the receiving line, they moved toward the large room that had been prepared for the banquet. Alora took note of its proximity to the hallway she would need to traverse to gain access to the bunker.

"We're early."

Lainey's eyes darted around the room. "My grandfather detonated the nukes before this dinner. He's most likely already in the bunker now."

"We each need to make our way down the hallway where Gordon is waiting at the end," Alora said. "Hold your head high and appear confident. I'll go first. See you all there." Floating through the throng of people, Alora trailed toward the restroom, body buzzing with adrenaline. At the last moment, she took a turn and headed down the hallway, understanding Liam had set the cameras on loop and she wouldn't be detected.

Suddenly, a hand gripped her wrist, and Alora gasped, turning to find a stone-faced Secret Service agent.

"The bathroom is this way, ma'am," he said in a firm tone.

"Oh, I must've gotten lost. Thank you, sir." Tugging her arm from his grasp, she hurried away, back around the corner and to the bathroom. Once there, she stared at her reflection, thankful the agent hadn't questioned her. Steeling herself, she vowed to try again.

Several women filtered in the door, and Alora slipped back into the hallway, noting the various people milling in the distance. Deciding to go for it, she zipped down the hallway, around the corner, toward the doorway where Gordon awaited.

Sensing a presence behind her, she pivoted to find Hunter hot on her tail. Lainey and Eli appeared shortly thereafter, and they approached Gordon where he waited by the door, legs wide, fists crossed above his belt.

"Hello, Gordon," Alora said as he opened the door for her.

"Fuck you, bitch."

What a dick. Alora hoped his wife discovered his dalliances and kicked him out on his ass.

"The security cameras are on a loop?" Hunter asked Gordon.

"Yes. For ten minutes. Liam has it covered."

"Got it," Hunter said, waving them in. "Let's go."

Gordon accompanied them as they hurried down the darkened walkway. Eventually, they came to the large metal doors Ronald guarded. The agent scowled at them as he unlatched the doors and ushered them inside, locking them closed after they entered.

Alora's shoulders tensed at the sound. "Was he supposed to lock us in here? I don't remember that being part of the plan."

Hunter's gaze was worried. "It's conceivable Victor already knows every detail of our plan, but we knew that was possible. Too late to stop now."

They quickly traversed to the point on the concrete wall Lainey indicated. "This is as far as I can go and postulate the time machine will still work correctly."

Quickly arming themselves, Hunter gave Lainey a kiss on the forehead. "Make sure that thing's fired up. Once we've stopped Randolph, we'll need to transport immediately."

Lainey grabbed his lapels and pulled him to her for a passionate kiss. "I love you."

"Let's save the world, duchess." Placing one last peck on her lips, he turned and gestured for Alora and Eli to follow.

They advanced to the end of the hallway, arriving at a door that had a window showcasing the bunker. Scanning inside, Alora could make out President Randolph pacing back and forth, appearing frustrated and unstable as he ran his hands through his brown hair.

"What is he saying?" Alora whispered.

"I don't know," Eli said, "but our ten minutes are eroding quickly. We need to bust inside."

Hunter drew his gun from his waist. "Ready?"

Alora and Eli drew their own weapons. "Ready."

Hunter tested the knob, turning it, and slammed through the door. The three of them lifted their weapons, aiming at the four occupants.

"Step away from the nuclear football, President Randolph," Hunter commanded. The nuclear football was a briefcase that held all of the authentication codes and information Randolph would need to detonate the nukes. One call from the secure phone in the bunker with the authorized codes, and the entire world would change.

Edward lunged for his gun, aiming it high as Alice screamed. "How did you get in here?" he asked. "Where are the agents?"

"They're alive and unharmed," Alora said. "But you're not setting off the bombs today, Randolph. Put the gun down."

Edward fired a bullet, causing them to crouch before Eli rushed him, firing. Edward bent below the table, pulling Alice down with him, trying to hide from the spray of bullets. Terrence Stapp, the Secretary of Defense, pulled his gun from his belt but was quickly wounded as Hunter shot him in the shoulder. Screaming in pain, he dropped to the ground. Hunter aimed his gun at the Vice President Andrew Salerno, who stood in the corner, hands up. The man appeared terrified, and it comforted Alora that he was shaking like a leaf. It was about time these assholes felt true fear.

"Don't make me shoot you," Eli snarled, knocking Edward's gun out of his hand before grasping his shirt and tugging him to stand. Pressing the barrel of the gun to his neck, he held him hostage. "Do you understand how much pain and death this one decision will cause? How many lives will be ruined?"

"Yes!" Edward wheezed, fear evident in his expression. "But I have no choice."

"What do you mean?" Eli said, shaking him. "Turn yourself in. Identify your associates. Surely, they will give you some immunity for identifying the others."

"They'll kill him if I don't detonate the nukes," Edward sputtered.

"Who?" Eli asked. "Who will they kill?"

"Great question, son." Heads snapped to the door as Victor Hernandez walked through, a man entering behind him who was...also Victor Hernandez, although many decades younger.

Elder Victor lifted his gun and shot a single bullet through the Vice President's head as the man still cowered in the corner. He fell to the ground, lifeless, as Hunter asked, "Did you hurt Lainey? I swear, I'll kill you right now if you touched one hair on her head."

"Relax," Elder Victor said, appearing unconcerned, as if he'd lived this scenario a thousand times. Hell, maybe he had. "We tied Lainey up in the hallway. The Secret Service will eventually find her and most likely send her to jail. I have a latent fondness for her that precludes me from killing her. Unfortunately, I don't feel the same for the rest of you."

Alora could see Eli's struggle as he questioned whether to shoot his father or keep his gun aimed at Randolph.

"This is impossible," Eli said. "You're dead."

"I was never dead," Elder Victor said, inching forward, seemingly unconcerned that his son was on the verge of shooting him. "Powerful men never truly die. Isn't that right, Victor?"

"Yes," Younger Victor said with a tilt of his head, his own gun held high.

"I faked my death when I realized the future timeline was out of control. Eventually, I made my way to Australia, where I... *encouraged* Nelson to rebuild his Sphere."

"By threatening Lorna, I'm sure," Alora gritted through her teeth.

"Yes, that's right. I threatened to slit her pretty little neck open, and he sent me to 2035 and my associate Sebastian to the early 2000s so fast I could barely blink." Giving a sneer, he asked, "How's your family, Alora? Well, I hope—oh, wait..." He rubbed his chin, eyes narrowing. "No, they're probably still dead. Slaughtered like the Colombian trash they truly were."

Alora remained still, refusing to be baited by the awful man.

Straightening, Elder Victor sighed. "Well, this is all quite fortuitous, isn't it? What we've all been waiting for?" Taking another step forward, he assessed the room. "What none of you realized is that Edward always had a change of heart. Although he toyed with detonating the nukes, he never had the strength to carry out the plan. Only after we recognized we needed to...*urge* him along did he comply. We've assured him we will murder Lewis unless he follows our instruction to the letter."

Pulling a pad and pen from his pocket, Victor slid them across the table. "Sit down, Edward. My son will let you go because he's never really had the constitution to murder innocents, although I'm not sure if that's what you are. Quite a waste, if you ask me."

"No fucking way," Eli said, clutching Edward tighter.

"Shoot Alora," Victor said to his younger self.

"No!" Eli called, pushing Edward toward the desk. "Sit down and write whatever he wants you to write."

With shaking hands, Edward pulled the pad close and wrote the words Victor dictated. Words explaining his actions and that he was attempting to save humanity from itself.

"Good," Victor said, nodding. "Now, my son is going to hand his gun over, Edward, and you're going to shoot Alice and Terrence. Then you're going to shoot yourself."

"Please," Edward said, shaking his head as he pleaded. "I don't know where this went so wrong, Victor. I only wanted to help those who were worthy."

"Worthiness is not for you to decide!" Alora said, clutching her gun, still aiming at Elder Victor but wary of Younger Victor out of the corner of her eye. "Worthiness is intrinsic, and every person deserves a chance to thrive!"

Rolling his eyes, Elder Victor sighed. "Good god. How could you fall for someone so idealistic, Eli? I can't wait to murder your family in front of you again," he said, gesturing to his younger self. "I'll be counting down the days, you Colombian whore. How could you even *think* you're good enough to touch my son? Fucking bitch." He spat on the ground.

Alora told herself to remain calm although she wanted nothing more than to lodge a bullet in his brain. "It's over," Elder Victor said with an absent shrug. "Lainey can't operate the time machine inside the bunker. I'm going to set off the nukes and kill you all, just as I've done every single time this has happened before."

"How many times?' Lainey called from the doorway, palms facing forward as she tentatively stepped inside the bunker. "How many times have we done this, Victor?"

"Well done, my dear," Victor said, tone laced with reluctant respect as he arched a dark brow. "Who untied you? That worthless brat, Aiysha? I'm almost convinced she isn't worth the trouble I expended to ensure she was conceived."

"I had a knife wrapped in an asbestos sheet hidden in my dress. I'm determined to win this time, Victor. Mark my words."

"Get back outside, Lainey!" Hunter screamed.

"No!" she said. "I can't keep failing. I have to figure this out. Obviously, we're stuck in a terrible loop, and it has to end." Taking a step toward Elder Victor, she asked, "How. Many. Times?"

He blew a breath though puffed cheeks. "I've honestly lost count. Three hundred? Four? It doesn't matter anymore. You always fail, right here. I kill these three," he said, gesturing to Edward, Alice, and Terrence, "and then you try to escape to the time machine in the hallway. I set off the nukes and run to find you, but you've already vanished." He snapped his fingers. "It's a fate paradox. I've never figured out where you end up, but there have never been any older versions of you, so we assume you die every time." Shrugging, he continued. "I go into hiding, and Younger Victor forms the New Establishment. Lewis has you, Eli joins me, and we repeat the cycle over and over. It's maddening."

"Then let's create a new cycle," Lainey said. "There must be something you want—some other scenario that can prevent all this."

"I am the leader of the New Establishment, Elaine. I always will be. It's all I've ever wanted. The world will fear me, and I will instill systematic reign over every human on the planet." Lifting his gun from his belt, he aimed it at Edward. "Sorry, old friend, but it's time to die."

* * * *

Elle exited the Starbucks bathroom, now fully clad in the ballgown she'd shoved into her bag. Thankfully, it was made from some fancy material that wouldn't wrinkle. She'd ensured that when she purchased it from the consignment shop. Approaching the White House gate, she showed her invitation and ID to the guards, taking measured breaths so her hands wouldn't shake. They verified her name on the list, and she continued on the walkway and up the front steps to the mansion.

Aiysha met her, and they fell into the routine they'd previously rehearsed.

"Elle," she said, giving her two quick pecks, one on each cheek. "You look stunning."

"Thanks for the invite, but I've torn my dress," she said, pointing at the rip in the fabric she'd made herself only minutes ago. "Can you lead me to a bathroom?"

"Of course." Turning to the security staff, she said, "Let me get Ms. Huber cleaned up, and we'll let you formally announce her." The two brawny men nodded, and Aiysha whisked her away.

They meandered through the herd of dignitaries and socialites, blending in as they weaved their path to the bunker hallway door. Facing Aiysha, Elle gave her a quick hug.

"Gordon and Ronald will grant you access," she said, gesturing to the agent standing at the end of the hallway. "Here," she said, surreptitiously handing Elle a gun. "Good luck."

Elle clenched it tight. "Thank you."

"When I campaigned for Edward and helped him win the minority vote, I kept telling myself it was for the cause. *This* cause. You have to win, Elle." Splaying her hand over her distended abdomen, she seemed firm with resolve. "Kick their asses."

Elle covered the woman's hand, giving a supportive squeeze, and then bounded past Gordon and down the hallway. Ronald opened the metal doors, and she breezed through, noticing the mini-Sphere lying open in the hallway. That meant Lainey must be inside the bunker. Pushing away every fear that threatened to drown her, Elle approached the bunker, hearing the sound of voices—one of which sounded very much like her father's.

* * * *

"Victor!" Lainey shouted.

He grunted, glancing at her over his shoulder.

"There has to be something you want. Something that can appease you so we can save millions of innocent lives. Please," she pleaded, her maple-colored eyes full of emotion.

"Enough," a female voice said from behind the table. They all turned to look at Alice as she held the secure phone to her ear, clutching the authorization codes. "I'm tired of this, Victor. Edward, finish the letter so I can detonate the nukes."

Lainey's eyes grew wide. "Alice?"

Alice rolled her eyes, appearing disgusted. "None of you ever even contemplated that I could be the biggest threat of them all. Little ol' Alice, fucked over by her shitbag husband with that *whore* Vivian Elders." Releasing the papers, she backhanded Edward, busting open his lip as blood began to trickle down. "I was

133

recruited into the regime years ago. I'll always be dedicated to the New Establishment and will always ensure the nukes are detonated." Alora tensed on the trigger, ready to kill Lainey's grandmother.

"I wouldn't do that, Alora," Victor said. "Alice has a gun hidden underneath the desk—don't you, dear?"

Detaching the gun, Alice held it high, aiming at Alora. "I always do at this very point in every timeline. Lainey's failure to contemplate that *I* could be the ultimate foe is always her downfall."

"Grandmother," Lainey called softly.

"Oh, now I'm *Grandmother*?" she asked, spittle exiting her mouth. "I married into this family because I craved greatness, but instead, I was saddled with a cheating waste of a husband and a son who shuns our name. Shuns our *power*. Not anymore." Picking up the phone and thrusting it at Edward, she said, "I'm calling command, and you will read the codes and detonate the nukes, Edward. *Now*."

Lainey appeared utterly defeated as she shook her head. "I didn't postulate a scenario in which Alice was a traitor. Why didn't I see it?" Sympathy welled in Alora's chest as her friend fell down the chasm of regret and self-doubt.

"You tried your best, Lainey," Alora said. "Hopefully, next time around, we'll anticipate Alice's deception."

"Shut up!" Alice screamed, jerking the gun as crazed fury lit her eyes. "My son will die in this cycle before Elaine is ever born. Good riddance. This time, it will end once and for all." Staring down at her husband, she commanded through clenched teeth, "Prepare to recite the codes." Situating the phone between her ear and shoulder, she began punching the buttons that would connect him with command.

Suddenly, a shot fired from the doorway, and Alice gasped, her eyes growing wide before she crumpled to the ground behind the desk. Two more shots exploded, and Alora turned to see Elle stepping over Younger Victor's now lifeless body and striding toward Elder Victor, who lay gasping on the floor.

"Hello, Father," she said, crouching down and sticking the gun into his cheek. "It's nice to finally meet you."

"Father?" Eli asked, his confusion mirroring Alora's own.

"It's true," Elle said, roughly scraping the gun over Victor's face. "One of Victor Hernandez's favorite conquests was my mother. He would pass by and use her, always telling her he would return one day and make her whole. Instead, he left her with a bastard daughter and no means whatsoever. Isn't that right?"

"Who the *fuck* are you—?"

Elle pistol-whipped him, cutting off the words. "You always saw yourself as above the lessers in society. Those of us who had to work and scrape and, yes, prostitute ourselves to climb out of the gutter. You wanted us eliminated, but you failed to see that *we* are the strong ones. We are the ones who will always prevail.

Yes, Victor, your insignificant *whore* daughter from your insignificant *whore* lover is the one who's going to end your life, asshole." Staring into his eyes, she pressed the gun into his forehead. A muscle clamped in her jaw as her nostrils flared...and then she pulled the trigger.

Victor expelled one long breath, open-eyed as the life left his body.

Crumpling into a ball, Elle buried her face in her hands and began to sob.

"It's okay," Hunter soothed, lifting her into his strong arms. "We've got to get the hell out of here, guys."

Edward fell to the ground and ran his hand over Alice's face, frozen and expressionless. "I never realized she knew the affair was with Vivian," he said, sadness in his tone.

"We have to go, Grandfather," Lainey said, seeming to comprehend she was seeing him for the last time. "I'm sorry we had to meet like this. I wish things could've been different."

Edward stood and gathered the scattered papers on the desk, stuffing them back into the briefcase that comprised the nuclear football. "As do I," he said, crumpling into one of the chairs. "Go on," he said, waving his hand. "It's done. The Service will be here to arrest me and Terrence soon." The Secretary of Defense also lowered into a chair, seemingly overcome with shock.

Lifting her chin, Lainey called to the president. "You still have time to change, Grandfather. I hope you choose to do so." Pivoting, she gestured toward the hallway. "Come on, guys. We have to go. *Now.*"

They ran out of the bunker, huddling around Lainey as she furiously pressed buttons on the mini-Sphere. Stepping back, the wormhole grew, and she ushered Hunter inside.

"Go through with Elle."

Hunter departed, Elle in his arms, and Lainey urgently waved at Alora, directing her to step through next. "Come on, Alora."

Before Alora could step into the portal, she whipped her head around, counting at least eight agents running toward them. Understanding Lainey's importance and how close they were, she shoved her friend in the wormhole.

"I'll follow. You go first!"

Lainey nodded and jumped through, vanishing in the dark orb.

"You go next!" Alora yelled over her shoulder to Eli as she aimed her gun at the rapidly approaching men.

"Not before you." He stepped in front of her and lifted his gun. "Get in the damn machine, Alora!"

"No!" she said, firing a few shots at the thighs of the men running toward them, trying not to fatally wound them. A resulting shot hammered her in the chest, right over her heart, and she struggled to breathe.

"Damn it, Alora," Eli said, pushing her toward the mini-Sphere. "Go!"

She turned back to him and tried to pull him through.

"They'll need a scapegoat," he said, sadness and determination in his handsome features. "Someone to be the face of the intruders and come up with a plausible excuse for why everyone else vanished into thin air. I'll stay behind. There's nothing for me here."

"No!"

He shook his head. "We did this once before, and I'm not doing it again." A bullet flew by his head. "Unless there's a reason for me to go, I'm staying behind. I'll be more useful that way."

Alora knew what he was asking her as the men grew so very close in the dim hallway. Could she give him a reason? Was she willing to love him back? Unable to make the commitment, she wavered, still struggling to breathe from the bullet lodged inside her protective vest.

"Goodbye, Alora," he said, spreading his palm over her chest and pushing her through the wormhole.

Her arms flailed as she tumbled through darkness until she slammed into a wooden floor with an *oomph*.

"Where is Eli?" she asked, sitting up and looking around, taking in the hardwood floor of the hallway she now resided in. A living room sat to her right, with a brown leather couch and matching chairs, and a kitchen was to her left. "Are we at the house in Boonsboro?"

"Yes," Lainey said, clicking buttons on the mini-Sphere to shut it down. "It's almost six o'clock on September fifth, and Eli didn't come through," she said, sounding frustrated. "They most likely arrested him. He's more valuable to them alive, so they can interrogate him."

"Damn it," Alora said, pounding the floor with her fist.

"But guess what?" Staring at the group, she said, "Although I'm frustrated and pissed Eli was left behind..." She lifted her arms, an expression of wonder across her face. "I think we just prevented the apocalypse, guys."

"Holy shit," Hunter breathed.

"Amazing," Elle said.

Lainey strolled toward Elle and cupped her cheeks. "You were our X factor, Elle. Holy crap, I didn't see it at all. Your connection to Victor and Alice's deception were the only two unknowns I hadn't postulated. Thank you. I mean, you should've told me you were Victor's daughter, but wow. You saved the day."

Elle nodded, her eyes still swollen. "I was dedicated to the cause, but I also vowed I would kill Victor. It was ultimately why I asked to travel back with you. I felt it was important to keep my connection to him secret in case this time was different. And it was," she whispered, overcome with the gravity of the situation

"You're remarkable, Elle," a voice chimed from the living room.

"Zach!" Running toward him, she threw her arms around his neck and placed fervent kisses over his face as he clutched her tight.

"Glad to see you all made it," Lainey said, addressing Zach, Marie, Sara, and Luke as they all shared hugs. "In other news, I think Alora was shot."

"It was stopped by the vest," Alora said, pulling the covering from her body as she rubbed her chest. "Still hurts like hell though."

"Come on, Superwoman," Lainey said, offering her hand and pulling Alora to stand. "We'll figure out where he is," she murmured. "I promise."

Alora gave her a nod, both hopeful and terrified Eli was alive and unharmed.

After many hugs and expressions of disbelief that they might have finally prevailed, they settled into the cabin on the outskirts of the quiet town. Turning on the TV, they confirmed Speaker Anita Rohan had been sworn in as President, and former President Randolph and the Secretary of Defense were being held in a secure location for questioning. Cyrus also called to confirm the news and congratulate them for finally succeeding. After all the cycles and all the pain, they had finally saved the world.

"Although I'm beat, Hunter and I need to head to 2039," Lainey said, addressing the group as they sat around the large living room. "I want to finish our mission so I can destroy the time machine. I don't want to leave any possibility that it might fall into someone else's hands. When we return tomorrow, I'd really like to hear more of your story, Elle, if you're open to telling me."

Elle nodded, looking pensive but brave as Zach sat beside her clutching her hand.

"Ready, Hunter?"

"Ready, duchess," he said, rising and pulling her from the couch.

"We'll return tomorrow at twelve noon. I'm going to make several visits to Eli in 2039 and some a few years afterward. A few months might pass for Hunter and me, but it will only be a day for you all. If I return with extra wrinkles, you'll know why."

"You'll still look sexy," Hunter murmured in her ear.

"I'm keeping him, guys," Lainey said, hugging him tight.

They all headed outside and observed Lainey power up the mini-Sphere before she and Hunter vanished along with it. Left with her team—minus Eli—Alora walked inside, her exhausted mind craving sleep.

Chapter 24

The next afternoon, Elle analyzed Lainey's reaction, Hunter and Zach beside her at the kitchen table, and she steeled herself to recount her story. "First of all, I want to say that I'm sorry I didn't tell you I was Victor's daughter. I felt in my bones that it was pertinent to keep it close to the vest, especially since I'd decided to kill him and knew that might upend whatever space–time continuum you felt should remain intact."

"I want to understand, Elle," Lainey said. "I promise, there's no judgement here."

Puffing her cheeks, she blew out a breath. "My whole life has been about this mission, whether I wanted it to be or not. Much like Eli, I really didn't have a choice. I was steered into the cause by my mother when I was very young. Grandpa Will ingrained the significance of ensuring Luke's letter got to the hub safely on the exact date it needed to arrive."

Sitting forward, she rested her elbows on the table as her fingers fidgeted together. "But what I didn't realize until years later was that Victor had met my mother. He'd passed by our rural home, and she was smitten by his attractiveness and confidence. She didn't realize at first who he was. She only knew his name was Victor. They shared some time together, and then he left, promising to come back when he passed through again."

"But he never came back?" Lainey asked.

"Oh, he came back," Elle said, her hands clenching together so tight the veins were blue. "Once we'd moved to the house outside Terrum, he would pass by with his soldiers. By that time, Grandpa Will had died, and times were tough. Victor was at the height of his power and realized she'd been prostituting herself. Feeling he deserved to take her without paying since he'd already been with her before, he was quite rough with her. I would watch through the slits in my bedroom wall, not understanding why he was hurting her. And then he would offer her to his soldiers. It was...tough to watch."

Zach slipped his hand over hers, squeezing to offer comfort. Elle smiled, so thankful for him, hoping she hadn't blown everything by lying.

"For some reason, she deluded herself that he would return. That he would pay her the money he owed her and retire from the New Establishment. As I've told you, she wasn't well. Eventually, she told me he was my father. It was shocking. After all, we'd known of Victor and the New Establishment through Luke's letter, and it was all rather unbelievable. And then he passed by one last time." Sucking in a breath, she hesitated.

"Go on," Hunter said, his tone encouraging.

"He came searching for my mother. By this point, he was quite deranged as well. Two lost souls intent on torturing each other. He dragged her to the river that flowed near our house along with a few soldiers. She didn't even fight. I think she still held out hope. I watched behind a tree as they used her." She swiped the tear that ran down her cheek. "The soldiers eventually dispersed, and she tried to reason with Victor, told him they had a daughter and that I needed food and support. He didn't believe her and called her a whore, and she struck him. A physical altercation ensued, and then he..." She broke off, covering her face in her hands as she sobbed. Zach was there immediately, scooting his chair over so she could lean into his firm body. "He drowned her in the river. And I just stood by, frozen. I didn't help her." Burrowing into Zach's chest, she relived the memories, not used to crying but overwhelmed with emotion.

Lainey shook her head. "That's just awful, Elle. I'm so very sorry."

"I dragged her body from the river and buried her after he left. I was so ashamed I didn't help her. I vowed that day that I would kill him. I would deliver the letter to you at the hub, convince you to bring me back, and I would kill him before he could ever hurt her in this new timeline. I didn't really care about anything else. Until I met Zach." Lifting her face, she gave him a warbled smile as he caressed her cheek.

The room was quiet for several moments before Lainey spoke. "I understand. We all are motivated by awful moments in our lives. Those terrible memories make us strive to do more; endeavor to secure better outcomes. I wish you'd told us from the start—it honestly would've probably made me admire you more—but you had your reasons, and it's water under the bridge now."

"It was so strange meeting Eli. Knowing he was my half-brother. I found myself wanting to know him, to search for similarities between us. And then I fell in love with Zach," she said, palming his cheek as he squeezed her, "and I realized I might actually have connections—might have a purpose—once I killed Victor. *If* I killed him.

"Aiysha approached me when I left the health clinic the day I went in for my exam. She informed me she was Cyrus and Claire's daughter and that she was intent on ensuring this cycle was the last one. She'd been spying on both Victors as they met and understood there needed to be someone who would infiltrate the bunker after Alice showed her deception. We devised a plan that I would be that person and hopefully kill my father. Killing him was bittersweet though." She rotated her hands, studying them. "It's been my only focus for so long."

Zach placed a tender kiss on her forehead. "Then we'll find a new focus. Together."

Tears clouded her eyes. "I'd really like that."

"If you all are done takin' up space in my kitchen, I'd really like to get back to work," Marie interrupted, entering the room. "I knew the second I saw the girl, she was Victor's kid. Some observational skills you all have for a bunch of scientists." Reaching into the cabinets, she banged some pots and pans around as she continued to mutter.

"Well, your plan worked," Lainey said, grinning. "I firmly believe that you were the extra piece we needed to fall into place to win, Elle. It might've been a bit messy, but the outcome is all that matters. I'm so sorry for everything you experienced. I'm pretty sure Zach is eager to ensure your future is much brighter than your past."

"Damn straight, I am," he said, smiling when Elle placed a sweet kiss on his lips.

"Thank you for telling us your story. I'm sure it wasn't easy," she said, standing and stretching her arms above her head as she yawned. "Now, if you'll excuse me, I'm exhausted from months of time traveling, although it was only a day for you two, and I want to spend some time with this man who's somehow convinced me to marry him." Beaming, she extended her hand to Hunter.

"She begged me to marry her, guys," he said, holding his hand to the side of his mouth and whispering loudly. "I always told her she was dying to marry me—"

"Shut it," she said, slapping her palm over his mouth. "Take me upstairs before I change my mind."

"Gotta go," Hunter said, clutching his woman's hand and dragging her from the room so fast Elle thought she saw smoke curl from his heels.

"You okay?" Zach asked, stroking her hair.

Elle nodded. "Are you mad at me? For not telling you?"

"No way," he said, shaking his head. "Haven't you figured out that there is literally nothing you could do that would make me mad?"

She scrunched her nose. "That's a bit obsessive. There has to be something."

He shrugged. "Maybe. Guess we'll have to spend lots of time together to figure out what it is."

Sighing, she relaxed into his body. "Guess so."

His lips found hers, the resulting kiss so wistful and full of promise, and Elle finally understood that every ounce of heartache and pain had led her to this man whom she loved so dearly. Excited for the future they were sure to build, she kissed him back until Marie shooed them from the kitchen. Feeling lucky for the first time in her life, Elle embraced the hope that swelled in her heart.

* * * *

That evening, once it was dark outside and the moon shone bright, Lainey gathered them around the mini-Sphere. Holding the thick end of a wooden baseball bat, she aimed the handle at Marie.

"Well, Ms. Elders," she said, smiling. "Want to do the honors?"

Marie suspiciously eyed the bat. "Nothing's going to jump out at me, right?"

Laughing, Lainey shook her head. "I already removed the uranium pellet and wrapped it in the zirconium rod Nelson and I fashioned for disposal. Hunter buried it several feet deep at the base of that tree, where it will rest in perpetuity. Come on," she said, gesturing with the bat. "I know you want to beat the hell out of the time machine, Marie."

Grinning, she took the bat, a sparkle in her eye as she tested the weight of it in her hands. "I'm not going to go easy on the thing. You know that, right?"

"We have to destroy it, so we might as well make it fun."

Cackling, Marie lifted the bat over her head and began to beat the contraption with skillful strokes. Gears and levers threw in the air as the crew looked on. After a full sixty seconds, she stood back and swiped her arm over her forehead.

"Whew, that was cathartic. Someone else give it a go." Turning she handed the bat to Alora. "I think you need this as much as I do."

Alora took the bat and proceeded to whack the machine before each member of the team followed suit. Finally, Lainey took the bat from Sara's hand and shook her head.

"You guys are monsters. I love it."

"Damn, that was awesome," Elle said.

"I don't have the constitution to demolish it myself, considering it was my life's work, but you guys did a pretty good job. We'll load the pieces into separate bags and deposit them at various dump sites tomorrow. Thanks for helping me destroy it."

"Even though the machine is destroyed, your work and accomplishments live on, dear," Marie said, sliding her arm around Lainey's shoulders. "You understand that, right?"

"I understand it here," she said, tapping her temple. "It might take a while to understand it here." She thumped her hand over her heart.

"Fair enough," Marie said, leading her inside. "Let the boys clean up the pieces. Elle, Alora, Sara?" she called. "Get your butts inside, and let's pour this woman a glass of wine."

Hugging the mother figure close, Lainey followed her, so thankful for her unwavering support.

Chapter 25

Eli heard the lock click at the door of his solitary confinement cell. Rising from the squalid bed attached to the wall, he waited to see who would enter. So far, he'd been visited by a few people, most of them high-ranking officials on President Rohan's staff and FBI agents looking for answers. He'd stayed silent—yet another skill his father had taught him long ago. No amount of torture could make him talk, although they'd treated him quite well for the three days he'd been sequestered. Squaring his shoulders, he watched the door swing open.

"Thank you," Alora said to the guard before walking inside.

"Five minutes, Ms. Castillo," the guard said.

She nodded as the door closed behind her. Turning to face him, her eyes roved over his orange jumpsuit. Arching a brow, she said, "Not really your color."

"How did you gain access?" he asked, understanding they didn't have much time.

"Aiysha. She's extremely well-connected and will continue on as President Rohan's Press Secretary."

"That's good to hear. One of our own on the inside. Learning Aiysha was Cyrus and Claire's daughter after the White House tour was surprising enough, but realizing Elle is my half-sister shocked the hell out of me. Holy shit."

The air between them was thick as her melted brown irises darted between his. "Lainey has visited seven-year-old you in the future and returned. The time machine has been destroyed. At this point, we're all vestiges of a world that never existed, left to build our own lives."

Everyone but him. No, he'd chosen to be a martyr, and now he was screwed. But what did it really matter? He hadn't planned on traveling back anyway, so who really cared if he wasted away in a staid D.C. prison?

"Well, I wish you the best," he said, giving her a nod, "building your new life. How the tables have turned. You must be elated that you're now the one visiting me in a cell."

"I'm not elated at all," she said softly, shaking her head. "I want to help you escape."

"Why?"

"Because you don't deserve to be locked up like an animal."

He scoffed. "But I am an animal, right? It's what I'll always be to you. The man who allowed your family to be murdered. Someone evil whom you can never trust."

"That's too simplistic. I think you have good qualities, Eli, but you ask me to forget things I never will."

Stepping forward, he jabbed his finger at her. "I *never* asked you to forget that day," he said, angry that she couldn't find some small sliver of forgiveness toward him. "I want you to remember every second. Every way I tried, and succeeded, to save your life!"

"At the expense of my family?" she asked, knocking his arm away. "I would've rather died."

"No!" he said, grasping her upper arms and shaking her. "Letting you die was never an option. Somehow, I knew even then that you would become the center of my world. All I ever asked of you was to give me a chance to prove I could be the man my mother raised me to be. Hell, I'm not sure if I'm proving it to myself, or you, or to both of us. But I just want you to open your heart this much." He lifted his hand, showing her his thumb and index finger as he held them a centimeter apart.

Her nostrils flared as she glared up at him. "Let go of my arm," she gritted.

"You just can't do it, can you? You can't find one ounce of compassion that compels you to love me back."

"I can't see a way." Her shoulders softened as the barest hint of wetness glistened in her eyes. "I'm sorry," she whispered.

Huffing a frustrated laugh, he released her. "You know what? I'm done. Fuck you, Alora. Just leave me alone."

Turning his back to her, he leaned his palms on the far wall, furious he'd all but begged her yet again and she'd reacted with such indifference to his feelings.

"Eli—"

"I don't need you to save me. I'm pretty damn resilient. You keep reminding me what a monster I am. Believe me, I've been in worse situations than this. I'll find a way."

"Lainey thinks—"

"I don't care," he said, pivoting and slicing his hand through the air. "I'm over all of it. You, Lainey, the fucking team that I was never really a part of. I'm glad you saved the world. I truly am. Now, just let me figure out a way to live or die in peace, on my own."

Her expression was filled with so much sorrow, he almost deluded himself she cared. Then he doused the hope that simmered in his gut. One lesson he needed to learn for good was that Alora would never forgive him and certainly never care for him.

"I don't want you to die, Eli."

"Honestly, Alora, I don't really give a shit what you want anymore." Shuffling past her, he banged on the door. The guard opened it, and Eli grabbed Alora's arm, all but yanking her out of the cell. "We're done here, officer."

"Don't manhandle me!" When she faced him, he saw the plethora of emotions cross her face. The ones she always showcased right before she lost control with him. He remembered so long ago, convincing himself that meant something. Now, he knew it just meant she hated him.

Palming the door with both hands, he pushed it shut, effectively pushing her out of his life. Sitting on the bed, he ran his hands through his hair.

"Holy hell, Hernandez," he muttered to himself. "How the mighty have fallen."

There, in the small cell with bare concrete walls, the once-revered, once-powerful Eli Hernandez accepted his life would end with a pitiful whimper, just as his father's had. He truly was his father's son. An irredeemable soul, lost and hopeless.

* * * *

Wracked with insomnia, Eli was doing push-ups in his cell when the key jangled in the lock. A tall, russet-skinned police officer entered, thick muscles filling out his blue uniform.

"You're being transferred, Mr. Hernandez," he said, hands on his belt, which was full of weapons and other gadgets. "Please put on your shirt and shoes, and I'll shackle your ankles and hands before we exit the cell."

"Sure, why not?" Eli sighed, wondering if he would be led to an interrogation room. Honestly, his life had turned to such shit lately, it might be a nice change of pace to have his face beat in since he'd decided not to answer any questions. At least he would feel *something*.

After he was clothed, the officer shackled him and led him from the cell down a long hallway toward a nondescript door. The officer gave a silent nod to the guard at the door, who nodded back and let them pass. Exiting into a parking lot, Eli noticed the dark sky above with only a sliver of moonlight. A broad hand covered Eli's head as he was pushed into the backseat of a police car. The cop sat behind the wheel and began to drive, giving the guard on duty a salute as the vehicle passed through the front gate.

They drove in silence for a while, and Eli realized there was something highly irregular about the trip. Not only was it the dead of night, but they seemed to be driving into an abandoned industrial park. Maneuvering behind one of the warehouses, the officer brought the car to a stop and got out, walking around to open Eli's door.

"Let's go," he said, jerking his head.

Eli stepped out—difficult with the shackles still on—and the officer lowered to one knee. Pulling out a key, he unlocked the restraints at Eli's ankles and then the ones on his wrist. Eli rubbed the chapped skin, trying like hell to figure out what was happening.

"I love my sister, so I told her I'd do her a favor this *one* time," he said, holding up a finger. "Apparently, you're involved in a scheme I don't want any part of. She's always been a bit more enthralled by Mom and Dad's stories than me."

Recognition began to form as Eli studied the man's features. Feeling his lips curve, he studied the man.

"You're Cyrus and Claire's son."

"Jamal," he said with a nod. "And all I've ever wanted to be is a cop. I don't do backdoor deals and shady transactions, and I sure as hell don't believe in time travel even though I'm pretty damn sure it was Lainey and not Mara who I spoke to in that alleyway a few months ago. Regardless, Elaine has assured me you deserve a leg up."

Eli's eyebrows drew together, a bit confused.

"You know her as Aiysha, but we always called her Elaine until she went to college. Can't bring myself to call her by her middle name, although I try. She says you're one of the good guys, and she asked me to bust you out."

Walking to the trunk, he opened it and pulled out a bag. "Everything's inside. Prepaid phone, cash, clothes. I have a friend in Florida who was looking to sell his boat, and my parents bought it and put it in the name of an LLC. All the documentation is inside. It's docked in Miami. I'd suggest taking the train down there—less traceable. The FBI will look for you, but they have a bigger shitshow on their hands now that Randolph has been outed as a traitor. They're much more interested in tracking down his associates and cleaning up Washington. You should change your name though. They have that information."

Eli nodded. "Hernandez never really did me any favors anyway. It's probably time for a change. How are your parents doing?" Eli had briefly met Cyrus and had never met Claire but knew that Alora and Lainey loved her dearly.

"Dad's okay. Mom's another story," Jamal said, his gaze falling to the ground. "She has cancer."

"I'm really sorry to hear that."

"She's tough as hell though. We expect her to go into remission. She's fighting with everything she's got."

"Please tell them I said thanks. This is extremely generous and quite unexpected."

"I will. Mom wants me to pass along a message to you."

"Okay."

Squinting at the sky, he said, "All right, she told me I had to say it exactly like this." Lowering his gaze to Eli's, he shook his finger as he spoke. "You're an idiot for letting Alora push you away. Get your crap together and keep telling her you love her until she says it back.”

“Wow,” Eli said, rubbing the back of his neck. “That’s pretty specific.”

“Mom loved Alora. Still loves her. She wants her to be happy. I guess she thinks you might help her achieve that.”

“I’m not sure about that, man.”

Jamal’s lips twitched. “I’ve got to go. Good luck, Eli. I hope you enjoy Florida. Look me up in a few years once this all has died down. We can have a beer.”

“Will do. Thank you so much, Jamal.”

With one final tilt of his head, Officer Jamal Montgomery drove off, leaving Eli behind with the black bag filled with necessities to build a new life. Never one to squander an opportunity, Eli unzipped it and got down to business.

Chapter 26

Several Weeks Later...

Alora hugged Zach so tightly she felt his heart beat beneath her own. Placing a wet kiss on his cheek, she wiped away the lip gloss left behind.

"I'll miss you so much," she said, worried for him to make his way in the unknown world as if he were her own child. But, alas, they hadn't prevented the past to bury their heads in the sand, and there was a whole life out there to live, especially for ones so young. "Please be safe."

"We will," Zach said, placing his arms around Elle's shoulders. "We rented the RV for a whole year and are going to explore as many parts of North America as possible. We're able to run our IT and website design company from anywhere, and hopefully we'll survive on the income from that. If I'm lucky, I might even convince this one to elope with me."

Elle beamed up at him. "We're thinking of tying the knot above the Grand Canyon, or maybe on the beach in Tulum. There are so many possibilities."

"I want to be at your wedding," Lainey said, frowning as she hugged Zach. "Please try to send us notice. I know you two are obsessed with each other, but you're my family, Zach."

"We'll let you know, Lainey. Promise," he whispered in her ear.

After releasing him, she hugged Elle and murmured, "Please take care of him."

"I will," she said, nodding into Lainey's hair.

They climbed into the huge RV, Zach behind the wheel, and waved as he honked the horn. Exhaust puffed from the muffler, and they were off, arms flailing out the windows as they waved goodbye.

"I give 'em ten minutes before he springs a flat tire," Marie harrumphed. "Who taught him how to drive anyway?"

"I gave him lessons," Hunter said, slightly grimacing. "He was, uh, okay?" His voice ended on a higher note, questioning Zach's skills.

"And who taught you how to drive, boy?" Marie asked, rapidly blinking her eyes as she gave him a sardonic glare, hands fisted on her hips.

"My grandfather had a four-wheeler on his farm. It was awesome. Come on, I'll tell you all about it." Sliding his arm around her shoulders, he led her inside the house they were now renting in Virginia. They'd left the Boonsboro home behind, understanding it was smart to stay mobile for a while.

"Everyone's leaving me," Lainey said, smiling at Alora.

"Did Sara and Luke get settled in San Diego today?"

"Yep," Lainey said, lifting her phone from her jeans pocket and shaking it. "She texted me an hour ago. Luke's new construction job pays double time, and she's excited about nesting. Must be a baby thing. Good for her."

Alora sighed, already missing her friends. "She's had a thing for San Diego forever. Used to talk about it when Lewis recruited her as the hub's nurse years ago."

"She saw pictures in one of my mother's albums from a trip she took with Dad, and she was hooked. I hope she and Luke find happiness there."

"Me too," Alora said wistfully, staring off into the distance.

"Come on. Let's sit on the porch rockers. Might as well use them before Hunter and I move to Argentina."

"I can't believe it," Alora said, trailing up the steps beside her before they lowered into the wooden chairs. "You're going to be so far away."

"The land we found was amazingly cheap, and it's within driving distance of fourteen wineries. We'll build a house and finally settle down in one place. Holy shit, Alora," she said, shaking her head in wonder. "I'm going to be surrounded by so much damn Malbec, I might never be sober."

"You've earned it, my friend." Reaching over, she squeezed her hand. "You saved the world. All that effort. All the failures with the Sphere. All the pain. I'm so proud of you, Elaine Randolph, and so honored to call you my friend."

Lainey's chin trembled as she clutched Alora's hand. "So much pain," she whispered. "But we all got our happy endings, even Marie, although she'll bitch about it forever." They chuckled. "All of us but you," Lainey said, head resting on the chair as she gazed at her friend. "I can't move down there knowing you're not happy, Alora."

"I'm extremely happy, *amiga*," she lied. "We accomplished our goal. My family will no longer be murdered by a violent dictator and his son."

Lainey inhaled, staring at the blue sky as she contemplated. "So you can't forgive him? Not even with everything you know now? Everything that happened between you?"

"Sex is just a function—"

"I'm not just talking about the sex, Alora," Lainey said, shooting her a glare. "Although that has repercussions as well." When Alora didn't respond, Lainey's brows lifted in frustration.

"Oh, fine," Alora huffed, waving her hand. "Perhaps I came to care for him a tiny bit. But not enough to absolve him of his sins."

Silence stretched, and the longer it lingered, the more frustrated Alora became. "Just spit it out, Lainey. You obviously have more you want to say."

"What would it take?"

"For what?"

"To absolve him of his sins?" Lainey asked. "Saving you from dying along with your family? Ensuring Tanner didn't kill you when he captured you? Working with us to save the world? What the heck would it take, Alora, for him to be absolved of his sins?"

Alora let the tears well in her eyes as she contemplated. She'd never been a crier, but things had drastically changed over the past few weeks, and she let the feelings surface.

"I don't know."

"Absolution is extreme, my friend. That asks a lot when he's only human and did the best he could. Your hatred of him was formed when you didn't understand his motivations. Now, you do. Perhaps you could just try forgiveness instead of demanding absolution. I'm an atheist, but I'm pretty sure forgiveness is a big deal for Catholics."

"It is," she muttered, annoyed at how logical Lainey always was, most likely due to the scientific wiring of her brain. "Even though we're in a new timeline and my family will be safe if God allows,"—she looked to the sky and sent a silent prayer—"it doesn't erase the fact I saw them murdered before my very eyes. How do I reconcile that?"

"Day by day, with a lot of extreme patience and understanding."

Alora emitted a hearty laugh. "Have you *seen* Eli and me together? Patience is the antithesis of what we have."

"You have a passion and like-mindedness I've rarely seen between two people. He was by your side on the most important day of your life. Albeit not in the position either of you wanted, but it still tethered you together. He will be the only person who can truly ever understand what you experienced that day. Think about that, Alora. It's extremely significant."

She rubbed her hand over her face, suddenly exhausted by the entire conversation.

"I know it's tough, but you're on a timeline now," she said, her eyes full with the secret Alora had only entrusted to her. "You need to figure this out. I think you already love him but are stubbornly holding back from admitting it to yourself. Don't waste time. It's a lesson I had to learn too. Every day I wasted pushing Hunter away is one I won't ever get back."

"Okay, *amiga*," she said, wringing her fingers together in her lap. Ingrid's ring shone back at her, still so pretty upon her finger. She'd meant to leave it with Eli the day she visited him in jail, but he'd pushed her out the door so fast she never got the chance. "How do I find him?"

"I don't know," she said, shrugging. "But I know someone who used to be really awesome at reconnaissance and surveillance. Maybe she can help you track him down."

Alora scrunched her features. "You're a pain in the ass, Lainey."

Deep-throated laughter surrounded them. "That I am. Ask Hunter. I have no idea how he puts up with me."

"When will you get married, now that you're engaged?"

"I don't know. I'm not in any rush. Honestly, I'm only doing it because it's so important to him. So whenever he decides he's ready, I'll be ready. I don't need the ceremony of it all. I just want him to be happy."

"You never got a chance to tell me what happened when you visited Kara in 2063. I imagine it was strange seeing her in person."

"It was so surreal," she said, "meeting the woman he loved when he was so young. She had such a great energy about her. I told her I was a psychic and that she needed to be extremely careful on April 9, 2063. Most people would've told me to fuck off, but she just thanked me and looked at me as if I was slightly insane." Rolling her eyes, she gave a *pfft*. "Me, a psychic? It's absurd."

"But it was such an amazing gesture," Hunter said, appearing behind them and placing a peck on Lainey's cheek. "You amaze me every day, duchess. Saving the world was just the beginning."

"Eh, I'm okay," she teased, shrugging.

"Well, I think I'll help Marie prepare the chicken," Alora said, standing and wiping her palms on her jeans. "It's my last night here before I head to Colombia, and I want to spend some time with her."

"Have you decided what you'll do when you get there?"

Alora shook her head. "I just want to visit my home. Smell the air and remember the place where I was happy so long ago, before I ever understood what murder and pain were."

"Remember, you can't come into contact with your parents in their younger versions. It will create a paradox that could upend the world."

"I know, Lainey. You've only told me a million times. But I think you know how hard it is to stay away from those we love the most." She arched a brow, reminding Lainey they both had traded secrets no one else knew.

"Is this a girl-code conversation?" Hunter asked, confused. "What am I missing?"

"Forget it. Take my seat. I'll see you inside."

Later that evening, the four of them ate Marie's succulent meal, the older woman lamenting the time she dated a two-timing Argentinian in the past. She made it clear she wasn't thrilled with Lainey's choice of relocation, but she'd swallow it so she could keep an eye on her and make sure she didn't waste away.

That night, as Alora fell asleep, she contemplated everything she and Lainey had discussed. Was forgiveness possible? Could she allow herself to love Eli? God forbid, did she already love him deep in her heart?

Yes.

The word pulsed in her brain as she rested her hands over her abdomen and fell into a dreamless sleep.

Chapter 27

Alora walked along the wooden pier, her boots tapping in tandem with her brisk steps as she pulled the coat tight across her abdomen. She'd always thought Florida was warm, but January obviously had other ideas. Forcing her teeth not to chatter, she spotted him in the distance.

His broad shoulders were covered by a bulky sweater over khakis, and his back was to her as he circled a rope around a metal hook on the third boat from the end. She didn't know a lot about boats, but it looked quite large. Closing in, she saw his body tense ever so slightly as her heels clicked on the wood.

Annoyed, she crossed her arms. "I know you saw me, Eli," she said, tapping her foot. "Stop being a coward and face me like a man."

Straightening, he placed his hands on his hips and looked to the sky, most likely praying for patience. Once finished, he slowly turned, the forgotten rope left behind.

"Hello, Alora."

She arched a brow and gritted her teeth, preparing for a fight. She always felt most alive when they sparred and ached to unleash her temper on him.

"Hello."

His eyes raked over her long brown coat and jeans above the knee-high brown boots. "You fit right in with 2035 fashion. But I would've expected nothing less."

"2036 now," she corrected.

He nodded, placing his hands on his hips again. After several moments of silence, he sighed. "Well, this has been fun. I've got to get back to work. Thanks for stopping by." Dismissively turning, he bent down and fussed with the rope again before heading toward the door that led inside the boat.

"Hey!" Jumping onto the vessel, she grabbed his arm and tried to swing him around. "I came here to speak to you. The least you could do is listen."

He shrugged off her arm and glanced at her over his shoulder. "I think we've said everything that needs to be said. I know I did. Good luck with whatever you've decided to do with your life. Now, leave me the hell alone."

His tone worried her, so unlike the Eli she'd come to know. He'd always been passionate with her once they'd begun to truly become friends, and his attitude of annoyed indifference was so worrisome she wondered if the damage was too deep.

Had he closed his heart to her so completely that she didn't stand a chance of swaying him?

"*Mierda*," she breathed, unwilling to accept defeat. Stomping down the stairs, she found him at a small sink, washing his hands as if he had nothing else to do in the world. As if she didn't even exist. Stalking toward him, she felt the anger well within, threatening her control as it always did around him, and mentally commanded herself to stay calm.

He shook his hands over the sink and reached for the towel, drying them as she imagined strangling him. Bastard. Determined to force him to face her, she waited. He clenched the counter, knuckles white, as he stared straight ahead out the tiny window over the sink.

"I'm not going to fight with you, Alora. I know that's what you want. It creates a power imbalance where you can paint me as the bad guy afterward." Turning, he crossed his arms over his chest and leaned back on the sink. "But it's not happening, so you might as well leave."

His calm nature shook her to her core, and a thousand images ran though her mind of slapping his handsome face.

"Go ahead. You want to punch me—it's written all over your face." Shrugging, he taunted her. "I just don't care, Alora."

She huffed a frazzled breath. "Then was it a lie when you told me you loved me?"

His deep brown irises lowered to the floor before returning to hers. "Why are you here?"

"I want an answer!" She stomped her foot, furious.

The man rolled his eyes as if she were some insignificant waste of space and shook his head. "I don't have time for this," he muttered. Pushing away from the counter, he headed back outside and resumed fiddling with the damn rope.

She followed him, about five seconds from pushing him overboard, and punched him directly in the spot where he'd been grazed by the bullet all those months ago. Turning to glare at her with fury, he rubbed his upper arm.

"You fucking witch."

A laugh escaped her throat, and she thanked God above that he was pissed. Anger meant emotion, and emotion possibly still meant love. Praying with every ounce of her soul it was true, she forged ahead.

"There you are," she said, batting her eyelashes as her lips formed a sardonic smile. "I was worried you'd lost your damn mind for a minute."

"Damn it, woman, you're infuriating. You want anger? I'll fucking give it to you." Closing in, he slid his palms over her neck, tilting her face to his. "I tried to make things right," he said through clenched teeth, "but I'm irreparable to you. You made that abundantly clear. I don't know why you're here, but whatever the reason, I'm not interested."

The warmth of his hands seeped into her skin as she swung for the fences. "You once told me not to lie to you. What if I asked the same of you?"

"I don't owe you anything. I'm done paying for sins I can never atone for. And you're an asshole to keep throwing them in my face." Releasing her, he ran his hand through his hair. "Get off my boat, Alora."

"How did you afford this?"

He scoffed. "None of your fucking business."

Reaching forward, she grabbed a fistful of his sweater. "I'm making it my fucking business," she said, teeth clenched so hard she thought they might disintegrate.

"Oh, yeah? And what makes you think you have the right to show up here and ask me questions, sweetheart?"

She tightened her grip. "Because I don't want my child's father to be a criminal. I'm hoping you came into possession of this boat legally, or you're going to have to get rid of it. *Se entiende?*"

Confusion swam in his eyes as they darted between hers. "What?" he whispered.

"You heard me!" she snapped. Slowly releasing the crumpled fabric, she stepped back and slid her coat open, revealing her slightly distended abdomen.

Eli just stared at her, his face a shocked mask of disbelief. "How?"

She gave him an incredulous look. "Really? Do I need to tell you how babies are made? Every good Catholic girl knows the pull-out method is iffy at best. Somehow, your swimmers found a way, determined little bastards."

His gaze fell to her stomach, laced with reverence, before lifting back to hers. "Holy shit," he breathed.

"Yes, *mi amor*," she said with a derisive laugh. "Holy shit is right."

Thrusting his fingers through his hair, he roughly scratched his scalp as he contemplated her. "Well, what the fuck do we do now?"

Sighing, she placed her hands in the pockets of her coat and looked across the water. "That depends on you."

He stood silent for so long she was forced to turn back. His gaze was hooded, his full lips forming a slight frown.

"I don't know what you're looking for here, Alora."

Feeling her throat close, she realized she was going to have to beg him. Son of a bitch. She'd never begged anyone for anything in her damn life. But eventually, everyone had to eat crow at some point, right? At least she could get it over with and move the hell on.

"I didn't want to tell you about the baby until we could talk. But you were being extremely difficult," she said, scowling.

"Difficult?" he exclaimed. "I think you invented the word, honey."

Her eyes narrowed. "Don't lie to me, Eli. You told me you loved me the night we made this baby. I want to know if you still do."

A harsh laugh escaped his lips. "That's incredibly unfair—"

"Don't lecture me about unfair!" she interrupted, slicing her hand through the air.

"I'm not lecturing you," he said, calm and firm. "But I'm not putting my heart out there again so you can stomp all over it. It's not fucking happening."

Sighing, she glowered, hating she had to grovel but understanding the end result would be worth it. Inhaling deeply, she said, "I didn't want to tell you about the baby before I told you I loved you back. But you were supposed to tell me first, and then I'd tell you...and *then* I'd tell you about our daughter. I had it all planned in my head," she finished, circling her hand in a frustrated gesture.

His lips quirked as he stuffed his hands in his pockets. "Sounds really nice."

"It was," she said, scrunching her face at him, "until you ruined it."

Breaking into a full-on smile, he withdrew his hands from his pockets and slid them around her wrists. "Tell me how it goes again," he murmured.

"You say you still love me," she said softly.

Gently, he tucked a wayward strand of her silky hair behind her ear. "I still love you," he said, emotion shining in his eyes as he gazed down at her.

"That's good," she said, clearing her throat. "Much better."

He chuckled. "I think it's your turn to say something now?"

She glared at him. "You're enjoying this."

He closed his eyes, his face awash with satisfied joy. "So damn much." Lifting his lids, he cupped her face in his hands. "Go on."

"I love you, okay?" she said, rolling her eyes.

He squinted one eye shut. "Was that really how you said it in the scenario you imagined?"

Turning her face, she bit his hand.

"Ouch," he said playfully. "Sheathe your claws, woman."

The words were from the first night he'd touched her, all those months ago, causing affection to well in her heart.

"I love you," she whispered, standing on her toes to place a kiss on his lips. "I have no idea how it happened, but it's so real, Eli."

A ragged breath exited his lips as he placed his forehead upon hers. "Alora," he breathed. "You have no idea..." The words drifted away, lost to the sea as they embraced. She held him so tightly, safe in the knowledge their child was nestled between them and they were going to be okay.

Lifting his head, he palmed her cheeks. "It's a girl?"

She nodded. "It's a girl. I found out the sex last week and was so sad you weren't there. I'm so sorry." Gliding her hand over his jaw, she said, "I hated you for so long, I didn't know what to do when it turned to love. Hell, I still have no idea what to do. Part of me is so torn, wondering if I'm betraying my family by loving you." Pain entered his eyes, and she shook her head. "I'm not saying that to hurt you, but you deserve honesty, and I'll do my best to give it to you. There will be times when the old scars flare to life, and you're going to have to be patient with me. It's not going to be easy, but I think you already know that."

"I don't need easy. Arguing with you is hands down my favorite pastime."

Her eyebrow arched. "Well, you're in luck because my hormones are raging."

Overcome with laughter, he rested his lips against hers. "Bring it on." Pushing her lips apart with his own, he plunged his tongue inside her mouth. Alora met him full-force, sliding her tongue over his, aching to remember his taste. Groaning, she pierced her nails into his neck.

"God, I've missed those claws, sweetheart. I want them *everywhere*."

"Everywhere?" She cupped his straining shaft through his pants.

"You little she-devil," he murmured into her mouth. "What am I going to do with you?"

"I think it's time you married me for real." Bringing her hand into view, she wiggled her fingers, Ingrid's ring sparkling. "I kept it safe for you."

He pulled her palm to his lips, softly kissing the ring. "Thank you."

"I'm honored to wear it," she said, running her thumb over his lip. "And maybe one day, we can pass it down to her." Alora placed her hand over her abdomen.

Eli covered her hand with his. "I love that idea," he whispered.

"I love you," she said reverently, cupping his jaw as she finally set the feelings free, unable to hold back any longer.

Although the cold wind whipped around them, they were warm from the glow of their love and the child they'd created before they'd done the impossible and saved the world. So thankful to be back in her husband's arms, she swayed with him under the blue January sky until he carried her downstairs and made love to her on the very comfortable bed of the boat he'd somehow managed to procure. She still wondered how, but there was time to hear that story later. Even though time had been their enemy for so long, it was now their ally. Thankful for every turn her life had taken, even those that had once seemed so tragic, she now understood all the pieces had to fall in order to form the life she now had. Clutching her husband close, she said a silent prayer, excited for their uncharted future.

Epilogue

Late December, 2040, Argentina

Cyrus studied his wife from the doorway as she frowned in the mirror. Rubbing her fingers over the peach fuzz on her mostly bald head, Claire sighed and picked up the wig. As she combed it with the brush, rotating it to smooth out all the strands, he approached, sliding his arms around her waist. Green eyes met his in the reflection as she smiled.

"Purple today?" he asked.

"Yep," she said, examining the wig as she twirled it in her hand. "It felt apt since I had purple hair when I last saw them. Should help jog their memories, although I look quite different now." Her smile faded, gaze fixed on the wig, and Cyrus nudged her temple with his nose.

"You look just as beautiful as the day we got married," he murmured in her ear.

"Oh, you just have to say that because you're my husband," she teased.

"And because it's true." His heart swelled when her grin returned.

"Well, thank you. When we said, 'through sickness and health,' who knew we'd end up here? You really stuck through that one, chief."

"Piece of cake," he said, squeezing her. "Being your husband is pretty damn awesome, Finch."

For silent seconds, they gazed at each other in the mirror, slightly swaying as he embraced her, his broad body bracketing her back. Lifting her arms, she secured the wig atop her scalp, turning her head to inspect the result in the reflection.

"I think it looks pretty good."

Stepping back, he gave a tilt of his head. "Sure does. Jamal and Elaine both called this morning. They're so excited for us to see everyone. The grandkids want to video chat on Christmas Eve."

"Oh, that will be lovely."

Cyrus noticed her eyes becoming glassy, and he clenched her hand. "Although we already said goodbye in person, it will be nice to see them before the holidays— on video at least."

"Yes," she whispered, eyes swimming with tears at the words they didn't voice. They'd said goodbye to their children and grandchildren knowing the hugs they'd bestowed would be the last for Claire.

"You made the right decision, sweetheart," he said, clutching her hand. "Four rounds of chemo was enough. When you went into remission again five years ago, it was a miracle. Our bodies can only take so much. It's time you let yours rest."

Sniffling, she swiped the tear that escaped down her cheek. "Well said, old man." A laugh filtered through the emotion, the sound melodious to Cyrus. "You'd know better than anyone."

Chuckling, he leaned forward and placed a soft peck on her forehead. "I would. Ready to go?"

With a deep exhale, Claire straightened her spine and nodded. "Ready. I'm freaking dying for all the updates. I mean, Lainey is finally married, which I never expected she'd actually do, but she didn't stand a chance with Captain Hotness."

Cyrus's lips twitched. "Should I be jealous of Rhodes? You speak an awful lot about how sexy he is."

"Oh, posh," she said, swatting his chest. "He's nothing compared to you, chief."

"Don't forget it." He gave her a playful wink.

"And Alora and Eli," she continued, lifting her hands in wonder. "I'm dying to hear that whole story. And I haven't seen Zach in so long. God, Cyrus, it's going to be amazing."

"Well then, let's get on with it." Glancing around the hotel room they'd rented near the airport knowing they'd need to crash after last night's late flight, he took one last inventory. "Everything's packed. It's about an hour's cab ride to Lainey and Hunter's place."

"Let's do it." Excitement sparkled in her eyes, confirming they'd made the right choice of how to spend Claire's final moments in this timeline. They'd debated spending them with their children, but they'd already shared so many years of love and laughter, and Claire wanted the grandkids to remember her as vibrant and strong. Jamal and Elaine had fully supported her decision to spend some of her final days with the people she loved so much and hadn't seen in several decades.

Cyrus mostly thought of time in decades now. He had just entered his eighth, and Claire was more than halfway through her sixth. Funny how a block of ten years could symbolize so much and allow for such growth and reflection. He and Claire gathered their belongings and headed outside to wait for the cab. Their bodies were slower now—hell, his damn ankle still hurt like the devil some nights—but they ambled along well enough.

When the taxi arrived, they loaded the suitcases into the trunk, and Cyrus opened the door for her.

"Ready?" he asked, gesturing her into the car.

Lifting her hand, she cupped his cheek. "Ready," she replied, running her thumb over his jaw.

Covering her hand, he slid it over his lips and placed a sweet kiss on her palm. As he helped his wife into the cab, Cyrus let the excitement wash over him, reveling in the pulsing emotion, which was rare for his stoic demeanor.

Soon, he would get to hug Lainey and all those he held dear from the squalid yet so very important years he'd spent at the hub. Threading his fingers through Claire's, their joined hands rested atop his thigh as they forged ahead to reconnect with their family.

* * * *

Lainey held the curtain open, heart pounding as the taxi toiled down the dirt driveway. "They're here! Hunter, they're here."

"Be right out, sweetheart," he called from the kitchen. "Go on outside, and I'll meet you there."

Lainey had to stop herself from bolting to the car as Claire and Cyrus exited, grabbing their suitcases from the trunk. "Claire," she warbled, already feeling the tears overwhelm her.

Claire turned, her smile so wide, and began inching forward on her cane. Lainey's heart cracked wide open at her frailty—god, she was so thin—but she forged ahead, needing to hug her beloved friend.

"Hey, Lainey," she said, opening her arms.

Lainey pulled her into a smothering embrace, trying like hell not to cut off her airway but unable to control her arms. "God, Claire," she whispered into her fake purple hair. "I missed you so much."

"I know," she said, nodding into Lainey's shoulder and sniffling. "It's been so long. There's so much."

"Yes," she said, pulling back and palming Claire's cheek. "So damn much. I want to hear it all. Everything."

Claire beamed. "Well, spoiler alert: I'm in love with Cyrus."

Lainey chuckled through her tears, wiping them from her face. "I figured that one out. Even before you left the hub?" she whispered.

"Yep," Claire said. "But I never thought he'd love me back."

"She's never realized she's way too good for me," Cyrus said, appearing behind Claire and placing a kiss on her head. "I hope she never does."

"He's the best husband," she said, staring up at him, love crossing every inch of her expression. "And the best father. Well, you've met the kids. We have four grandkids now too. Elaine just had her second child. A girl."

"Amazing," Lainey said, enfolding her hand and leading her toward the house. Cyrus picked up their luggage before trailing behind. "Can't wait to hear all your stories. In the meantime, you'll never guess what I have waiting to pop open during dinner."

Claire's eyes widened. "No! You waited until now? Seriously? That's some intense patience."

Closing her eyes, Lainey said wistfully, "The 2005 Vina Cobos Marchiori Estate Malbec. I got my hands on a bottle, and we're finally going to drink it."

"Well, hot damn," Claire said, biting her lip. "Can't wait to try it."

"Me neither," Lainey said, leading her up the stairs, where Hunter was waiting. He embraced Claire and then gave Cyrus a friendly elbow.

"Hey, Montgomery. Nice to see you after all these years."

"Hey, Rhodes. You taking good care of her? I'm still not above breaking your neck if you aren't."

"Oh, stop," Claire said, slapping her husband's chest. "He's just jealous because I might have mentioned how hot you were a time or two this morning," she whispered to Hunter conspiratorially.

Cyrus scowled as Hunter chuckled. "Well, thank you, Claire. I never did figure out if you snuck a peek at my chest all those years ago from the outdoor showers."

"A lady never tells," she said, making an X across her heart.

"Okay, okay," Cyrus muttered. "Where should I put the bags, Lainey?"

"This way," she said, waving him inside. "I've got the downstairs guest room all prepared for you guys. There's a dedicated bathroom, so Claire won't have to climb any stairs."

"Thank you," she whispered, giving a sad smile. "I wish I felt better. Hell, I wish I looked better."

"You look beautiful," Lainey said, sliding her arm across her dear friend's shoulders. "Come on. Let me give you the tour. Eli, Alora, Zach, and Elle will arrive later this afternoon, and we'll all video chat with Luke, Sara, and their kids one night while everyone is here."

"I'm so excited to see them."

"Me too, Claire. So damn much."

Glued to each other's side, they entered Lainey's home.

* * * *

Eli helped his wife and daughter out of the car, holding Carolina's hand as they walked across the grass toward the large home. Situated on many acres of land, it appeared serene and peaceful.

Suddenly, his daughter released his hand and ran toward the approaching couple. "Aunt Elle!"

Laughter rang across the meadow as Elle picked her up, swaying back and forth. "How's my favorite niece?"

"Good! Daddy let me sit by the window on the plane even though it was really his seat."

"Well, how thoughtful," she said, smiling at her half-brother. "Well done, Dad."

"Thanks." Leaning down, he kissed her cheek and then gave Zach an elbow. "How's life on the open road treating you guys?"

"Good," Zach said, taking Carolina from Elle's arms and giving her a hug before setting her on her feet. "We still love it. Hi, Alora."

"Hello, *parce*," she said, hugging him before pulling Elle into her embrace. "It's so good to see you both."

"Mama, there are llamas over there!" Carolina said, pointing to the fenced-in area. "Can I go pet them?"

"I think they're alpacas. And yes, but only if Daddy agrees to wash your hands afterward."

Carolina stared up at Eli, eyes wide with anticipation. "Go on," he said, jerking his head. When she ran off, he pulled his wife to his side. "Witch," he murmured in her ear.

Chuckling, she threaded her arm around his waist. "Is everyone inside?"

"Yes, and Lainey's busting out the Malbec," Zach said, excitement in his expression. "Finally. Come on."

"I'll watch her," Eli said, urging Alora to follow them by patting her ass. She shot him a heated glare, which he returned in kind, confirming that wouldn't be the last time he'd touch her gorgeous ass today. Not by a long shot. She licked those luscious lips and winked before following Zach and Elle inside.

"His name is Jeff," Carolina informed him, petting an alpaca as he approached.

"Oh? Did he tell you that?" She nodded, and he huffed a laugh. "I wasn't sure alpacas spoke English."

"And Spanish too. Like me."

"That's fantastic. Hello, Jeff. It's nice to meet you."

"He only talks to people who are younger than five. He told me that too."

Eli realized his daughter had inherited his excellent fabrication skills. They'd have to work on that one day so she understood lying was wrong—in most cases, at least—but there was time for that. For now, he enjoyed her adorable embellishments, enthralled by the other things Jeff had supposedly passed along.

Finally, they headed inside for family dinner, reminiscent of all the dinners they'd previously shared in cramped quarters before they'd saved the world. Lifting her glass, finally full with succulent Malbec, Lainey toasted to their happiness and to Marie. The night was filled with memories and laughter as they ate the amazing feast Hunter had prepared.

"I can't believe you learned to cook, Rhodes. You're making Eli, Zach, and me look pretty bad here," Cyrus said.

"My husband is a wonderful cook," Elle said, beaming up at Zach.

"*My* husband is terrible, but he has other skills," Alora said, batting her eyelashes at Eli.

"And by that, she means I'm great at cleaning the fish we catch. She won't touch the damn things until I debone them."

"But they taste fantastic."

"Seems like you all have it worked out," Hunter said, chuckling. "Since Lainey saved the world, I figured she deserved an early retirement. Culinary school down here was pretty awesome, and I love my job as a chef at the local winery's restaurant. Plus, she really enjoys the leftovers."

"I think I've gained ten pounds since he started working there," Lainey said, shrugging. "Marie would be thrilled, although I need to start jogging around the property again. One day soon."

"She says that every day," Hunter teased.

Lainey smacked his chest before he grabbed her wrist and nipped it. "And *retirement* is a stretch. I'm writing a dissertation on time travel and the equations that ultimately got the Sphere to function correctly. Once I'm done, I'll publish it and make sure Dad gets a copy at the university. Science should be shared by all, and I feel an obligation to disseminate it throughout the scientific community. Of course, it will be presented as theoretical. No one will know it actually works."

"Let's hope they never have cause to use it," Hunter said, squeezing her hand.

"I hope not," Lainey said, glancing around the table. "We broke the cycle, guys, and each of you were integral to our success. Even Cyrus and Claire, who had the foresight to gather intel on the Knights of Washington and build up an impressive financial portfolio so we could pay off Liam Downey's debts."

"We worked hard and earned every penny," Claire said. "I really enjoyed being a P.I., and Cyrus worked so many late shifts at his security jobs. When I decided to fast-track my biology and chemistry degrees before ultimately earning my forensic science degree, we knew we'd need a lot of money to fund my education."

"Becoming a forensic investigator was perfect for Claire because she could combine science and investigative work," Cyrus said. "But I think, deep down, she sometimes missed discussing physics and time travel."

Claire scrunched her nose. "Maybe a bit, but believe me, I had enough at the hub. The career I fashioned was perfect. I never felt guilty about investing wisely to aid the mission...*and* to send the kids to school." She grinned at Cyrus. "Yale and Howard aren't cheap. Did we have a tiny inkling which investments would succeed? Yes. But the returns helped the cause, and we were able to buy that fancy tactical gear for you guys when you infiltrated the White House."

"I thought that was from Lewis's stockpile?" Eli asked.

"We were close to running out, and Cyrus and Claire offered to contribute so we'd each have a little left once we disbanded," Lainey said. "I figured if we succeeded, we could thank them in person."

Everyone lifted their glass and gave a toast to the couple, who beamed in return. Finally, after so many failures, the team shared a poignant moment basking in their success.

After dinner, they walked outside to the pretty thatch of land Marie had designed herself. Encircling it, they each held a candle—Eli making sure Carolina's didn't singe her fingers—and Lainey pulled out an envelope.

As they stood around the soft mound of earth with the headstone that read *Marie Elizabeth Elders*, Lainey sighed and gave a reverent smile. "As you all know, Marie instructed that I should read this letter once we were all together again. Can you guys hear me?"

Luke and Sara waved, their image on the screen of Zach's cell phone. "Loud and clear!" Sara said.

Unfolding the paper, Lainey began to read aloud.

"Dear Family,

If you're reading this, I croaked—and it's about time. I mean, for the love of all that's holy, I tried to die so many times in so many timelines, I'm still not sure I'm really dead. But we'll assume I am so Lainey can read on and you all can go back to your new lives.

It was an honor to be part of your family. Lewis found me after the apocalypse and had a burr up his ass that he wanted to protect me. Pretty bizarre coming from a complete stranger, but he was adamant, so I let him whisk me to the hub, where we became fast friends. It was only later that I realized he was probably my half-brother.

My mother, Vivian, was involved with Edward Randolph when they both were very young. She never told me who my father was, and I never really cared much. When you have a mom as awesome as mine, she's the only parent you need. When I figured out our possible connection, I never mentioned it to Lewis, nor did he to me. By that time, our bond had already been formed, so it wouldn't have mattered anyway. Still, I want you to know, Lainey, that I'm proud to call you family, as I am each and every one of you ragamuffin stragglers that make up our team. Families aren't always made from blood. Some are forged just as ours was, through war and failure, peace and success.

I know Claire is sick, and she'll probably be the first to go, so I'd like to let her know I'm saving her a seat. That might seem morbid, but it's the truth, and there's no point in pretending it doesn't exist. You're not alone, sweet girl, and ol' Marie will be here ready to give you a hug and tell you how ridiculous your hair looks."

Claire laughed, swiping a tear as Cyrus smiled down at her, love encompassing his every feature.

"Now, go on and let this old lady rest. It's been a long life, and I don't want you to mourn me. Remember me with love and remember to love each other. You did the impossible: you

Tears streamed down Lainey's face along with most of the others, and Eli pulled Alora close as she smiled up at him, wet cheeks glistening in the moonlight.

"Daddy," Carolina said, tugging on his pants. "Why is everyone crying?"

"Because our friend Marie wrote us a really emotional letter. She was part of our family."

"And she died?"

Nodding, he stroked her hair. "Yes, sweetheart."

She gnawed her lip for a moment before asking, "Can I draw her a picture? I'll make sure it has rainbows so she can slide on them in heaven."

Alora squeezed him, acknowledging their daughter's endearing words, as he nodded. "That's so thoughtful. You can draw it first thing in the morning." Her resulting grin almost burst his heart wide open.

Later that evening, he and Alora covered Carolina with blankets as she slept on the couch in the large room Lainey had prepared for them. Arm in arm, they stared down at her as she slept, mouth open and slightly snoring.

"She gets that from you," Alora whispered.

"I do *not* snore," he murmured.

She snickered. "You absolutely do." When he opened his mouth to argue, she lifted a finger. "Careful, dear husband. We were having such a nice day. Do you really want to argue with your wife?"

He nipped her finger. "Fine, woman. But once I have you alone, we'll debate this again."

She waggled her eyebrows. "Can't wait."

Tugging her toward him, he slid behind her, threading his arms around her waist as his front bracketed her back. Resting his chin on her shoulder as they gazed at their daughter, he said, "She's the best of us, Alora."

"Yes." She clutched his forearms, leaning into him. "Our second chance."

"No more time machines. Just one shot."

"I like our odds," his wife whispered, gently rocking in his arms.

"Me too."

Once the lights were dim, Eli crawled into bed and spooned her tight. "Did you see the car lights that kept appearing over the horizon during Marie's ceremony?"

Her body stiffened slightly. "Yes."

"Should we be worried? Lainey said no one lives within several miles."

"We can't live in fear. All the time machines were destroyed. The one in Australia, the one at the hub, and the mini-Sphere."

"If I were my father, I'd ensure there was one more somewhere along the way."

Alora shivered. "Your father is dead. *Every* version of him in every timeline."

"How certain are you today?" It was a game of sorts they often played as they fell asleep, gauging how sure they were that the team had actually prevailed.

"Ninety-five percent," she said softly.

"Eighty-five for me. Seeing everyone together...I don't know. It should reassure me, but it actually had the opposite effect."

"Go to sleep." She snuggled into his frame. "Tomorrow, you will have a different answer."

Listening to his wife, he closed his eyes and inhaled her scent as he drifted to slumber.

* * * *

Outside, under the bright full moon, a man kept watch over the house. Assured that everyone was asleep, he started his pickup truck and drove back to the small farm he kept by himself. Stepping inside the house, he picked up the arrowhead the woman had given his son over a year ago. It was nondescript and seemed to hold no value, yet the woman he'd traced to this remote part of Argentina had visited Florida and given it to his son.

Testing the weight of it in his palm, his mind raced to discern what could've possibly motivated her. Determined to find out, he fell into bed, exhausted. Tomorrow was another day, and he would resume solving the mystery then. For Victor Hernandez had always been a sucker for a great mystery, and this one was too meandrous to give up now.

<h1 style="text-align:center">Thank You!</h1>

Well, my friends, they saved the world! Was there every any doubt? Of course, I had to end on a *tiny* twist! I hope it leaves you thinking about these characters who stole my heart for a little while longer. Thank you so much for taking this journey with me. I adored writing this series and can't wait to bring you more.

In the meantime, if you'd like to try another one of my books, check out **The End of Hatred**! Inspired by my love of J.R. Ward and Nora Roberts novels, it's a fantasy romance series with a Metallica-loving Slayer princess and a sexy, stoic Vampyre king. Their attraction is forbidden, but they both crave peace. Happy reading!

*** * * ***

Please consider leaving a review on Amazon, Goodreads, and/or BookBub. Indie authors survive on reviews and they are so appreciated. Your friendly neighborhood author thanks you from the bottom of her heart!

*** * * ***
<u>Books by Rebecca Hefner</u>

<u>Prevent the Past Series</u>
Book 1: A Paradox of Fates
Book 2: A Destiny Reborn
Book 3: A Timeline Restored

<u>The Etherya's Earth Series (Fantasy/Paranormal Romance)</u>
Book 1: The End of Hatred
Book 2: The Elusive Sun
Book 3: The Darkness Within
Book 4: The Reluctant Savior
Book 4.5: Immortal Beginnings (in the ***Untouched Heroes*** anthology)
Book 5: The Impassioned Choice
Book 5.5: Two Souls United
Book 6: The Cryptic Prophecy
Book 6.5: Garridan's Mate (in the ***Hearts Unleashed*** anthology)
Book 7: Coming soon!

Acknowledgments

I'm so proud and elated to be finishing my second series! Although the Etherya's Earth series is not yet complete, I always knew the Prevent the Past series would be a trilogy. Writing a time travel series is exhausting. If I never have to look at an age calculator again, or my notebook full of scribbled notes upon notes, I'll be just fine! Of course, I say that now, but I really do love time travel, so who knows if a new series will pop into my head in the future? Only time will tell (perhaps Future Me is already writing one in her own timeline!).

Thanks to all of you who took this journey and fell in love with these characters like I did. I appreciate each and every one of you who take the time to leave a review on Amazon, Goodreads, and/or BookBub. Reviews are so important to indie authors and they help motivate us to write when we want to cuddle with our cats and watch Real Housewives instead (who, me?).

Just a few notes on this book. I used Boonesboro as one of the locations as a shoutout to all my fellow Nora Roberts lovers. I think her readers will enjoy this series if they stumble upon it, and, hey, maybe even Nora will read it one day. If so, my life will pretty much be complete, but until then, we can all fangirl about her together.

As a former medical sales rep, I also wanted to write a frank discussion about STDs in this book. Now, that might seem weird to some, but I've always found it strange that romance novels have so many instances of people boning but very few discussions on STDs! Of course, it's not really a "sexy" topic but I do believe having an honest discussion with your partner about your sexual history is really freaking sexy. It shows you care about that person and their health. I hope the conversation between Zach and Elle came off as genuine and refreshing, and I look forward to writing more discussions like this in future books.

As I spoke about in A Destiny Reborn, it was really important for me to make this series diverse, so the characters represent our connected humanity and multicultural world. Since Alora is Colombian and uses a fair amount of Spanish, I wanted to make sure I wrote her character, and all of the characters, with care. Thanks so much to Nini Aviles for performing the sensitivity read for this book. Her feedback and suggestions were excellent, and she really helped me develop Alora's character to represent her culture with authenticity. Working with her was a fantastic experience, and I'm so grateful we connected.

Thanks to my superhero team of Megan, Bryony, and Anthony. I'm so lucky to be surrounded by these amazing people!

And, lastly, can you tell I'm a big fan of male virgins? What did you think? Should I write more? (Hint: I'm probably going to write more—and maybe already have under my other nom de plume??) Here's hoping you find your Zach, Elle, Alora, Eli, or whomever will make your heart sing. If there's one thing we've learned from 2020 in general, don't waste an opportunity to seize happiness. Until next time, happy reading, my friends!

About the Author

USA Today bestselling author Rebecca Hefner grew up in Western NC and now calls the Hudson River of NYC home. In her youth, she would sneak into her mother's bedroom and read the romance novels stashed on the bookshelf, cementing her love of HEAs. A huge Buffy and Star Wars fan, she loves an epic fantasy and a surprise twist (Luke, he IS your father).

Before becoming an author, Rebecca had a successful twelve-year medical device sales career. After launching her own indie publishing company, she is now a full-time author who loves writing strong, complex characters who find their HEAs.

Rebecca can usually be found making dorky and/or embarrassing posts on TikTok and Instagram. Please join her so you can laugh along with her!

Follow Rebecca Here:

www.rebeccahefner.com